THE CLYDESIDERS

In the summer of 1914, as clouds of war gather over Europe, the Cartwrights of Hilltop House in the West End of Glasgow are secure in their life of wealth and privilege. Meanwhile the Watsons are fighting a losing battle against hunger, unemployment and poverty in the slums of the Gorbals. Their lives are changed forever by a chance meeting between Virginia Watson, a kitchen maid at Hilltop House, and Nicholas Cartwright, heir to the Cartwright fortune. Their illicit romance has hardly begun when war breaks out and Nicholas has to leave to face the horrors of the Western Front...

THE CLYDESIDERS

THE CLYDESIDERS

by

Margaret Thomson Davis

KGL

Magna Large Print Books
Long Preston, North Yorkshire,
BD23 4ND, England.

British Library Cataloguing in Publication Data.

Davis, Margaret Thomson
    The Clydesiders.

    A catalogue record of this book is
    available from the British Library

    ISBN   0-7505-2522-3

First published in Great Britain 2003 by B & W Publishing Ltd.

Published in Large Print 2006 by arrangement with
Black & White Publishing Ltd.

Magna Large Print is an imprint of Library Magna Books Ltd.

Printed and bound in Great Britain by
T.J. (International) Ltd., Cornwall, PL28 8RW

ACKNOWLEDGEMENTS

I'm very grateful to the kind friends who helped me with the research for *The Clydesiders*. Farquhar and Cathy McLay for trusting me with their book about John Maclean by his daughter Nan Milton. Molly and Joe Fisher for sharing their knowledge about John Maclean, and Joseph Latham for all the help he found for me on the internet.

The poetry in *The Clydesiders* is by Michael Malone.

1914

1

Virginia Watson wasn't allowed to be seen, far less talk to anyone – upstairs, that was. Down in the basement kitchen, talk was permitted to a certain extent. High up under the rafters, in the attic bedroom with Fanny Gordon, the scullery maid, she could talk as long as she could keep awake. Fanny didn't call it their bedroom. To her it was a dark and dismal cell. Fourteen-year-old Fanny, who was two years younger than Virginia and now shared the lumpy iron bedstead with her, had come from a cottage. There she had slept in an attic with her three sisters.

'All right, we were crowded top-to-tail in the one bed, but the attic there was bright and cosy. At night we had two candles. Not like here! Mrs Cartwright must have pots of housekeeping money, and fancy, she's had gas put in all her rooms, but we've to make do with one wee candle.' Fanny pouted. 'Rotten mean, that's what ugly old Mrs Cartwright is. I hate her, so I do.'

Virginia had no love for the Cartwrights either. She too resented the one candle which made it so difficult to read any of her books. But she worried about Fanny's reckless tongue. With a sigh she gave up brushing her long hair. She could barely see her reflection in the pock-marked and chipped mirror.

'You've hardly been here ten minutes, Fanny, and you won't last much longer if anyone hears you talking like that.'

'I'm not daft. I'm not likely to march up to Mrs Cartwright and tell her what a mean old tyrant she is. Ugly as well. Her and her long nose and beady eyes.'

Virginia shook her head. She was seriously concerned for Fanny's job. Mr Gordon's rheumatism, Fanny had confided, was getting worse and the Gordon family were worried in case he lost his job. If he did, it would mean losing his tied cottage. Then where could Fanny go? It was a miracle she'd got the job in the first place, with her cheeky pimply face and wild frizz of mousy hair that looked none too clean.

'Listen,' she told the girl. 'You'd better watch the upstairs servants as well.' The upstairs staff consisted of two house-maids, a parlour-maid, the lady's maid and the butler. 'They're all right but you never know. Better to be safe than sorry.' It wasn't a rule that came easy to Virginia but she had discovered it was necessary for survival.

'Think yourself lucky you've got a job and a decent room to sleep in.'

'What? This horrible cell, you mean?'

'If you saw what I came from, Fanny, you'd think this was a wee palace.'

'Go on,' Fanny scoffed. 'The Gorbals can't be that bad.'

Virginia regretted her words because they could be construed as being disloyal to her parents who were decent, hard-working folk. 'Don't get me wrong,' she said hastily. 'My mum and dad did the best they could. Anything bad about the houses in the Gorbals is the landlords' fault.'

She could understand Fanny's hatred of Mrs Cartwright. She felt the same emotion at the mere thought of the people responsible for the Gorbals slums. Putrid, evil-smelling places that she was sure had been the cause of her sister's death from tuberculosis. She remembered with horror the cramped ground-floor one-room-and-kitchen flat – or 'house' as all tenement dwellings were called in Glasgow. Although it had no bathroom, no inside lavatory, no hot water, her mother worked tirelessly doing her best to keep the place clean. The worst thing to cope with was the common lavatory in the dark tunnel of the close. A damp sickening smell clung everywhere – the room, the kitchen, the close, the lavatory. Her mother tried to ventilate the house by keeping the windows open, even on the coldest days of winter, but nothing made any difference.

'The master seems alright,' Fanny said.

Virginia knew she must mean young Master Cartwright, because Mr Cartwright senior had been away on business since Fanny arrived.

'And how would you know anything about him?'

'I saw him on the stairs when I was taking up the coal this morning.'

'You didn't!' Virginia exclaimed, aghast. It was an iron rule at Hilltop House that downstairs servants must not disturb the family.

'Well, how was I to know he'd be up and about so early?' Fanny's eyes widened with excitement. 'I gave him a smile.'

'You didn't!'

'He smiled back. That's why I thought he seemed alright. Must take after his daddy in looks. He's certainly not ugly like his mammy.'

'All very well for him to smile,' Virginia said. 'He's got plenty to smile about. Not like some folk.'

In actual fact, much the same thing had happened to Virginia only the other day. He had smiled at her but she had not smiled in return. She had lowered her head and bobbed a brief curtsy. 'Easy for him to smile,' she'd thought bitterly, seeing in her mind's eye the difference between his situation and that of her brothers. However, despite her bitterness – or maybe because of it, she couldn't banish his handsome face from her mind. Once, she'd caught a glimpse of him in his smart army uniform. He was training to be an officer. According to the gossip in the kitchen, he had gone into the army rather than into his father's business. However, the parlour-maid insisted that his father wanted him to join the army, and that it was his mother who wanted him to go into the family business.

Nobody was very sure what the family business was, but it meant Mr Cartwright travelling a lot and whatever it was, it certainly made him a lot of money. The lady's maid said that what Mrs Cartwright wanted more than anything was a title, and no amount of money could buy her that. However, she had engineered a friendship with Lady Forbes Linton and encouraged the long-standing friendship between Lady Linton's daughter, Fiona, and her own son, Nicholas. Fiona and Nicholas had been friends since childhood, and the lady's maid said she was sure Mrs Cartwright had set her heart on an eventual marriage between the two young people.

Virginia had once asked Mrs Tompkins, the cook, what Mr Cartwright's business was, but the cook had told her to mind her own business. Virginia had suffered a lot from Mrs Tompkins during the year she had been working in Hilltop House, but it was mostly when Mrs Tompkins was drunk. She was a solid mountain of a woman with the strength of an elephant. Unfortunately she had a weakness for drink and had regular bouts of drunkenness, much to the terror of all the staff, including Mrs Smithers, the house-keeper, and even – Virginia suspected – Mrs Cartwright. The latter kept well clear of the kitchen area during these lapses, discreetly warned no doubt either by the housekeeper or the lady's maid. Had any other member of staff behaved in such an outrageous manner they would have immediately been dis-missed. But thanks to Mrs Tompkins, the mistress was renowned and envied for miles around for her luncheons and dinner parties. If Mrs Cartwright had let Mrs Tompkins go, there would have been plenty of Mrs Cartwright's friends and acquaintances only too ready and willing to snap Mrs Tompkins up. After all, despite her obvious failings, she was a superb cook, even when she was drunk. The other members of staff were not so fortunate, several had been dismissed, and for very minor offences. Mrs Cartwright had a temper, not hot and noisy like cook, but cold and hard as ice.

Virginia kept her head down to avoid any trouble. She had learned how important this was in her last job as a maid of all work in a Glasgow villa. There had been no other staff and, even more than the back-breaking work, it was the isolation and loneliness she experienced there that still haunted her. It had been such a shock after the crowded conditions of her Gorbals home where, day and night, she was never alone. In the villa, she had been expected to do everything, be everything – char-woman, house-maid, nurse, parlour-maid and cook. She never had any help with anything from the daughters of the house, or from the mistress. They were too busy going out shopping, or visiting friends, or playing the piano, or doing cross-stitch or crochet. Virginia had to get up at five o'clock every morning. Every night – usually around midnight – she simply fell into bed aching with exhaustion. All she had to keep her going was looking forward to her one afternoon off a month, although even then she had to be back by ten at night.

Sometimes, by the time she'd cleared the lunch things and washed the dishes, she didn't get away until after two. She suspected the family purposely took longer over their lunch on her afternoon off, just out of spite. She hated them all right. Oh, how glad she'd been to move to Hilltop House. At least she had the company of other servants. She'd hoped to work her way up from kitchen maid to perhaps a parlour-maid, or something in the upstairs staff. But Mrs Tompkins said the mistress would never allow such a thing.

'Why not?' Virginia had asked, 'I'm a hard worker.'

'I know, hen.' Mrs Tompkins replied sympathetically.

She too had dragged herself out of the Gorbals and, when she was sober, their shared background made her feel more kindly towards Virginia than towards the other members of staff. 'But your trouble is you're too nice looking. Mistresses cannae thole a pretty lassie near them. It makes them look bad, you see.'

'I could hide all my hair under my cap.' Virginia had taken it for granted that her hair was the problem. So many people had told her what lovely hair she had, so glossy, such a warm golden colour.

'Och!' Mrs Tompkins shook her head. 'It's no' just your hair, hen. You cannae hide your bonny face. Or these bright blue eyes. And just look at your wee nose compared with the mistress's big beak. No, she'll never let you be seen anywhere near her.'

Virginia wanted to know if all mistresses in big houses were the same about looks. After all, she had no intentions of slaving away in the kitchen and the long dark corridors in the bowels of Hilltop House for the rest of her life if she could avoid it. Perhaps eventually she would be forced to try for a better position in another household.

'Maybe no,' Mrs Tompkins said without

18

conviction. 'It aw depends. If the mistress is young and pretty, she might no' mind sae much, but there's no' likely to be many as bonny as you, hen. You've a real drawback there. Your best bet is to find a decent fella to marry you.'

Most of the female servants, Virginia included, dreamt of escape from drudgery into marriage. Maybe the volatile and gigantic Mrs Tompkins and the prim and petite Mrs Smithers had once nursed such a dream. If they had, their dreams had come to nothing, for although it was the custom to address the cook and the housekeeper as Mrs, neither woman had ever married.

There didn't seem much hope in Hilltop House even for the younger servants. The brief time off once a month didn't give them a chance to meet anyone outside their immediate family. At work the only male employees were the butler who was quite elderly, the chauffeur who was already married, and a gardener who seldom set foot in the big house, except to make sorties into the basement to catch rats.

Fanny hadn't had time to formulate any dreams, at least about marriage. Working in the big house that she'd only glimpsed from a distance through the trees before was still exciting to her. She had no fears for the future. Her only dream was to be rid of her mass of pimples. Her only fear so far was of

Mrs Tompkins who, in her last drunken rage, had hurled a ladle at Fanny. Fanny had just managed to dodge it in time, before taking to her heels. Even so, she had giggled about it afterwards.

'She couldn't hit somebody the same size as herself, far less somebody as fast on their feet as me. Her aim's that rotten, ugly old cow!'

Virginia was thinking of this episode while she was walking in the nearby woods later that day, gathering mushrooms for Mrs Tompkins. It was a warm summer's day and she had taken her starched cap off and let her hair tumble loose over her shoulders. There was no danger of Mrs Cartwright seeing her here. Mrs Cartwright was off in her motor car visiting a friend in Glasgow. Anyway, she would never deign to go near such a wild place as the woods. For one thing she might damage her shoes or get the hem of her dress dirtied. As she strolled along, Virginia began to sing to herself, and to the tall trees and tangle of bushes and colourful wild flowers. Sun dappled the ferns and flowers with a shimmering glow. She felt the heat of the sun bathing her face, slowly melting her cares. The insidious buzzing of insects seemed to carry her mind gently out of herself to drift free as the motes of dust suspended in the golden light. It was wonderful to escape for even a short time from the exhausting rigours of her other tasks.

After a time she stopped singing so that she could listen to the birdsong instead. Then softly singing again, she began to gather more mushrooms. Her fingers scrabbled in the musty smelling earth as she plucked the soft cold stems. Then she brushed off the clinging soil and placed the mushrooms carefully into the basket that she carried over one arm. It was almost full but she intended prolonging her freedom as long as possible.

Suddenly she was startled by a loud clapping. She whirled round and struggled to her feet at the unexpected sight of the young master of the house. Nicholas Cartwright smiled with his eyes as well as his mouth.

'You've a voice as lovely as your face. What is your name?'

Virginia lowered her eyes. 'Virginia Watson, sir.'

'May I walk with you, Virginia? I would appreciate your company.' Virginia thought he must have gone mad. She nodded, unable to think of what else to do, and they began strolling side by side. For a time there was silence, only broken by the faint crunching of their feet on some broken twigs and the melodious song of the birds high among the trees. Virginia took deep breaths of the fragrant air.

At last Cartwright said, 'Have you heard

the news? By the looks of things war is going to be inevitable.'

'Are you sure?' Virginia was surprised and confused by this unexpected pronouncement. All the servants had been talking for weeks about the possibility of war, but surely, she thought, it could not really happen?

He sighed. 'Don't you ever read the newspapers?'

She felt a surge of bitterness and anger. Wasn't it just like someone of his class to be so ignorant of the life she and her fellow servants led.

'Well,' she said, forgetting to sound subservient, 'I don't have much time. I get up at five o'clock in the morning and never stop working until nearly midnight. It's a wonderful treat for me to be allowed out like this. And by the way, I couldn't afford to buy any newspapers for myself.' She nearly allowed her bitterness to run completely away with her and add 'on the pittance of a wage your mother pays me', but she controlled herself in time. As it was her heart had begun to thump with fearful apprehension. She knew her outburst had been more than sufficient to result in her losing her job.

Cartwright stopped walking and turned towards her. 'I'm sorry, Virginia. I've obviously no idea what goes on downstairs. That's my mother's province and in any case I've been away from home for most of my life – from boarding school onwards. Do forgive me.'

She gave him a nervous smile. Clearly, he was mad, but quite nice all the same. 'It's all right,' she said. 'I'd heard rumours about the trouble between us and Germany. Mrs Tompkins is always saying we can't trust the Kaiser, even if he is related to the King.' She paused for a moment, then asked, 'If there is to be a war, does that mean you'll have to go away again?'

Now she noticed that he looked terribly sad. His dark, deep-set eyes were clouded with unhappiness. 'I expect so. If it does happen. The Colonel of my regiment is a real fire-eater – he'll be sure to want his men in the thick of things right from the start. After all, it's what we've been training for, and as an officer and a gentleman it's my duty to fight for my country, whenever the need arises.'

She thought then of her two brothers and felt afraid for them, but surely they wouldn't think their country worth fighting for. What had it ever done for them? They'd had to work like slaves when they had work, and starve when they hadn't.

'Since the Austrian Duke and Duchess were killed by that damned Serb,' Cartwright was saying now, 'I've thought war was pretty much inevitable. The Germans have been looking for any excuse to challenge the

23

British Empire. And now they've got it. God alone knows where it will all end.'

Virginia failed to see why her brothers, or even Nicholas Cartwright, should risk their lives over some foreign duke or duchess in some far away land of which she knew nothing. But she refrained from saying so. Instead, seeing the obvious distress in her companion's face, she impulsively touched his arm and told him earnestly,

'I'll remember you in my prayers tonight. I'll ask that you be kept safe.'

'Oh, Virginia,' he said, and stepped close to her. Before she knew what was happening, he had taken her into his arms. She was too shocked to resist as he held her firmly to him and kissed her, long and tenderly.

2

He held her gently for some time, his head resting down on hers. She felt the heat from his body and the beat of his heart. At first she was fearful and horrified at such an unexpected turn of events. If anyone found out this would certainly cost her her job. She would lose a decent roof over her head, enough food in her belly and the few shillings she was able to give to her mother.

Good jobs weren't easy to come by, especially for a girl who'd been dismissed.

Then, equally unexpectedly, her fear was swamped by tenderness. Poor young man. She drew back a little to gaze up into his face. In his eyes, she could see as he looked down at her that he was just a sensitive human being. His black hair was rumpled, making him appear very young and vulnerable, although she thought he must be at least twenty. She put up a hand and stroked his hair back. 'Shhh,' she soothed as if he was weeping.

'You're very kind, Virginia,' he said. 'I shouldn't be burdening you with my worries. You'll have more than enough of your own to cope with.'

'No, it's all right. I mean, I'm not really working every minute of the time.' She felt guilty about her exaggeration now. There were quiet spells between meals, especially when it was just family meals. Not luncheons and dinners with lots of guests. At quiet moments, she did manage to slip out like this for a wee while. She seldom had to work until midnight in Hilltop House – usually it was just until ten o'clock, sometimes even a bit earlier. It was different for the lady's maid. She always had to wait until the last minute to help Mrs Cartwright undress in the large, stuffy bedroom. A fire had to be lit and kept burning in Mrs Cartwright's bedroom winter and summer, then the lady's maid had to lay out the clothes that Mrs Cartwright chose to wear next morning. After that, she had to fetch the hot cocoa. Mrs Cartwright always liked a cup of hot cocoa in bed.

'I manage to come here quite often, sometimes just for a few minutes, but it's worth it. It's so beautiful and peaceful.'

'Yes,' Nicholas agreed, and he looked around. 'I used to come here as a boy when I was on holiday from school. Sometimes I brought a book and I would sit under one of the trees and read in peace.'

Virginia could guess what lay behind his words – read in peace. Mrs Cartwright had once caught Nessie, one of the house-maids, dipping into a book in Mr Cartwright's library while she was dusting. Mrs Cartwright had been furious and warned Nessie that if she was caught reading any of the books ever again, she would be instantly dismissed. Her final comment on the matter – 'Books are not for reading!' – was the source of great hilarity when Nessie later re-enacted the scene for the benefit of the other below-stairs staff.

'Isn't that jist like that wuman!' Mrs Tompkins said to Mrs Smithers. 'Books are jist for dustin', accordin' tae her. For aw her airs and graces, that wuman's pig ignorant.'

The pinched sallow features of Mrs

26

Smithers had warmed at this. 'Now, now, Mrs Tompkins, I can't allow you to speak of the mistress in those insulting terms, especially in front of the staff.'

It was fortunate that Mrs Tompkins had been sober at the time. Otherwise she wouldn't have allowed Mrs Smithers to remain vertical.

Virginia could quite easily imagine Mrs Cartwright seeing her son's interest in reading as a wicked waste of time. It was a miracle that Nicholas Cartwright had turned out as well as he had. His mother was a cold, domineering woman. Obviously not everyone who was an only child was spoiled and smothered with love. Virginia couldn't imagine Mrs Cartwright ever showing the slightest affection to her son.

Nor could she understand how any mother could banish a young child of seven to the austere regime of a typical English boarding school. Virginia hadn't been at Hilltop House in those days, but Mrs Tompkins had and she told her how Nicholas had been sent away to England.

'To England of all places, and him jist a wee laddie of six or seven. He used to slip down here to the kitchen when his mammy was oot, I'd give him one of my home-made biscuits and we'd have a wee blether. He came to say goodbye to me, the wee soul, before he was sent away. He was always that

27

polite, a perfect wee gentleman.'

Lucky him, Virginia had thought at the time. Plenty of books and marvellous food and comfortable rooms at a place of learning. One of the best in Britain. How her beloved brothers, self-educated and well-read thanks to books borrowed from the public library, would have relished the chance of such advantages in life.

'Do you mind if we sit down for a few minutes?' Nicholas asked. 'This is such a lovely spot.'

It seemed very odd to have one of the Cartwrights (or anyone) treat her like a lady and ask her permission to do something, instead of ordering her. It made Virginia feel good and secretly grateful to Nicholas Cartwright for the experience.

She sat down on the soft, sweet-smelling grass, laid her basket of mushrooms aside and tidied her dress over her legs and feet. He sat beside her, stretching out his long legs and leaning back against the tree. He remained in thoughtful silence for a few minutes before saying,

'I probably shouldn't have gone into the army, you know. Of course I'll be glad of the opportunity, if it comes, to serve my country. But I've come to the conclusion – rather too late unfortunately – that Sandhurst and an army career was not the right choice for me.'

'What would you rather be doing?'

He hesitated. 'Don't laugh.' He gave a short laugh of embarrassment.

'I won't laugh, I promise.'

'I'd like to be a poet, or at least some sort of writer.'

'But that's wonderful,' Virginia cried out in genuine delight. She'd always had a great admiration for writers. Not that she'd ever known one personally, but oh, how she'd always loved reading. And how she treasured books. Her Auntie Sarah, who had married an office worker and was comparatively well off, had given her a book of poetry on her fifth birthday. On her sixth, she'd presented her with a copy of *Robinson Crusoe*. On her seventh, she'd received *Treasure Island*. Every year until Auntie Sarah died, she'd given Virginia a book on her birthday. Sometimes it was a slim volume of poetry, sometimes a novel. Sometimes even a play. Virginia had been enchanted by writers as varied as Balzac, Jane Austen, Shakespeare, the Brontes, Dickens and Dostoevsky. She'd especially enjoyed reading the biographies of writers. All the books that Auntie Sarah had given her were second hand, and some of them very dog-eared. Probably Auntie Sarah had picked them up from one of the barrows in Clyde Street but what did that matter? They were wonderful books and her most prized possessions. She'd be forever grateful to her

Auntie Sarah for opening up such a magic world to her.

In between birthdays, she was a regular visitor to the public library. It was only since she'd left school to go to work at the Glasgow villa that she no longer had time to go to the library or even to read her own books.

'Do you really think it's so wonderful?' Nicholas asked.

'Of course I do. What have you written so far?'

'Oh, only a few poems. I shouldn't think they're very good. But I've started work on a novel. It's not easy finding the time to get on with it. Especially now. Perhaps if things clear up and the war doesn't last long, then I'll resign from the army and really give it a go.' He gave a short laugh again. 'Although my mother and father won't like it.'

'You mustn't listen to them,' Virginia cried out passionately. 'It's your life and it's your duty to make the most of the talent that God gave you.'

'Don't worry, I'm going to write no matter what anyone says.' He smiled. 'Although I'll probably end up starving in a garret – that's if the Kaiser and his Generals ever give me the chance!'

'I'd love to read something you've written.'

'Do you really mean that?'

'Of course I do.'

His eyes immediately lost their sad,

resigned look. Virginia's enthusiasm seemed to have raised his spirits and filled him with a new optimism.

'I'll give you a couple of poems as soon as we get home.'

It was then that Virginia realised that for a short but magical interlude, they had been in a world of their own. Now that moment had come to an end.

'Heavens, do you want me to be dismissed? If your mother or anyone else saw us together...'

'I'm sorry. I see what you mean. I don't want you to get into any trouble on my account.'

Virginia brightened again. 'Perhaps if you left your poems discreetly somewhere where I could collect them later without anyone seeing.'

He brightened too. 'Good idea. How about under that big Chinese vase in the hall?'

'That would be too difficult for me. I don't often get the chance of going anywhere near the main hallway, but there's a bowl of pot pourri just near the door that leads to the servants' quarters. That would be easier.'

'Splendid. That's what I'll do then. I'll do it right away.'

'I'll run back first.' Virginia struggled to her feet. 'You wait here for a few minutes.'

It didn't seem a bit odd any more to talk to him as an equal. She believed, strange as

31

it might seem to anyone else – either of his class or hers, that they were friends now, no longer master and servant. She turned to wave to him before starting to run, her fair hair streaming out behind her, the basket bobbing on her arm.

'Virginia, wait!' Nicholas called. 'When will I see you again?'

She stopped in her tracks and thought for a minute. 'I'll try to manage tomorrow at the same time. After we get all the lunch things cleared up, cook goes to her room for a rest.'

'Same place?'

'Yes, and I'll tell you what I think of your poems.'

'Oh God!' Nicholas groaned. 'I hope you won't be too hard on me.'

She laughed. 'Don't be silly.' Then off she flew, feeling so happy she could have soared up through the summer's air like a bird. She longed to tell somebody – everybody – all about her exciting experience but at the same time, she wanted to hug it to herself, to cherish it and share it with no-one.

She had also acquired an intense feeling of loyalty to Nicholas Cartwright and that alone would prevent her confiding in anyone.

Just in time as she neared the back of the house, she remembered to pin up her long hair and tuck it under the starched cap that she'd been carrying in the bib of her apron. She tidied her apron and her dress and took a deep breath, and walked sedately the rest of the way.

Soon she was descending into the kitchen via a basement back door. It led down into long, dark and airless corridors. Off the warren of corridors was the larder, cool and dank with a floor of brick and shelves of slate. There were also doors leading to the living quarters of the butler, the housekeeper, and the cook. There were also the still room, the wine cellar and some other store rooms. These dark cellars were infested by beetles, cockroaches and mice. Too often there were rats as well. It was the terror of Virginia's life, as well as Fanny's, to scrub the floors down there. The butler's room, the housekeeper's room and the cook's room were up a few steps at the other end of a passage near the kitchen, and they at least had the benefit of more light, but even those rooms did not escape the occasional infestation of cockroaches. The gardener was called in from time to time to help in the fight against the rats. He was the only one who could boast of some success in the ongoing battle with these relentless vermin.

Virginia helped prepare the vegetables for the evening meal, then she and Fanny washed the pots and pans in the scullery. After that, they tackled the hundred and one other jobs, including washing the dishes that were brought down from the dining room, though knives and silver were cleaned in the butler's pantry. Up to their elbows in soap suds, they were sweating by this time. The hot water and the steam billowing up from the deep wooden sink added to their discomfort.

Despite the irritation of her clothes sticking wetly to her skin and the strands of hair escaping down over her face, Virginia still felt happy and excited. She could hardly wait for an opportunity to slip upstairs and collect the poems.

But every now and again – despite the heat, despite the excitement – she shivered. She was all too well aware of the danger of the situation, and of what would certainly happen to her if she was caught.

3

They met every day, sometimes very early in the morning when the wood was sparkling with dew and the sunlight was just beginning to filter through the high branches overhead. Sometimes they met late at night when they could barely see each other, with only the moon's pale gleam to light their path. If it was early in the morning, Fanny covered for her as best she could, even suffering the terrors of being alone down on her hands and knees scrubbing the warren of dark basement passageways, with scrapings and scurryings threatening her from every shadowy corner.

Virginia had spun a tale to her about secret meetings with a lover, knowing that Fanny would never in a million years guess that it was Nicholas Cartwright she was meeting. Fanny was grateful for any excitement to break the monotony of her working days. Virginia had also promised to read Fanny a story every night from one of her books. Most times, luck was with Virginia and she didn't need Fanny's help. When cook was having her afternoon nap, it was possible to race through any jobs she'd been left to do and then slip out, and away. What made it easier was the lack of lunches and the resulting pile of dishes and pots and pans to be washed. Mr Cartwright was still away on business, although he was expected back very soon. Mrs Cartwright was taking advantage of his absence by dining out with friends in Glasgow and indulging her passion for shopping. The chauffeur kept carrying in piles of boxes containing expensive outfits, hats and furs, all of which caused the lady's maid extra work. Not that Mrs Cartwright would give a thought to that.

Virginia quickly became accustomed to leading a double life. One part – the most important part – was so beautiful she could hardly believe it to be true. Each time she saw Nicholas waiting for her, it was like another miracle. Each time he came towards her, hands outstretched, eyes eager, she ran joyfully towards him. He always brought poems and they earnestly and enthusiastically discussed them. She could see that with each poem he was improving, and told him so. The first poem had been short and clever. He called it a 'haiku', which he said was a Japanese form of poetry. It all sounded very exotic and romantic, and she listened attentively as he read.

Milk's last droplet stains
Forgiven, the past is past
But not forgotten.

Later he began producing more personal poems and she liked them better. She remembered what Coleridge had said: 'What comes from the heart goes to the heart.'

She told Nicholas this too. He said she was his inspiration and his encouragement. He said he owed everything to her. This was despite the fact that she often criticised his work and he hotly defended it. They had many lively, sometimes quite noisy arguments. Then she'd feel guilty and remind him that after all, she'd never written any poetry herself.

'What do I know?' she told him. 'Don't pay any attention to me.'

'Nonsense, you're a wonderful critic. You do know what you're talking about and I value your opinion.'

He wrote,

Cup your hands gently
Keep warm the cradle of skin
Within rests my heart.

Whenever she could she would fly to meet him in their secret place in the woods. He would catch her and joyfully whirl her round and round while she squealed with laughter.

One of his poems was entitled 'You'.

Your laughter tickles
  my ears
Your smiles caress
  my eyes
Your joy fills
  my heart
Your words touch
  my soul
You have the essence
  of an angel
The touch
  of a butterfly
The spirit
  of a tigress.

Every moment she could manage, she reread her own treasured books of poetry. She wanted so desperately to be able to help Nicholas, as well as to enjoy informed discussions with him. Once Mrs Tompkins caught her sitting in the kitchen shelling peas but with a book on a chair beside her, on which she was concentrating more than on the job in hand. Mrs Tompkins promptly hit her over the head with the book with such force it caused immediate dizziness and then a throbbing headache for the rest of the day. However she forgot about the pain as soon as she saw Nicholas.

By now she felt as if she'd known him all her life. She knew of his boyhood loneliness as if she'd suffered it herself. She knew about his hated boarding school as if she'd been there with him, hating it too. She saw the military college, heard the shouted commands. Viewed the immaculately uniformed cadets in her mind's eye, thanks to Nicholas's wonderful talent for description. She also knew that the lifelong ambition of his parents was for him to marry Lady Fiona Forbes Linton, the daughter of a wealthy titled friend of Mr Cartwright's. Lady Fiona and her parents had been regular guests at the Cartwrights' luncheons and dinner parties, and the Cartwrights were regular guests at the Forbes Lintons' stately home.

But Virginia didn't want to think about that.

'You should be writing your novel,' she told Nicholas. 'You're going to be a famous novelist one day. I feel sure of it.'

'Darling,' he said softly, and she could see the love in his eyes.

It was then for the first time that she realised she loved him too. He kissed her gently – on her brow, on her cheek, in the curve of her neck, on her lips. She responded with a passion she had not realised she was capable of. In bed that night, after Fanny was safely asleep, Virginia wept. She knew that any normal and lasting relationship between the son of such a wealthy family and the kitchen maid was impossible. It would never be countenanced, either by his parents or his class, or indeed by her family or her class. Neither she nor Nicholas voiced this reality. It went without saying. They simply went on being happy in their own secret world where nothing or no-one mattered except each other.

Then war was declared and everything changed. For Virginia, though, the outbreak of war was a dim worry compared with the immediate terror she faced. She had missed a period, something that had never happened before. She had never been even a day late since her periods started when she was twelve years of age. She knew she was pregnant.

At first she didn't say anything to Nicholas. She tried to blot the knowledge out of her mind. It was too dreadful – too disastrous – to contemplate. She was plunged into a nightmare of apprehension and terror. If Mrs Cartwright found out she was pregnant, she would immediately dismiss her. She would think that the father would be some other ne'er-do-well servant. If she knew the truth, she would throw Virginia out without a halfpenny of her wages and make sure she never got a job anywhere else. Virginia had always been a good hard worker, but she could well imagine Mrs Cartwright giving her the reputation of a lazy, immoral slut to all her friends and acquaintances. There would be no limits to Mrs Cartwright's malice.

The workhouse loomed large in Virginia's mind. It was what every person she'd ever known dreaded beyond anything. She vividly remembered how the anxiety of it had haunted her grandmother. It was the reason her mother had struggled to keep Granny with the family in the room and kitchen in the Gorbals until the day she died in the set-in-the-wall bed in the kitchen. Granny had shared the bed with her mother, herself and her sister Rose. Rose used to take bouts of coughing in the middle of the night. One night, Virginia had got up to fetch her a cup of water when she suddenly became aware of how still and cold Granny was. The main thing she felt was relief that the old lady had died safely in bed with her family. They all thanked God that she had escaped the workhouse.

The day before Nicholas left to join his regiment, he gave Virginia a poem to keep. The beauty of it overwhelmed her.

It was entitled 'To my Mentor'.

Here within your bridge of feathers
I bathe in your mind's lambant light.

We soar the skies together
Glide on a cloud of thought,
Ride a current of fascination.

You, sometimes pushing
Always eager
Never harsh.

I feel the warm air
Lift my feathers
And pray that I prove

Deserving
Of the strain
Of your sweat.

'It's beautiful,' she said. 'Thank you, Nicholas. I'll always treasure it.' Then she wept broken-heartedly.

'Please don't,' he pleaded. 'They say the war will be over by Christmas. I'll be back in no time.'

'It's not just that,' she sobbed. She did not want to tell him of her fears for herself – it seemed so selfish when he was marching off perhaps to his death. But she found herself blurting out the truth. 'I'm pregnant, and once it begins to show, your mother will throw me out and I won't know what to do or where to go. I can't go home and be an extra burden to my family. They're nearly starving as it is.'

There was a silence while he held her close and stroked her hair. Then he said, 'I'll tell my mother the truth and say that she must allow you to stay at Hilltop House as long as you wish.'

'Oh no, you mustn't.' Virginia pushed him away in alarm. 'She mustn't know it's you. She'd be furious at me. She'd send me packing immediately.'

'I'll insist on it, Virginia. Then when I return, we'll work something out. I won't allow you to suffer in any way on my account.'

She was collapsing inside as if she was already bereft and alone. She realised that despite everything they had shared, he had no understanding of her life, her world. He had no conception of the harsh and cruel reality that awaited her. They said their goodbyes before returning separately to the house in their usual way.

'It won't be for long,' Nicholas said. 'We'll see each other again soon.'

But she knew that their magic world had gone for ever. She saw his future quite clearly and it wasn't with a kitchen maid from the Gorbals. It would be Fiona Forbes Linton waving him off on the train the next day, and it would be Fiona waiting at the station for him when he returned. Virginia accepted his future life with Fiona and she knew Nicholas did too. It was only right and proper. It certainly did not make her love him any less. She would always wish him every happiness and fulfilment.

That night, her day's work over, she climbed the dark winding stairs to the top of the house. She looked at the attic's grey distempered walls, the bare floor boards, the chipped wash basin, and she knew that this would be the last night she would spend here. Mrs Cartwright would wait until Nicholas was safely away and then she would summon her.

Virginia went down on her knees at the side of her bed and prayed to God for mercy. Fanny arrived while she was still down on her knees.

'Oh sorry,' Fanny whispered, putting an apologetic palm against her mouth. 'I didn't mean to interrupt your prayers.'

'It's all right,' Virginia said, rising. 'I'm finished.' There was an ominous ring to the words. She immediately resented their wider implication. She'd be damned if she'd let somebody like Mrs Cartwright finish her off. She wasn't finished by a long chalk.

Her mouth hardened as she climbed into the high lumpy bed.

'Good night, Fanny,' she said. Then she closed her eyes and began mustering enough courage to face the coming day.

4

The day was not made any easier by the cook getting drunk. Thankfully she had still been reasonably sober when all the staff were lined up in the driveway to curtsy and wave goodbye to Nicholas. In the motor car sat Mr and Mrs Cartwright, Nicholas and Fiona. Mrs Cartwright and Fiona were splendidly attired. Mrs Cartwright wore a huge-brimmed, black velvet hat trimmed with large, curling feathers, a high-necked white blouse and a tailor-made costume in striped suiting. Fiona's black straw hat had a tiny brim but was piled high at the crown with bows of pink ribbon. Her tunic dress was of grey silk but the upper bodice of sheer grey fabric revealed a pink under-bodice. Mr Cartwright was his usual sober self in a dark suit and waistcoat, wing-collared shirt and bowler hat. Nicholas was resplendent in his officer's uniform.

As all the servants waved and called 'Good luck, sir', Nicholas smiled and raised a hand in return. None of the others deigned even to glance in the direction of the servants. The motor car gradually disappeared down the long drive between the avenue of trees. The servants turned back into the house. Proto-col was temporarily abandoned because of the stress of the parting with the most popular member of the family. Upstairs and downstairs servants sat together in the kitchen for a comforting cup of tea. All of them, except Virginia, shared their memories of Nicholas. The butler even remembered Nicholas as a baby and toddler. He recalled Miss Kane who had been Nicholas's nanny. The old man shook his head.

'Very severe, she was. Never liked that woman. God alone knows what the poor wee lad suffered, locked up alone with her in that nursery.'

'Sheila knew,' Mrs Tompkins moaned. 'Remember Sheila, the nursery maid. Oh, the tales she used to tell me!' Mrs Tompkins began to weep copiously – the drink often had that effect on her – and wiped at her heavy-jowled face with her apron. 'Aw, the

45

poor laddie. Aw, the poor wee soul.'

Mrs Smithers tutted. 'He's hardly a wee boy any more, Mrs Tompkins. He's a grown man of over six feet tall.'

'Aw, shut up, ya wee nyaff.' Mrs Tompkins growled, as she continued to drown her sorrows with yet another drink. 'He'll always be a wee boy tae me. That's how I'll always remember him.'

Mrs Smithers' small mouth tightened with anger and disapproval, not about Mrs Tompkins drinking – she was well used to that, but at the insulting reference to herself in front of the other servants. It was essential in the disciplined running of any establishment for the staff to have respect for the housekeeper. Being called a wee nyaff did nothing to help Mrs Smithers in her already difficult task. She hesitated, unsure whether to give Mrs Tompkins an immediate reprimand or wait for a more suitable moment when the cook was sober. She decided on the latter, and instead turned on the upstairs maids.

'Don't just stand there. Get upstairs at once and get on with your duties.'

She followed them smartly from the kitchen and left Fanny and Virginia at the mercy of Mrs Tompkins. The butler, fearing one of Mrs Tompkins' drunken rages, had hastened to his own room as quickly as his tottery legs could carry him. For most of the servants, there wasn't much to do just now as Mr and Mrs Cartwright and Fiona were dining in Glasgow after seeing Nicholas off at the Central Station. Then the Cartwrights were taking Fiona home to Campsie Castle. They were due to return in the late afternoon in time to dress for dinner. Already the lady's maid would be laying out the clothes and jewellery Mrs Cartwright had said she wished to wear that evening.

Mrs Tompkins was singing now, or bawling more like, as she staggered dangerously about the kitchen with a long knife, in preparation for cutting some chops. 'Ae fond kiss and then we sever, Ae farweel and then for ever, Deep in heart wrung tears I'll pledge thee, Warring sighs and groans I'll wage thee.'

Virginia couldn't bear it. She went through to the scullery where Fanny was shakily peeling potatoes. Fanny whispered to Virginia, 'I don't like the look of her with that knife.'

Too distressed to speak, Virginia nodded agreement and went through to the larder to fetch the milk that cook would need to make the custard. As soon as she arrived back in the kitchen with the big cold jug clutched in her hands, cook bawled,

'What the hell do you think you're doing?'

'You said you wanted it for the custard.'

Keeping a safe distance from the table

47

where cook was hacking at the chops with the knife, Virginia placed the jug on the dresser that stood against the far wall.

'Can you no' see, you idiot, that I'm no' nearly ready to make the custard. That milk'll be sour wi' the heat of this place before I'm ready for it. Can you no' do anything right, you glaikit wee idiot.'

Normally Virginia, like all the other servants, would have kept silent, even agreed with Mrs Tompkins, no matter what she said. Anything to try to placate her and escape a worse fate than just being called names. Today, however, Virginia knew she was going to be dismissed anyway. She had nothing to lose. She didn't care what Mrs Tompkins said or did. Mrs Tompkins couldn't make her suffer any more than she was suffering now.

'Don't you call me an idiot. I've more intelligence than you. I don't drink myself stupid, for a start.'

For a couple of seconds, Mrs Tompkins was stunned into silence. Then with a roar like a stampeding elephant, she lurched enraged towards Virginia, wildly stabbing at the air with her knife, her white cap tipping sideways over one ear. Virginia dodged out of the way, the knife missing her by inches. She felt the cold air of the blade and the smell of the blood from the chops.

'I'll kill you,' the enraged Mrs Tompkins

yelled. 'Stand still, you impertinent wee bisom.'

The two house-maids appeared briefly in the kitchen doorway before hastily retreating again. At each lunge, Virginia was too quick for the older and much heavier woman who eventually ran out of puff. Her huge bulk collapsed defeated into a chair, making it give a high pitched squeal of protest. Virginia lifted the jug of milk and took it back to the larder.

In the scullery, a chalk-faced Fanny said, 'Have you gone mad?'

Virginia shrugged and began helping Fanny to prepare the first lot of vegetables. As soon as they were peeled and cut, Fanny nervously carried them through to the kitchen, before retreating back to the scullery again. The icy water in the wooden sink had turned Virginia's hands red with the cold but she wasn't aware of the discomfort. She was thinking once cook either dozed off in her chair, or went to her room for a nap, she would go up the back stairs to the attic and pack her tin trunk. Then all she'd have to do was collect it, put on her coat and slip away. She didn't want to answer questions from any of the servants, or face the ordeal of a tearful goodbye from Fanny. They had become good friends, almost like sisters. They'd miss each other. Virginia had decided she had no choice but to go home to the

Gorbals. She'd make some excuse for being dismissed. Then she'd try and find another job, maybe in a factory. Hopefully it would be months before her pregnancy would show and by that time, perhaps she'd manage to save some money.

She didn't dare contemplate ending up in the workhouse hospital. She'd heard dreadful stories about how poor girls had been mistreated there and their babies taken from them. Virginia was determined to keep her baby. She didn't know how she could possibly manage it, but manage it she must. The baby was all she had left of Nicholas. She dreamt it would be a boy with Nicholas's dark eyes and black hair and gentle smile.

Eventually, when she and Fanny ventured back to the kitchen, it was to discover that somehow Mrs Tompkins had managed to prepare a big pot of soup, as well as the chops which lay on a platter waiting to be put under the grill. A steam pudding in a bowl covered with a cloth tied over the top was in a large pot of simmering water on the hob. Mrs Tompkins was nowhere to be seen.

Fanny gave a sigh of relief. 'Thank God. How about a cup of tea? The kettle's on the boil.'

'You go ahead and make it,' Virginia said. 'I've to go upstairs and do something. I'll be back in a few minutes.'

'Oh aye?' Fanny's pimply face broke into a

sly grin. 'Meeting that lover of yours again, eh?'

'Upstairs, I said, not outside.'

'All right, all right, there's no need to snap at me.'

'I'm sorry, Fanny. My nerves are a bit shattered. Mrs Tompkins nearly made mincemeat of me. It's lucky I'm so quick on my feet.'

'I know.' Fanny agreed. 'For pity's sake, don't do that to me again. I was afraid you'd had it and I'd be left on my own with her.'

'I'll be back down in a few minutes,' Virginia repeated.

The attic was ice-cold in comparison with the stifling heat of the kitchen, where the 'Black Eagle' cooking range kept the whole room like a furnace. Virginia hastily flung her few possessions into her tin trunk and laid her coat and hat on the bed. The trunk would be awkward to carry but not heavy. It was with a heavy heart, though, that she returned downstairs to join Fanny in the stone-floored kitchen.

Fanny had two cups out on the table and tea already poured. A couple of biscuits balanced on each saucer.

Virginia smiled. 'Good job cook's asleep.'

They weren't allowed biscuits. Biscuits were for the family or for Mrs Tompkins and Mrs Smithers when they were on good terms and having a cup of tea together at the end of the day. Often the butler joined them. Being very elderly (nobody knew his exact age) he sometimes dozed off in the middle of their tea party. Mrs Tompkins and Mrs Smithers would sadly shake their heads. It was a miracle to them how he hadn't been dismissed long ago. Every day they expected him to be made homeless. He had no family and nowhere to go.

Mrs Tompkins said, 'Not that Mrs Cartwright would give a thought to that.'

Mrs Smithers pursed her lips and refused to utter a disloyal word about her mistress, but it was obvious that she agreed. Virginia guessed that the reason the old butler remained was the fact that he knew his job inside out and was still useful to the Cartwrights. No doubt he had been paid the same wage for many years. If he was dismissed, or 'let go' as it was sometimes politely put, Mrs Cartwright would have to pay a younger man much more.

Fanny chattered non-stop in between gulps of tea and mouthfuls of biscuit about how lovely she'd thought the hats and dresses of Mrs Cartwright and Lady Fiona were, and how smart the gentlemen looked, especially Master Nicholas.

Eventually, Virginia warned, 'Shh, I think I hear Mrs Tompkins moving about.' Immediately they both scrambled up to rinse their dishes and sweep away the tell-tale crumbs.

They had just finished in time when a bleary-eyed Mrs Tompkins appeared.

'They'll soon be wanting their dinner,' she said. 'Where's Maisie hiding herself now? I hope she's got that table set ready.' Mrs Tompkins had obviously forgotten her rage and the cause of it. Such lapses of memory were quite common with her. They had barely started on their various jobs when a breathless Maisie appeared.

'You'll never guess,' she cried out excitedly to Mrs Tompkins, 'who Madam wants to speak to in the drawing room?'

'Who?'

'Virginia.'

She turned to Virginia. 'What on earth have you done? Madam's in one of her furies. I can always tell.'

Virginia didn't reply but on an impulse she turned to Fanny and gave her an affectionate hug before leaving the kitchen. Going upstairs to the main part of the house, she steeled herself for what was to come.

Virginia entered the lofty-ceilinged drawing room. It had plush buttoned chairs and sofas, the panelled walls were covered with heavy, gold-framed paintings, a variety of tables were scattered around and the tops were cluttered with small ornaments and larger vases. Blinds were half drawn at every window, which had curtains looped and festooned about them. Virginia's feet sank

53

into the richly coloured carpet and made her think bitterly of the bare boards of the attic rooms. She faced Mrs Cartwright with dignity. The older woman's eyes glittered with hatred and disgust. 'You know why you're here.'

'Yes.'

'Yes, Madam.'

Virginia kept silent.

'How dare you!' Mrs Cartwright was even more enraged at this impertinent lack of respect. 'You will leave this house immediately. Immediately, do you hear? And I can assure you that I will see that you are never allowed to work in any other decent household.'

'Yes, you would do that, wouldn't you. Well, I would not want to work for such an ignorant and spiteful woman anyway.'

'You ... you...!' Mrs Cartwright was spluttering with rage now. She looked as if she might have a stroke.

With as much dignity as she could muster, Virginia said 'Goodbye,' and walked unhurriedly from the room.

5

Virginia collected her tin trunk and instead of going down the back stairs to the basement, along the passageways and out the back way, she went through the green baize door and into the main hall. She was still in her reckless, rebellious mood. Awkwardly clutching her trunk, she gazed at the wide carpeted stair and the ornate gas lamps that brightened them every evening. No dark, unlit stairs for the Cartwrights to find their way up and down. These stairs branched out on either side at the top of an oak panelled gallery hung with gloomy paintings of the family and their ancestors.

Virginia now saw all this for what it really was – the Cartwrights trying to ape aristocracy like the Forbes Lintons. The Forbes Lintons *had* illustrious ancestors, the Cartwrights had not. The Cartwrights, however, had money, something that perhaps the Forbes Lintons envied. A surge of hatred engulfed Virginia. What had the Cartwrights, or indeed the Forbes Lintons, done to deserve such a luxurious way of life. It was people like her father and her brothers – who slaved for wealthy people like these – who created their wealth. It was people like herself, slaving in the homes of such people who allowed them to enjoy lives of ease and comfort, and all the time the working class led lives filled with anxiety, poverty, ill-health and constant drudgery. Trembling with the unexpected strength of her emotion, Virginia turned away and left by the front door.

Outside she took one last look at the imposing mansion. She would never see it again. Nor did she want to. Hitching the tin trunk up to balance on her hip, she made her way down the drive and began the long walk to Glasgow. Mrs Cartwright, as she'd expected, had not given her a penny of the wages she was owed and so she had no money to pay for her fare to the city. For miles she tramped along between fields full of butterflies that settled and vanished when the sun went behind a cloud. Every now and again she sat down for a rest and listened to the robins and the wrens until their hectic twitterings encouraged her on once more.

During the night, there had been a nip of frost but now it was a balmy September day. Virginia was thankful for the weather. Had it been in the middle of winter, she might have perished on the journey – or so she imagined. It had been bad enough suffering the winter in the attic. She well remembered rising shivering each morning, then trying to wash in water that had a layer of ice on top of the jug, with the face flannel frozen solid. Then a hurried breakfast of tea and a slice of meat left over from the Cartwrights' dinner from the previous night, and a piece of bread.

Bitterness overcame her again when she thought of the different world Mrs Cartwright awakened to. The house-maids would trudge up and down the stairs with hot water for my lady's bath. The lady's maid would give Mrs Cartwright a cup of tea in bed, and after Mrs Cartwright had had her bath, the maid would help her to dress and do her hair. Mrs Cartwright, and Mr Cartwright if he was at home, and any guests who happened to be staying, would linger over a delicious breakfast – a choice of bacon and eggs, kidneys, cutlets, boiled chicken, omelettes and fish, according to their taste. Plus as much bread, toast, rolls, butter, honey and jam as they desired.

While the family gorged themselves, the maids would be struggling up the stairs with heavy buckets of coal to light the upstairs fires. Rumpled beds had to be made, baths cleaned. Chamber pots had to be covered with a cloth and carried discreetly down the back stairs to be emptied, to avoid offending the sensitivities of the very people who had filled them. Carpets had to be swept, furniture and ornaments dusted, every pane of glass and every mirror polished until they sparkled.

Virginia glanced down at her hands. They were red and roughened by the amount of scrubbing she'd had to do. She thought of the soft white hands of Mrs Cartwright and Fiona and all the pampered women like them, and the hatred in her heart kept her going and saved her from fainting with exhaustion.

She did sit down for a few minutes when she reached Kirkintilloch. It was a small town that went back to the time of the Romans. She gazed at the old parish church with its crow-stepped gables, and was tempted to go in and pray for help and strength, but she could pray just as well sitting here. She closed her eyes but found prayer impossible in the midst of the bitter turmoil of her emotions. There was nothing for it but to continue on her journey using only her determination and willpower to push forward one foot after another.

It was dark by the time she reached the city of Glasgow. Buildings menaced her on each side with their towering blackness. The gas lamps gave a feeble pool of ghostly light. A man was singing in a drunken moan, 'Keep the home fires burning...'

It reminded Virginia of the war and of Nicholas. Quickly she banished him from her mind. It was too painful to think of him.

At last she reached the Gorbals and Cumberland Street. Almost weeping with relief, she stopped inside the close. All the closes led up to the various flats on each of the three landings and also through to the communal back court, or yard, in which the shared wash houses and middens were situated. Her parents and brothers would be in bed asleep by now, and although she didn't relish the idea of waking the household she had no choice. If the close had been warm and dry, she might have sat down on her trunk, and leaning back against the door, tried to get some sleep until morning. But a cold wind was funnelling through from the street, making her shiver miserably.

She pulled the door bell, then rattled the letterbox for good measure. She listened. There was only the loud snorting and whistling sound of her father snoring. Then a clatter of sound and a cacophony of voices started outside. Virginia knew it must be the bin men but she went to look out the back close. Sure enough there they were in the back yard with candles strapped round their heads and flickering over their brows. String tied round each leg below the knee prevented rats or mice running up their trousers. They were heaving bins onto their backs and trudging out with them to their cart.

Virginia retreated back to pull the door bell again. This time she heard movement inside the house. As expected, it was her mother who came to the door. Her father and her brothers were heavy sleepers but her mother slept fitfully, and sometimes had to get up during the night and make herself a cup of tea in the hope it would settle her. Virginia remembered this from the time she shared the kitchen bed with her mother, and Granny, and sister Rose.

Her mother peeped round the door, then gasped at the sight of her. 'Virginia, come away in, hen. What on earth are you doing out at this time of night?' Clutching her grey shawl over her white cotton nightdress, she stood aside to allow Virginia to enter. It only took them a few steps to cross the shoebox of a hall into the kitchen. The hall had a row of hooks on the wall facing the outside door, suspended from which were a shabby collection of men's jackets and dungarees. The kitchen itself wasn't much bigger than the hall. From the edge of the built-in coal bunker and dresser to the fireplace was only a few feet. And from the sink at the window to the edge of the hole-in-the-wall bed measured only a few more feet. In the centre of this small area was crowded a wooden table, four wooden chairs and an armchair on either side of the fireplace. As a result there was hardly any floor space in which to move around.

Janette Watson lit the gas mantle above the fireplace, then turned it down low so that the light wouldn't disturb her sleeping husband. Then just to make doubly sure, she tugged one of the bed curtains further along to shield his face. After giving the fire a poke to bring it to life, she placed the kettle on to it.

'It was boiling just a wee while ago, it won't take a minute,' she whispered to Virginia. 'What happened? Are you all right?'

'Just tired,' Virginia said. 'I was dismissed. She never even gave me my wages and I've had to walk all that way.'

Janette eased the poker in and out of the fire again. 'It won't be long. You'll feel better after a cup of tea.' She fetched the teapot and lifted the tin caddy down from the fireplace.

'Don't you want to know why?'

'In your own time, hen.'

'I was impertinent.'

'Oh dear!' Janette's sigh betrayed her fear that this was bound to happen some day. Virginia had always been a spirited child.

'Well, she was a horrible woman. Nobody liked her.'

Janette nearly added, 'Even so, hen, she was the mistress,' but thought better of it.

Virginia had taken after her father, Tam Watson, as indeed had her brothers. Like most of the country, they used to be good Liberals, but gradually first Tam, then the boys, then Virginia, had developed an angry independent spirit and become socialists.

61

They'd even turned away from God and the church – at least Tam and the boys had. Janette partly blamed too much reading – and all the meetings and classes Tam went to, run by firebrands like John Maclean. Tam even went to meetings on Sunday afternoons. Now the boys attended them as well.

It wasn't that she didn't believe in education. She'd had a good education herself. She'd left school when she was twelve but her parents had always had books in the house and encouraged her to read. She enjoyed reading, but nice romantic or Christian stories. For one thing, she was far too tired with scrubbing out pubs and halls all day to be able to burden her mind with all this socialist stuff, although Tam kept on pushing high-brow books on her. She had to admit that she did enjoy some of them – but only if they were novels. Not the serious political stuff that he was so fond of. Tam had stuffed the boys' heads with wild ideas he'd got from books like *Merry England* by Robert Blatchford – which he claimed was 'the best introduction to socialism there is'. He'd even got hold of a copy of something called *Das Kapital* – a dreary-looking volume which remained, unread and gathering dust, on the mantleshelf.

Janette never objected, except in a gentle way, about Tam's worrying drift away from the church. It wasn't so much his turning away from church attendance and his criticism of priests and ministers that worried her. It wasn't even his sincerely held views about the unfair distribution of wealth – she knew as well as anyone that it was an unfair world, and when you lived in the Gorbals such an idea hardly came as a great revelation. But she did worry terribly about his hardening atheism. All right, there was a lot wrong with the church and you didn't need to go there every Sunday to be a good Christian, but the actual teachings of Jesus Christ were sacrosanct as far as she was concerned. She had always tried to instill this deep feeling into Virginia, though with how much success she could never be sure. When Virginia had been a child, she had told her stories and shown her picture books about 'gentle Jesus, meek and mild'.

Now, looking at her daughter and seeing the rebellious spark in her eye and bitter twist to her mouth, she doubted that her religious teaching had had much effect.

'I'll start looking for another job right away. Factory work maybe. Anything but service. That's just slavery.'

Janette sighed. 'You think factory work's likely to be any easier? I think you'll soon find, hen, that you didn't know how lucky you were working in that nice big house, getting your bed and board.'

'Och, mammy, you don't understand what

it was like, or what that Mrs Cartwright was like.'

'You're forgetting that I had a spell in service myself in my young days.'

'You were lucky. You got a nice unmarried Christian lady who treated you like a daughter. How often do you think that happens?'

'Well, maybe not quite like a daughter, Virginia, but Miss Hamilton was a very good Christian lady, right enough.'

'Well, Mrs Cartwright is anything but a good Christian lady. Although she probably thinks she is because she's a regular churchgoer.'

'Och well,' Janette soothed. 'You're here now. Drink up your tea. We'll talk about what you're going to do in the morning.'

'Where'll I sleep?'

'Oh aye.' Janette nibbled worriedly at her lip. It had been over a year since Virginia had slept overnight. She had only ever got a few hours off from Hilltop House. Sometimes she didn't come home on her time off so that she could save her fare and help out with the housekeeping money. She was a good wee soul, really.

'It's all right, mammy. The floor'll do. I'm so tired I could sleep on the edge of a knife. I'll lie down on the rug in front of the fire. It'll be nice and cosy.'

'All right, hen. And here's a cushion for a pillow. And I'll slip one of the blankets off the bed.'

'No, no, you might waken daddy. Your shawl'll do fine.'

'Will you put out the gas?'

'Yes, don't worry. Goodnight, mammy.'

'Goodnight, hen.' Janette gave a faint smile. 'Sleep tight and don't let the bugs bite.' It was something she always used to say when Virginia slept at home. She climbed carefully back into bed and eased herself between the blankets.

Virginia finished her tea, turned off the gas and then settled down in the darkness under the grey woollen shawl. She became aware of the smell of paraffin wax. The wood of the hole-in-the-wall bed had long been infested by bugs but her mother kept them at bay by constantly rubbing every hole and crack with paraffin oil. As Virginia snuggled further down under the shawl, as well as the smell of the wool, she could also detect that of her mother, warm and sweaty from her hard day's toil. The familiar smells comforted Virginia and helped her to relax into a dreamless sleep.

It seemed no time at all until her mother was saying, 'Come on now, hen. You'd best get up before the boys come through.'

'Are they working again?'

'Aye, a lot of folk are being taken on at the munitions factories. Ian's doing that. Duncan's been doing a bit of labouring here and there.'

Her father appeared in the kitchen. He'd been at the lavatory and was in his rolled up sleeves, with a white scarf knotted at his throat.

'I told Ian,' he said, 'that the German workers were his friends. It's the capitalists over there that are the real enemy of the British and the German workers. I told him, but it still hasn't sunk in.'

Virginia thought he looked quite ill. His cheeks were sunken and under his eyes was dark brown crepey skin almost the colour of his bushy moustache.

'It's a good job, Da,' Ian said, following his father into the kitchen. He was a lively eighteen-year-old with laughing blue eyes and curly brown hair. He'd always been popular with the girls. 'And we need the money,' he went on. 'What Ma earns barely gets us a piece and jam for our dinner. Oh, it's you Virginia,' he cried out in surprise and pleasure at the sight of her.

She'd already replaced the cushion on the chair and folded her mother's shawl. She had tidied her clothes and now she was pinning up her hair.

'I've been dismissed.'

Her mother, in an apologetic tone, explained, 'She was cheeky to the mistress.'

Ian laughed. 'Good for you, hen.'

'Will there be any chance of a job in the

munitions factory, do you think, Ian?'

'Aye, they're needing as many as they can get now.'

'Not you as well?' her father groaned.

Duncan's big frame filled up all the elbow room that was left in the kitchen. He was a year and a half older than Ian and much more serious.

'You'd be better to stay in service, Virginia,' he said, thumping down at the table.

'That's what you think!'

'Virginia, apart from anything else, service is not dangerous like working with munitions. And you won't like turning yellow either.'

'Yellow?' Virginia laughed. 'You're joking.'

'No, it depends where they put you. In some departments, dust and chemicals fly about and make everyone's skin and clothes turn yellow.'

'Well, I'll just have to hope they don't put me on that.' She shrugged. 'I might not get taken on at all, but I think it's worth a try. Like Ian says, we need the money.'

'It'll be dangerous no matter where they put you.' Duncan had always been the moody, pessimistic one of the family.

'I'm willing to take my chances,' Virginia said cheerfully. 'I believe in equality and if Ian isn't afraid of the work in the munitions factory, then neither am I.'

Her mother cast her eyes heavenwards.

That Pankhurst women and her suffragette friends had a lot to answer for. 'Equality,' she said. 'What next!'

6

At first Virginia thought it was great. Starting work at eight o'clock in the morning, instead of five or six. She could hardly believe her luck. It was all very exciting and interesting too. After clocking in to the large, one-storey building, she was given a fireproof overall and a cap that had to completely cover her head. Not one hair must show. Pins, brooches, rings or metal of any kind were strictly forbidden. Rubber shoes had to be worn. She was led down long corridors and into the huge room where she was to begin work.

When she saw the number of girls in the room, she was astounded. She had never in her life seen so many people all together in the one place. Hundreds and hundreds of girls – or so it seemed to Virginia – all dressed the same and standing intent on doing the same thing, or hurrying to and fro. She was given boxes of small brass parts for fuses, to be gauged and checked for rejects. It didn't take her long to learn how to do it and soon her attention began to stray a little. She saw notices stuck up on the dark grey walls. They told the workers where to go in the event of a raid by zeppelins or other aircraft.

Another thing that caught her attention was the fact that so many of the girls had their fingers bandaged. She soon found out the reason. The brass parts with which she worked had sharp edges which cut the fingers and before the day was out, she had to go to the surgery, nursing her hand and trying to catch the drips of blood to prevent them from falling onto her overall.

At the dinner hour, they could all go to a separate room, have a cup of tea and eat their pieces. She was shocked to learn that many of the girls had developed septic poisoning and had to attend the surgery every day to have their fingers dressed. In the light of this discovery, Virginia's euphoria of the morning quickly evaporated. She also soon discovered that the work was repetitious and standing for so many hours exhausted her. By the end of that first day, she was very weary.

'I told you,' Duncan said. 'It's not so great as you thought, is it? And you've already been injured.'

She tried to perk up. 'Oh, stop nagging at me, Duncan. And I'm just a bit tired, that's all. I'll feel all right after I've had something to eat.'

Janette had made soup with some bones, lentils, barley and vegetables. She ladled it out from the big iron pot on the grate. Afterwards, there were sausages and potatoes. Normally they had their dinner, as it was called here (in Hilltop House it was lunch) in the middle of the day but because Virginia, Ian and Duncan were at work all day, Janette had changed things around. She and her husband had their tea together at twelve noon. Tam was a moulder and every morning and afternoon, summer and winter, he went along to hang about outside the iron works in the hope of a job. Usually, if there was any work going it was given to a younger man. But Tam kept trying. Janette always said that it was that heavy work that aged Tam and ruined his health. Their tea was a simple meal of tea and bread and jam, and perhaps a scone or a pancake. Janette, despite working, managed to find the time and enough energy to bake once a week.

'There should be a canteen in that place, not just to serve tea but a decent meal,' Virginia said. 'I'm sure everyone could work better and not have so many accidents if they weren't so tired. A decent hot meal in the middle of the day would keep them going.'

'Aye, you're right,' Ian agreed. 'We've been agitating for that. There's a union meeting tomorrow night about it. Why don't you come along and speak up for the women?'

Virginia was taken aback. 'I couldn't do that.'

'Why not? You spoke up for your rights to Mrs Cartwright, by all accounts.'

'Oh, but that was different. Anyway, it got me dismissed. I don't want to lose this job if I can avoid it.'

'You won't, not if you join the union and get that behind you. Come to the meeting tomorrow and see what you think.'

'I'll see.'

'Good.' Ian grinned and stuck up his thumbs.

Her father nodded. 'Good for you, lass.'

'I never said I'd go. I never said I'd do anything. I'll maybe think about it, that's all I meant.' She continued eating her meal in silence while the men began a heated discussion about the importance of the unions. Ian was all for them, but Duncan and her father argued that the union leaders were too closely associated with the Liberal party. As were the great masses of the workers. But whatever their differences, her father and both her brothers saw socialism as the only way forward.

'If for no other reason,' Duncan told her when the meal was finished and she was helping her mother clear the table, 'you should go and hear John Maclean. He's an inspiration, that man.'

This was something the three men totally agreed on. At the mere mention of John Maclean's name, it was as if a light came on, beamed from their eyes and animated their features. Even Duncan was affected in this way. It made Virginia curious.

'Is he going to be at the meeting?'

'Yes, he'll be one of the speakers.'

'How he gets to so many meetings beats me,' Duncan said. 'He works during the day for five days a week as a teacher. Then every night and at weekends, he's travelling here, there and everywhere – all over Scotland – giving brilliant talks in halls, or at street corners, or at the work gates. And there's the Sunday classes he takes for workers, or anyone who wants to learn. He teaches economics and Marxist principles and industrial history. I'm telling you, his intellect and his energy are superhuman.'

Virginia couldn't help being impressed but Janette was thinking, 'What's his wife and family doing while he's tramping around the country educating the workers?' Although she had to admit that he had done quite a lot of good, if not for his own family, then for other folks. According to Tam, Maclean had once written a pamphlet called *The Greenock Jungle*. It was based on the famous novel by Upton Sinclair called *The Jungle*. The pamphlet exposed the criminal traffic in diseased carcasses by a number of Greenock butchers. It resulted in an enquiry by the local government board and a meat inspector was appointed for the town's slaughter-houses. Maclean had also agitated for, and had been successful in getting, the school boards to feed and clothe and provide free books to children who, because of the unemployment of their parents, would have starved.

So Janette listened patiently and without criticism to her menfolk's passionate enthusiasm for John Maclean. She wondered what Virginia would think of the man. She had no doubt that the girl would go to the meeting. Already she could see a gleam of interest in her daughter's eyes. She sighed to herself. It would only lead to more trouble. Although she loved her family and was proud of them, she wished they could be more contented. They worried her. Sometimes they even embarrassed her. They stirred things up. They not only argued amongst themselves, they argued with friends and neighbours. Sometimes she didn't know where to put her face.

But they seemed to thrive on these arguments and confrontations. She secretly hoped and prayed that Virginia would be different. As she washed the dishes in the black iron sink with its brass swan-necked cold water tap, she murmured to Virginia who was drying the dishes, 'You don't need to go, hen, if you don't want to. Never mind them.'

'Mammy, I'm perfectly capable of making up my own mind.'

'Aye,' Janette sighed, defeated.

Virginia glanced round. Her mother's face was drawn and tired. Her eyes were dull, her hair pinned back in a bun. According to Tam, it had once been 'such a bonny yellow'. It was all faded now and streaked with grey, and she wasn't yet forty.

'Must you go out scrubbing, Mammy? Now that you'll have my wages – I'll give you as much as I can, even though I've got to try to save something. I mean, these days you never know what's going to happen.' Except that she did know. Virginia quaked inside at the thought of the baby. It was just an invisible embryo at the moment but the time would come when it would be obvious and her mother and everyone would know. Her mother would be ashamed of her, and disappointed. She would be branded a fallen woman by everyone else, and regarded as a disgrace and a shame to her family. She could just imagine her father and brothers being ashamed of her. But somehow she would have to survive what everyone would say and think of her.

'Och aye, you're quite right,' Janette said. 'You should save as much as you can, hen.'

'But must you work so hard Mammy?'

'I'm like you. I believe in putting away a few pennies when I can. The boys could be out of work again, and then what would we do? You're a good girl, Virginia. I always appreciated what you gave me. Many a time it saved the day.'

'We're away, Ma,' the boys called out. 'Are you coming, Virginia?'

Virginia grabbed her jacket and the bread and jam her mother had wrapped in a piece of newspaper.

'Cheerio, Mammy.'

'Cheerio, hen, and you be careful in that place. I'm always telling Ian.'

'Yes, yes.'

Duncan soon headed off in a different direction, while Virginia and Ian continued to trudge along side by side. They didn't take a tram to work so that they could save the money for their fare. Coming home, however, Virginia was too tired to face the long walk. On each return journey, she was glad to take the tram. Every night her mother made her the bed in front of the fire with the cushion for a pillow and one of the blankets from her bed. It was cosy enough although it would be a different matter when the colder weather came and icy draughts blew under the doors from the close. The rag rug did nothing to cushion Virginia against the hardness of the floor. She was so stiff and sore each morning, she could hardly struggle to her feet. At night, as she lay trying to sleep, trying to ignore the racket of her father's snoring, she would think of Nicholas. She couldn't help it. She missed him.

During the day, for safety's sake, she had to concentrate on nothing but her work. But never a night passed but she missed him. She missed the sight of him, the sound of him, the touch of him. Over and over again, she relived their meetings. She remembered the joy on his face when he saw her approach. She felt his strong, hard arms around her, his hungry mouth on hers. His hands caressed her breasts, her thighs. He pulled her down beside him onto the sweet smelling earth. They undressed each other and made love. She felt him move inside her now, and she trembled with passion at the vivid memory. Oh, how she longed for him. She remembered how, still naked, they had moved in a dream dance together. She could see the morning mist clinging to the trees, making their white naked figures ghost-like and unreal. Yet it had been so beautiful. And she had loved him. She had believed that he loved her.

It had not been his fault that his mother had got rid of her. He would not know anything about it. Only sometimes she would wonder sadly if indeed he had not, as he'd promised, told his mother to keep her at Hilltop House. He had certainly told her about the pregnancy. Perhaps he'd even done so in order to get rid of her, knowing that his mother would certainly oblige. But it was only in her most exhausted states that such thoughts were able to take hold of her. For the most part, in those quiet times lying in the dark and silent kitchen, she was able to cling to the memories of their love.

On the way to work, she would determine once more to forget all about Nicholas Cartwright. What good did thinking about the past do anybody? She had to get on with her life. She attended several meetings at which John Maclean was one of the speakers. And she discovered that he was indeed a most charismatic man.

It wasn't so much his physical appearance. He was a stockily built man and wore a dark suit, neat collar and tie and a dark homburg hat. It was something about his face with its wide mouth, broad features and prominent cheek-bones. But it was his eyes that were the most compelling thing about him. They were beacons of passion, burning with enthusiasm and sincerity. The whole man was charged with such energy that it was infectious.

He was a masterly speaker, even at – or especially at – rough street meetings in the middle of the clatter of traffic, and with crowds of casual listeners constantly changing and being renewed. At meetings in halls, he could have the audience jumping to their feet and cheering, as he made the air around him spark with the electricity of his presence. Virginia couldn't help being impressed.

He had started to have regular meetings in Bath Street, even in Renfield Street, and not only attracted large numbers of socialists, but also passers-by. The streets became so packed that a child could have walked across the heads of the crowd. People became riveted by John Maclean's passionate speeches. A vast body of men and women would stand for hours in tense silence listening to him. Especially when he talked about the war, the unfolding tragedy that seemed to have cast its dark shadow over all their lives.

At the foot of the street, the tramway office was plastered with poster appeals to men to join the army. And there was John Maclean, standing on a table eloquently exhorting men not to join the army under any circumstances. The war, he told them, was not an accident. Indeed, it was the very nature of capitalism to engender warfare.

'The men you are asked to shoot,' he insisted, his face tense and drawn with earnestness, 'are your brothers. They have the same difficulty as you to find the rent for their miserable dwellings. They have to suffer the same insults from their gaffers and foremen. Do not forget that when the Scottish miners were on strike, they often received financial help from the German miners.' His eyes burned into the crowd. 'The main thing for you to know is that your real enemy is the employers. As long as turning lathes, ploughs, coal cutters, looms, ships – all the tools of wealth production – are possessed by a small class of privileged people, then so long will you be slaves. To get free from this slavery is your main concern. Victory can only be with the assistance of your brothers in other lands. For socialism cannot triumph in one country alone. The victory of social-ism must be worldwide. The only war worth waging is the class war.'

Walking home with her brothers after listening to the speech, Virginia felt shattered. She knew that Maclean had affected every-one. Duncan's fists were pushed deep into his jacket pockets. The buttoned jacket was of thin, cheap material and too short and too tight for him. On his head was a cloth cap pulled well down.

'What courage the man has!' Duncan exclaimed, 'To stand up for his beliefs like that. But I reckon he'll pay dearly for those brave words. They'll find some excuse to send him to prison.'

'For goodness sake, Duncan, surely not!' Virginia had protested.

'Right enough,' Ian agreed, 'the greedy bastards that are taking full advantage of the war don't want someone like him stirring up trouble. And there's plenty of folk who'll take his side now they're making us work longer and longer hours and not paying us enough to survive.'

'Aye,' Duncan said. 'It's only too true what Maclean said about industrial slavery under the Munitions Act. I'm with him a hundred per cent. And I'll fight against the capitalist class any day, rather than join their bloody army and murder German workers in the name of King and Country.'

'I'm with you all the way,' Ian fervently agreed.

Virginia had never seen her brothers so fired up. Having listened to John Maclean, she understood how they felt. At the same time, she began to understand her mother's concern and wondered where all this would end.

1915

7

After a few weeks Virginia was moved to a machine shop. There she had to use a heavy industrial press to finish the detonators. It was a task that demanded great care and attention to detail. She had a box of twelve detonators and she had to place one at a time inside a metal cup, put it into the machine and pull a lever. On one occasion a slightly faulty detonator nearly cost her her life, the only thing that saved her was that she had taken the precaution of closing her box of twelve before operating the lever. If the uncut detonators in the box had exploded, she would have gone up with them. As it was, only her hands had been injured.

Later her mother asked anxiously, 'Do you think they've moved you in there out of spite because you've joined the union?'

'No, it's nothing to do with that. Lots of other girls have been moved there in the past. It's what happens. Everybody gets moved from one place to another. I suppose it's so we learn all sides of the job.'

She had been reluctant to join the union at first, and especially to take such an active part in its work. Not because she didn't believe in what it stood for or what she'd argued for. It was just because of her pregnancy. She would have to leave once she began to show. Then, once the baby was born, the chances were, even if her mother looked after it, that they wouldn't take her back. What was the use of getting too involved? Yet, despite these misgivings, she had stood on a soapbox outside the works and rallied all the girls to approach the foreman and demand a canteen. They elected her to speak for them, and gave her their full support. She explained to the foreman and a manager who also appeared on the scene that it would be to everyone's advantage if the girls were able to sit down and have a decent meal. They'd be able to work harder as a result and so produce more. The girls shouted that if they didn't get a proper canteen that sold decent hot food at dinner time, they'd down tools. Whichever argument it was that won the day, one way or another they got what they wanted. Even so, when they got their canteen it was as much as they could do to afford to eat there, but still it was worth it.

Virginia had been four months pregnant when she was moved to the machine shop. Five months into her pregnancy she was moved to the spinning room. It was here that the springs of the fuses were tested. It was the most exacting job of all, requiring good eyesight and constant vigilance to ensure the accuracy of the spring. This procedure caused a fine haze of dust and chemicals to drift about the room, and Virginia soon discovered that it made her skin and her clothes turn yellow. This in turn made her mother's rag rug, her cushion and her blankets turn yellow. Everything Virginia touched took on a yellow hue. Virginia kept apologising but her mother always just said, 'Never mind, hen. As long as you're safe and well.'

She hadn't told her mother – and had warned Ian not to mention it either – of the two most recent accidents in the machine rooms. A man in Ian's room had two of his fingers cut off by an automatic machine. Then a girl who had bent down to pick up some work she had dropped got her cap and her hair caught up in the flywheel of her machine, and was scalped. It was only too true what Duncan had said. The munitions factory was a very dangerous place, and the long hours and exacting work were taking their toll. Virginia began to wonder how much longer she could stand it.

Six months into her pregnancy the chemicals began affecting her skin, not only turning it yellow. Her face, neck and legs began to swell. On being examined by the works doctor, TNT poisoning was diagnosed. The skin broke and fluid escaped. She was bandaged and told to go home and stay there for ten days. For the second time since she went to work there, Virginia was lucky to survive. TNT poisoning often proved fatal and many of those she worked with were not so fortunate. Her mother was in great distress by this time.

'Look hen, that place is killing you. Nothing is worth risking your life for. Certainly not for the pittance they pay you at that place.'

But it wasn't fear for her own life that made Virginia decide not to go back. There was her unborn child to consider – she had no right to risk its life.

'I know. Once I've recovered, I'll look for something else.'

After about a week, she began healing nicely and was beginning to think about going out to search for another job when she was surprised by the sudden appearance of Fanny Gordon in the house. She was in fact more than surprised. She was astounded when her mother, after going to answer a knock on the door, appeared back in the kitchen accompanied by the frizzy-haired scullery maid.

'Fanny!' Virginia gasped. She had never given Fanny or any of the staff her exact address. They knew she came from the Gorbals, that was all. Anyway, why would Fanny want to seek her out, especially during working hours?

'The mistress sent me. She found out that we were pals.'

Virginia gazed at the girl in puzzled bewilderment.

'The mistress sent you?' she echoed incredulously.

Fanny nodded. 'Och it's terrible, so it is. Even I'm feeling sorry for her. She went as white as a sheet and had to lie down. The lady's maid had to give her smelling salts.'

'I don't know what you're talking about, Fanny.'

Janette interrupted, 'The kettle's on the boil. I'll make a nice wee cup of tea.'

Fanny said, 'Oh thanks, Mrs Watson. I feel terrible, so I do. So does everybody in the house.'

'About what?' Virginia cried out in desperation.

Tears welled up in Fanny's eyes. 'It's the young master. A telegram came to say he'd been killed in action. Cook's awful upset. So is Mr Cartwright, but Mrs Cartwright's the worst. In a right state she is. I mean, we couldn't help feeling sorry for her.'

Virginia couldn't talk. Her voice was trapped in the lump that was growing in her throat. Her mother was saying, 'Poor woman. There's nothing worse in the whole world than a mother losing a child. And the poor young man. Och, this war is a terrible thing. All those boys dying out there and for what?' She paused for a moment, lost in thought, before recovering herself and asking, 'Why did she send you here, hen? Was it just to tell Virginia because Virginia used to work there?' Janette looked puzzled.

'No,' Fanny said, 'it was to bring her back with me. Mrs Cartwright's going to their holiday house down the Clyde somewhere for a few months – to see if it'll help her, I suppose. She wants to take Virginia with her. She'll probably take some other servants as well. I hope she takes me.'

The puzzlement still clung to Janette. 'But why Virginia, I wonder?'

'Och, maybe she feels guilty now about sending her packing the way she did, and she's trying to make up for it. The loss of her son has made her see things different maybe. Anyway, she said I was to bring Virginia back.'

'Well, there you are,' Janette addressed her daughter. 'She must have been fond of you after all.'

'Fond of me?' Virginia gasped. 'Mammy, you don't know her like I do...'

'I know the poor woman's lost her only son and must be in need of help and comfort.'

And I've lost my only love, Virginia was thinking broken-heartedly. She wanted to be on her own so that she could weep but she knew no amount of weeping would bring either help or comfort. Fanny was telling Janette he was such a nice fellow. 'Always ready with a smile, so he was. Nice looking as well. It's a shame, so it is. I left Mrs Tompkins – that's the cook – crying her eyes out. Oh, come on Virginia, you can't say no. Anyway, think of the nice long holiday you'll have doon the watter.'

Janette brightened. 'That's right, Virginia. It'll do you a power of good. It's just what you need. Come on now, I'll help you pack your trunk.' Then to Fanny, 'She's been near death's door herself, you know. TNT poisoning. She's been working in that awful munitions factory. It hasn't being doing my Ian's health any good either, I can tell you. I'll be losing him if he doesn't get out of there. I worry myself sick about him.'

'I'd be scared to work in a place like that,' Fanny said. 'You could be blown up at any minute, so you could.'

Janette had hauled Virginia's tin trunk from underneath the hole-in-the-wall bed, had taken Virginia's uniform apron, dress and cap from the dresser drawer and packed them neatly into the trunk.

'Good job we washed and ironed these after you came home.'

'Mammy, you don't understand. I can't bear the thought of going back there.'

'Fanny says Mrs Cartwright's going down

the Clyde to her holiday home so you won't
be going back to the house for long.'

Virginia was seeing Nicholas in her mind's
eye and thinking, 'Please God, don't let him
have suffered. I can't bear the thought of
him suffering.' She became more and more
distraught and less and less able to stop her
mother and Fanny forcing her to leave.
Fanny picked up the trunk, Janette helped
Virginia on with her jacket and buttoned it
up as if her daughter was a child again.

'Now on you go, hen. I'll feel so much
happier if you're away getting some nice
fresh air into your lungs instead of all that
poison. I'll miss you, of course, but as long
as you're all right, I'll be all right.' Then to
Fanny, 'How long did she say?'

'A few months.'

'Och well, you won't be able to come
home on your days off, Virginia, but you will
write, won't you, and I'll look forward to
seeing you when you get back. All right,
hen?'

In a daze of distress, Virginia felt herself
being hustled out of the kitchen and out of
the house. All she could think of was 'Oh
Nicholas, Nicholas! Oh my love!'

An anger at God began to fill her heart and
mind. How could He destroy such a beautiful, talented young man. It was too cruel,
too senseless. Then bitterness rose to the
surface. God, if there was a God, had noth-

ing to do with it. It was the men who had started this bloody war who had destroyed Nicholas. She wanted to weep and sob and howl against the generals, the politicians, the capitalists. She hated them all. She felt mad with hatred, hysterical with it. She shivered and shook with it.

'Are you all right?' Fanny asked.

'No,' Virginia said. 'I'm not bloody all right.'

'Och, don't worry. Mrs Smithers gave me money for our fare. So we don't need to walk all the way. We should be in time for our dinner. And Mrs Cartwright'll be all right to you, you'll see. She wouldn't have asked you to come back if she wasn't sorry for throwing you out as she did.'

Fanny half pushed, half lifted Virginia onto a tram car. 'I know there'll be a bit of a walk at the other end. But we can take plenty of rests.'

Virginia stared blindly out of the tram window, lost in a nightmare. It was impossible for her to return to the place that held so many memories of him. She couldn't face it. Yet she sat on in helpless despair, unable to resist whatever fate had in store for her.

8

The meal in the kitchen of Hilltop House was a gloomy one. Hardly anyone spoke. Eventually Mrs Tompkins said, 'It just shows how bad the mistress has taken it when she sent for Virginia. Virginia of all people. The poor woman's gone right off her head.'

This roused Virginia to say sarcastically, 'Oh thanks very much.'

'You know what I mean, hen.'

Virginia wasn't sure that she did.

'She never liked you before.'

That was true enough.

Maisie spoke up then. 'I don't think liking comes into it with her. I don't think she likes any of us. She probably never even thinks of us. Not as human beings anyway.'

'I think she feels guilty about Virginia,' Fanny said. 'Fancy throwing her out like that, without even a minute's notice.'

Maisie shook her head. 'She doesn't normally show signs of guilt. Remember poor Mary. She never showed any guilt or remorse about what she did to her, and Mary with that invalid mother depending on her as well.'

'Aye, but it's different this time.' Mrs

Tompkins sighed. 'That's what I'm trying to say. She's been knocked off balance with the terrible news. Her nerves are all to pot. Her feelings are running away with her.'

Maisie looked doubtful. 'She's not taking hysterics or anything. She's just sitting up there as if she's frozen solid. Mr Cartwright's trying to put a brave face on it but you can see he's awful cut up.'

'Poor souls,' Mrs Tompkins said. 'You cannae help feelin' sorry for them.' Then turning to Virginia, 'You'd better away up. It's nearly the time she said.'

Virginia felt more like lying down in bed in a dark room to try to sort things out in her mind. It was urgent to find some way to control her inward hysteria, to find a brave face that she could put on. The last thing she needed was to stand before Mrs Cartwright.

'Away you go,' Mrs Tompkins repeated, this time with an impatient edge to her voice. 'Don't just sit there.'

As if sleepwalking, Virginia made her way upstairs and into the hall. She knocked on the drawing room door.

'Enter!' Mrs Cartwright's voice sounded as cold and as hard as ever. Despite her own sadness, Virginia was shocked at the change in Mrs Cartwright. She seemed to have aged ten years. Although it was only a few days since she had received the fateful telegram, her cheeks were sunken, making her nose look even longer and sharper and her mouth smaller and tighter. Her features reminded Virginia of a picture of a vulture she'd seen in one of her books. But in Mrs Cartwright's small beady eyes there was a look, not just of suffering, but of madness.

Mr Cartwright was sitting in one of the deep buttoned chairs at the opposite side of the fire. He said,

'You have been told about the death of my son?'

'Yes, sir,' Virginia said.

'Naturally we are extremely distressed at the loss of our only child.'

Virginia said, 'All the staff are very distressed as well. He was a very well respected and admirable young man.'

'Thank you, Virginia,' Mr Cartwright said. 'Now my wife and I have a proposition to make to you.' He hesitated. 'This is most difficult and distressing for us both but it's got to be done. You are pregnant with our son's child.'

'Yes.' Virginia's voice turned wary.

'Our grandson.'

Virginia made no comment. It was now occurring to her what they were after, why they had sent for her. She felt faint. Surely they couldn't try to take her baby away from her? Even though they were wealthy and powerful, surely she had the right to keep her baby. They couldn't do this to her. She wouldn't let them.

'If you are suggesting,' she managed in a cold voice, 'that you have any claim to my baby, Mr Cartwright...'

'The child is all we have left of our son.' Mrs Cartwright spoke up for the first time.

'That does not alter the fact, Mrs Cartwright, that the baby I give birth to is my child, not yours.'

Mr Cartwright said, 'We could give him every advantage in life. We would deny him nothing. What could you give the child, Virginia? I know where you live. I know the mortality statistics. Do you? What do you imagine the child's chances are of surviving even his first few months?'

'I'll love him and do my very best for him.'

'Oh yes?' Mrs Cartwright spat out the words. 'Like you've been doing already. We know all about how you've been exposing yourself to filthy infections. God alone knows what harm you've done to the child already.'

Virginia felt confused. Had they been having her watched? Had they been asking about her at the factory?

'You talk about love, Virginia,' Mr Cartwright said. 'Did you love my son?'

Before Virginia could answer, Mrs Cartwright cried out in bitter disgust, 'Love? Love? How can you even mention the word in the same breath as that immoral creature's name?'

Virginia was fighting back her tears now. 'Yes, Mr Cartwright,' she managed, 'I loved Nicholas very much indeed. And I believe I knew him better than either of you. Did either of you know he wanted to be a poet?' Her voice cracked. 'That's all he ever wanted to do. He didn't want to go into your business, or to go into the army. He just wanted to be a writer. You didn't know that, did you?'

Virginia's outburst was followed by a long silence before Mr Cartwright sighed and said, 'No, I knew nothing of this.'

'And you wouldn't have understood it even if you had. I was the only one who helped and encouraged him. For a short time at least, he was happy. That's what I have of him, as well as his baby. The memory of his joy at being able to write. It wasn't me that made him happy, it was his writing.'

Another silence.

'You say you knew him,' Mr Cartwright said. 'Do you really believe he would want his child brought up in a slum in the Gorbals. Would he really wish on his child the real dangers of illness and death there. You must try to face the truth of this, Virginia.'

She had been trying for months now not to face the truth of this. She knew in her heart that to love someone – to truly love them, meant giving them up as she had done with Nicholas. She had loved Nicholas, and still loved him – would always love him – and she had been happy for him to get the best out of life in his work, in his marriage, in his proper place in society.

'Do you realise what you are asking?' she said. 'You are asking a mother to give away her child. How can I do that? It's too cruel.'

'To you perhaps.'

'There's no perhaps about it, Mr Cartwright. I can't do it.'

'But what about the child? Think of the child, Virginia. You're young. You will no doubt get married eventually to someone of your own class. You'll have other children. Think of this child, Virginia. Nicholas's child. If you loved him, if you love the child, you would want him to have a good life. You would want him to claim his birth right. Nicholas's child does not belong in the Gorbals, Virginia. He belongs here.'

Virginia twisted her hands together. She felt ill. The baby was kicking and moving inside her as it had never done before. She imagined that it was urging her to do the right thing, that it was desperately trying to tell her not to deny it this chance.

Mrs Cartwright spoke up. 'You would come with me right away. You would stay in our holiday home in Helensburgh. For the few remaining months until the baby is born, you will live like a lady. I will engage temporary staff there who do not know you. You will enjoy fresh air, good food, every care and attention so that you will be sure to have a successful delivery of a healthy child. This is a once in a lifetime opportunity for you. You must realise that. The chance to live like a lady for a few months. Who else of your class would ever be able to enjoy such good fortune?'

Virginia felt like killing the older woman. It was as much as she could do to keep her hands off her. 'Enjoy such good fortune?' Virginia had never felt so grief-stricken, so distressed, so lacking in good fortune, in her life. 'How can you talk about me enjoying good fortune when you are asking me to give up my child?'

Mr Cartwright rose and stood, hands behind his back, his back to the fire. 'Look, Virginia, we could take this to law. Is that what you want? And do you really believe that any court of law, any judge, would decide that the child's best interests would be served by allowing it to remain with you? Compared with all the advantages we can bestow. I hardly think so, do you?'

And of course, Virginia thought bitterly, the Cartwrights had friends in high places. They had many powerful and influential friends.

Mr Cartwright said, 'Do you really want to endure a long and painful legal dispute over this?'

His wife joined in. 'We'll stop at nothing,

you know. We *are* going to have our grandson. He is all we have left of our son.'

Oh, they'd stop at nothing all right. Virginia was certain of that. She said, 'Anyway, what will everyone think if you suddenly appear with a baby? How will you explain it?'

'I have already told Mrs Smithers,' Mrs Cartwright said, 'that the daughter of my late cousin lost her husband in the war and she is expecting his child.'

Virginia could see that would sound believable enough. The telegraph boy was now a dreaded and all too frequent sight. Already he'd been twice to Cumberland Street.

'I have said,' Mrs Cartwright continued, 'that the sea air would do her good and we could help and comfort each other if she came to stay a few months with me there. When I return eventually with the baby, I'll simply say that my relation has died.'

'I see,' Virginia said. 'You have it all thought out.'

'Yes. Mrs Smithers will explain to the staff after I've gone. She will tell them that they have to remain here to look after Mr Cartwright. Also that my relation is bringing her own maid and cook/housekeeper. You are coming to skivvy.'

'I haven't said I'm going anywhere with you for any reason.'

Mrs Cartwright's hollow cheeks flushed with anger. 'The quicker my grandson is away from the pollution of that filthy Gorbals place, the better. Are you wanting to be the death of him before he's even born? Is that what it is, you ignorant malicious girl.'

Mr Cartwright put up a restraining hand. 'Now, now, my dear. Talk like that will not accomplish anything. I'm sure Virginia wants the best for the child. I'm sure she knows what she must do for the best.'

She did, of course, but she could still not imagine how she could, in the end, actually part with her baby. It was unthinkable, and yet.

She thought of her parents and brothers. Here was her chance to spare them from the shame of her condition.

Summoning her every last drop of courage, she said, 'Very well. I'll come with you. I'll go and fetch my trunk.'

'No,' Mrs Cartwright said. 'The chauffeur will take it out and put it in the boot of the car. But you will not need anything from it for the next few months. We must, for appearances sake, try at least to make some attempt to make you look like a lady. I will supply you with some of my old clothes. They can be adjusted to fit you where necessary. There will be a dressmaker in Helensburgh if you have not the skill to alter the garments yourself.'

'Very well,' Virginia repeated stiffly. She hated the woman. She had always hated her.

How she was going to live in close proximity to her for the next few months without murder being committed, she did not know.

9

Helensburgh was situated at the mouth of the Gairloch on a gently sloping hill. Most of the streets were lined with lush green trees. The houses were handsome villas that sat in large gardens shaded by trees and high bushes. The exception to this was the few central streets where there were shops, with respectable flats above them. There were also a few public buildings like the town hall and the hospital. A wide esplanade from which a pier jutted out ran along the seafront. There was also a public park, a recreation ground and a golf course which stretched across the old Luss road, commanding fine views of the Firth of Clyde. A walk or a drive along the Luss road opened up the wonderful vista of Loch Lomond, Ben Lomond and the grandeur of the mountain scenery beyond.

Virginia would have enjoyed her walks along the Luss road and the esplanade, had it not been for the stiff and silent company of Mrs Cartwright. Mrs Cartwright refused to allow Virginia out of her sight. Virginia had argued about it, lost her temper with frustration about it, all to no avail. She would have run away from the older woman in order to be alone to enjoy the beautiful scenery. Or even just for an hour or two's privacy. However, two facts made this impossible. Firstly Virginia was now swollen and clumsy and not able to run, secondly, Mrs Cartwright was a tall, strong and determined woman who would not have had any problem in physically detaining Virginia.

A strange relationship had been established between them. They were alone together practically every waking moment in the dining room, in the drawing room, in the garden, out walking. Virginia even suspected that Mrs Cartwright spied on her when she was asleep in the bedroom that adjoined the older woman's. Virginia believed that Mrs Cartwright's obsession was driving her close to the point of insanity. She kept anxiously asking Virginia if she felt all right. She had her regularly checked over by a local doctor despite the fact that the doctor kept assuring her that Virginia was a healthy young woman and that everything about the pregnancy was perfectly normal. Mrs Cartwright had given her a wedding ring to wear and had introduced her to the doctor as a poor relation whose husband had been killed in the war.

Mrs Cartwright had even called the doctor out when Virginia had suffered a bout of morning sickness. 'Even I know that morning sickness is normal during pregnancy,' Virginia protested to Mrs Cartwright. The doctor won't thank you for calling him out again, and over something so trivial.'

'I don't need thanks from the doctor. I pay him well and he knows he must come when I wish him to. And I too know about morning sickness. But it normally happens for the first two or three months. That has been my experience and that of all my friends. You could have developed some sort of complication.'

Virginia realised that all Mrs Cartwright's anxieties and concerns were not for her but only for the baby she carried, and her constant questions and anxious looks became almost unbearably irritating. She had no other conversation either with Mrs Cartwright, or with another living soul. Two daily women came in, one to do the cooking, the other to clean, but one way or another, Mrs Cartwright made it impossible for Virginia even to have a few words with them.

One evening, after more than a month of this torment and anxious nagging, Virginia's self-control snapped.

'How do I know that you're not going to give my baby the same unhappy life that you gave Nicholas?'

Mrs Cartwright's gaunt face turned a deathly grey, from which her eyes stared out in naked agony. 'Unhappy? How could he ever have been unhappy? We gave him everything money could buy!'

Virginia began to regret her outburst. There could be no denying the sincerity of Mrs Cartwright's grief, but she had undoubtedly neglected him. 'You never showed him any love or affection. First you shuttled him off to that nanny – a cold-hearted witch she was as well, according to what I've heard. You were always sending him away.'

'But ... but ... that's what everyone does. It was the proper thing. Everyone ... everyone of my class employs a trained nanny. It is for the child's own good. What else could I do?'

Virginia wanted to say, 'Look after him yourself,' but knew without being told that this was not the proper thing in Mrs Cartwright's world, so she kept silent.

Then after a time, Mrs Cartwright cried out, 'The boarding school was the best in the country. We thought we were doing the best for Nicholas. And as for the army – that was his decision ... his regiment was one of the finest in the land.' She paused in a vain attempt to regain her composure, as the tears began to roll down her face. 'If only he had listened to me, stayed at Hilltop House and gone into his father's business...'

Still Virginia kept silent. She had already told the Cartwrights about Nicholas's longing to be a writer. What was the point of repeating it now? Despite everything, she had no desire to distress Mrs Cartwright any further. She still nursed a simmering hatred of the woman, but she couldn't be malicious. She also couldn't help thinking that Nicholas would not want her to hurt his mother.

For the rest of that evening, they had sat opposite each other in the drawing room. Virginia continued as best she could with the baby's jacket she had been knitting. Mrs Cartwright's knitting lay on her lap while her long bony fingers twitched uselessly. The fire was sinking and instead of putting another log on the dying embers, Virginia said, 'I think I'll have an early night.'

'What?' Mrs Cartwright raised a distracted face.

'I'm going upstairs to bed.'

'Oh yes.' Mrs Cartwright rose, allowing her knitting to drop unheeded to the floor. She followed Virginia from the room. Later Virginia could hear her pacing the floor of her bedroom. She doubted that Mrs Cartwright had managed to get even one hour's sleep the whole night. She certainly looked dreadful the next day, so much so that Virginia said, 'You don't look at all well. I think we ought to call the doctor out to *you*.'

'What good can any doctor do me? He can't bring my son back.'

Virginia could not altogether understand the depth of the woman's grief. After all, she had hardly ever been in close contact with her son, far less shown the slightest sign that she loved him and cared about him, while he'd been alive. Unless of course Mrs Cartwright's real problem was guilt. Perhaps now she realised how she had treated her son and was suffering so acutely because she knew that it was too late to do anything about it.

That night Mrs Cartwright broke one of her long silences by saying unexpectedly, 'I did love him you know.'

'Yes,' Virginia soothed, 'I'm sure you did.'

'You don't believe me,' Mrs Cartwright cried out. 'Whatever else you do, don't you dare lie to me or patronise me.'

'All right,' Virginia said in exasperation. 'I can't see how you could have loved him. You didn't show any affection to Nicholas, did you? You never told him you loved him. Not when he was a child, not when he was a man, did you?'

Mrs Cartwright shook her head. 'I'm ... I'm not that kind of person. I've never ... my parents never...' Her voice tailed off, as she turned her face to the wall.

'She's remembering her own childhood,' Virginia thought, and for the first time she had a glimmer of understanding and sympathy.

Mrs Cartwright didn't know about love. At least she didn't know how to express it. She had probably never been shown love by her parents. Perhaps her life had been more bereft than Nicholas's. At least Nicholas had his dreams.

'Perhaps,' she chose her words carefully, 'Nicholas understood that.'

'What?' The tortured face turned back towards Virginia.

'Perhaps,' Virginia repeated, 'Nicholas understood how you felt and didn't blame you. I know he was a much more understanding and forgiving person than I am. And he loved you,' she added, although she did not in fact know whether Nicholas had loved either of his parents or not.

Mrs Cartwright's eyes filled with pathetic eagerness and hope. 'Did he? Do you really think he did?'

'Yes, I'm positive he did.'

'Did he tell you? Is that what he said?'

'Yes, he did. And he said those exact words.' Virginia felt uncomfortable lying like this but she felt obliged to continue for Mrs Cartwright's sake. The woman was desperate for reassurance.

Mrs Cartwright was visibly trembling now. 'Thank you, Virginia. Thank you for telling me.'

The rest of that evening passed in silence. Next day, however, the questioning began again. Virginia began to feel both their lives were becoming a charade. Mrs Cartwright wanted to know every word Nicholas had ever said about her. Virginia felt pressurised into building endless dialogues in which Nicholas expressed love and admiration for his mother, when in truth Nicholas had said very little – if anything – about her. Eventually, Virginia had to call a halt.

'Mrs Cartwright, I understand how you feel and how you want to know all this about Nicholas, but honestly I've told you all I can. I can tell you no more.'

'Of course, of course, Virginia. I understand, but if you just go over it again. That time he said...'

There was no escape. It began to exhaust Virginia and to distress her. She had intended putting the past – at least her memories of Nicholas – behind her. It was too hurtful to think of him and to remember what he had been like, to be with, and all that he had really said to her. Also to be telling so many lies about him, even with the best of intentions, began to seem like a betrayal of him. One day she burst into tears.

'Mrs Cartwright, I can't bear any more of this. Has it never occurred to you that for me to keep talking about Nicholas is upsetting. I loved him too, remember, and I miss him. If you won't – for my sake-stop tormenting me with so many questions, do it for the baby's sake. If you harm me, you'll harm Nicholas's child, remember. Try to think of it that way.'

'Yes, oh yes, of course.' Mrs Cartwright pressed her lips tightly together as if to prevent the escape of another single word. After that, they reverted to their long silences interrupted only by anxious queries about Virginia's health.

Then one night, two weeks earlier than the date the doctor had given them, Virginia went into labour.

10

Virginia let out a high-pitched scream.

'For God's sake, get the doctor.'

Mrs Cartwright's tall figure hovered by the bed.

'I telephoned him. There was no reply. I don't know what to do.'

'Try again,' Virginia gasped. 'Something's going wrong. I know it. It isn't the right date yet.'

'No, no.' Mrs Cartwright's voice was a low tight moan. 'Nothing must go wrong. I'll telephone again.'

She hastened from the bedroom in great agitation. In a matter of minutes she had returned.

'He must be out on another case.'

'Dear Jesus!'

Mrs Cartwright wrung out a face cloth from the basin of water on a nearby table. With a shaking hand, she wiped the sweat from Virginia's brow.

'Don't worry. I'll keep trying until I get him.'

'Don't worry? Don't worry?' Virginia screeched as another agonising pain gripped her. She grabbed at Mrs Cartwright, digging her nails into the older woman's arm. 'Dear Jesus!'

She clutched round Mrs Cartwright's waist and held tightly on to her. Awkwardly Mrs Cartwright patted Virginia's head.

'Everything's going to be all right.'

'How do you bloody know?'

'I've been through this. I know what labour pains are like.'

Another respite from agony came and Virginia relaxed thankfully into it. Mrs Cartwright continued,

'What worries me is the pains are coming so quickly. That could mean the baby's about to be born. I had a nurse and a doctor attending me. They saw to the actual delivery. I must try to contact the doctor again. I'll never forgive him if he doesn't arrive in time.'

She disentangled herself from Virginia's rough embrace and hurried from the room yet again. She returned distraught, mumbling half to herself, 'No reply. This is awful. Absolutely awful.'

As she entered the bedroom, she was stunned by the sight that met her eyes. The bedclothes had slipped from the bed and Virginia was lying, legs bent and knees splayed out, screaming and sobbing and panting with pain.

'Good God,' Mrs Cartwright cried out. 'I can see the head! What am I going to do?'

'You'll always be the same,' Virginia sobbed. 'You'll be the same with the baby. You won't know what to bloody do. You never will. You'll be bloody useless, just as you are now.'

Mrs Cartwright took a deep shuddering breath and went over to the bed. 'I was told to push. I remember. That's what you must do.' She spoke calmly now. Calmly and encouragingly.

'It's nearly there. That's right. Good girl. Good girl.'

Sweat was now pouring over Virginia's eyes. Eventually she became aware that the pain had stopped. The sweet relief of it. She was totally exhausted. She was faint and sinking into blackness with exhaustion, but when she heard the infant's cry, she struggled back to consciousness.

'My baby!' She tried to raise herself on one elbow.

The room was empty.

'Mrs Cartwright,' she called out.

Mrs Cartwright, flushed with triumph,

111

appeared in the doorway.

'I telephoned again. The doctor's on his way. But I did everything.'

Virginia nodded. 'Yes, you did very well. Thank you.'

'I helped my grandson to come into the world.' Mrs Cartwright was euphoric. 'I'll have the doctor check him of course but he seems a perfect, healthy little boy. A lovely little boy and he looks exactly like Nicholas when he was a baby. I'm going to call him Nicholas.'

Weak tears streamed down Virginia's face. 'I want to see him.'

'No.' Mrs Cartwright looked alarmed. 'It would be better if you didn't.'

'I want to see him,' Virginia repeated.

'You promised. You gave your word, Virginia. For the child's own good, remember. If you saw him, you'd want to keep him. I can't risk that. I can't risk you taking him to the Gorbals. I care for the child's safety and well being, even if you don't, Virginia.' She flushed slightly and tipped up her chin. 'And I will show him love and affection. I promise you. I will not make the same mistake with my grandson that I did with my son.'

'I won't take him away. I want what's best for him. But I need to see him and hold him just for a few minutes. Please, Mrs Cartwright.'

After a minute's hesitation, Mrs Cartwright said, 'All right. But I'm trusting you Virginia...'

She brought the baby in from the other room. He had been bathed and wrapped in a shawl that had once held Nicholas.

Virginia stretched out her arms. Then gently, tenderly cuddled the warm little body close to hers.

'He is beautiful.'

'Yes.'

'Could you do me one last favour?'

Mrs Cartwright looked wary.

'What?'

'Don't call him Nicholas. He needs to be his own person, loved for his own self.'

'What do you suggest?'

Virginia kissed the downy head. 'I don't know. Richard perhaps.'

'Richard.' Mrs Cartwright savoured the word. 'Richard Cartwright. Yes, it has a good ring to it. Richard it will be then.'

The sudden clang of the doorbell startled them both.

'That'll be the doctor,' Mrs Cartwright said. 'I'll put Richard back in his cot now.'

'Please, let me hold him until the doctor leaves.'

'He'll want to examine you. And the baby. You can't hold him while he's doing that. Quick now, give him to me. I must answer the door.'

She forcibly prised the child from

Virginia's arms before hurrying from the room. It was as if she had carved a piece of flesh from Virginia's body. Virginia moaned with the pain of it. To come to terms with her loss she tried to keep visualising the difference between Hilltop House and the room and kitchen in the Gorbals. She had to keep reminding herself of the unsanitary conditions, the stench of the overflowing lavatories. They were always becoming blocked and sending a stinking, germ-laden river down the stairs and through the close. She forced herself to think of the lack of space, the icy cold water, how the little boy would be deprived of every comfort.

Whereas at Hilltop House he would have everything he needed for his health and well being. She had no right to deny him these things. If she loved him she had to let him go. But, oh, the pain of it.

Mrs Cartwright left early next morning. She was standing stiff-backed in the bedroom when Virginia woke up. She was dressed in her outdoor clothes, a wide-brimmed hat decorated with ostrich feathers and ribbons, a long cut-away coat, gloves and button boots.

'I've told the housekeeper to look after you,' she said. 'I have given her another two weeks' wages. I have left an envelope for you on the dressing table. In it you will find enough money for your return journey and a little extra to tide you over until you can find work.'

'You're leaving now?' Virginia could not believe it. 'Right now?'

'There's no reason for me to stay any longer.'

There was an awkward silence. Virginia felt shocked. Mrs Cartwright's face was an expressionless mask.

'The housekeeper will take good care of you. There is no longer any reason for me to remain. And I see no reason why our acquaintance should be further prolonged. Richard is mine now, and I do not expect ever to see or hear from you again.' Mrs Cartwright's expression softened slightly. 'You have made the right decision, Virginia. Now get on with the rest of your life.'

Now, on top of Virginia's anguish about giving up her baby, she felt another layer of hurt. She chastised herself about it. Why should she feel hurt at Mrs Cartwright's sudden departure. How had she been expecting Mrs Cartwright to behave? What had she been expecting her to do? Nevertheless she did feel hurt. Hurt and used, disappointed and depressed.

For a few days, she couldn't even be bothered eating. She just turned her face to the wall and lay under a black cloud that was too heavy to fight against, even if she'd wanted to. Then she'd overheard a conversation between the housekeeper and the other servant.

The housekeeper was saying, 'I know, and the poor lady had to take the baby away to look after it. Of course, the girl has lost her husband.'

'So have thousands of other folk.' The other servant sounded indignant. 'I know five women in our street who've lost their men and they didn't lie about like her feeling sorry for themselves. They've had to get on with life.'

'Aye,' the housekeeper sighed. 'It's an awful business. I know a few poor souls like that myself. One woman, Mrs Spencer, has lost her husband and her two sons.'

'My God. Is that not terrible?'

'Aye. I saw her just the other day. There she was with the dignity of a queen and a smile and a brave nod for everybody. Wonderful woman. Her men would have been proud of her.'

Virginia felt ashamed. She struggled up right away, washed and dressed and rang the bell for a cup of tea and something to eat. Her anguish and depression did not go away but she began to fight against them. She had done the right thing for her son. Now she must, as Mrs Cartwright said, get on with the rest of her life. She could not force herself to have any conversation with the two women who continued to come in daily but at least she made herself get up every day, eat properly and go out for walks in the fresh air. By the time the house was due to be locked up and she had to leave, she at least felt physically recovered.

Returning on the train bound for Glasgow's Central Station, she began to think of what she could do to start earning some money. Mrs Cartwright had added a few pounds extra to the rail fare. The money meant nothing to her – all she cared about was that they would give a good home and a good upbringing to Richard. She had every confidence that they would do so, and that they would spare no expense, no trouble, to give their grandson every advantage in life. Hopefully they would show him plenty of love and affection too. He was a lucky little boy. She must cling to this thought for now and be glad for him.

Virginia realised that she could go back to the munitions factory. She did say this to her mother after she had been welcomed back into the family home. But her mother had become so distressed, she was forced to give up the idea. Although she secretly knew that if she couldn't find any other employment, she'd have no choice but to return there.

'I'm nearly distracted with worry as it is with Ian being in that place day and night.' Her mother said, 'He does as many night shifts as day shifts and it means I can't sleep for worrying about him now. There's been so many accidents in that place.'

'Ian's all right,' Virginia said, trying to cheer her up. But she knew that Ian was Janette's favourite and if anything happened to him it would destroy her. She looked like death as it was. She'd lost weight, and her face had a sunken look.

'Mammy,' Virginia said eventually, 'I think you should go and see the doctor. You don't look well. I'm worried about you.'

'Do you know how much it is to see a doctor?' Janette asked. 'You surely think I'm made of money.'

'I've got a wee bit extra with working in Mrs Cartwright's holiday home. I'll pay for the doctor. Please go, Mammy. I'll come with you.'

'Well, all right, hen. Just to please you.'

Virginia braced herself for the bad news that she feared the doctor would give them. But before they even reached the surgery, they heard other news that shocked not only them but the whole of Glasgow.

11

They heard the explosion. It was muted, far off, but they felt the tremor under their feet. As the tremor subsided, a pall of black smoke was rising in the distance. Instinctively, they knew what it meant.

'Oh no,' Janette's shoulders hunched and she tightened her shawl under her chin. 'Please God!'

'It might not be the works,' Virginia said but not very convincingly. It was the munitions works all right. She frantically prayed that Ian was not one of the casualties. Please God, no, she was thinking along with her mother. Please God, no!

They had been on their way to the doctor's surgery but were stopped in their tracks. Janette leaned heavily on Virginia's arm. She said, 'We'd better go back.'

Virginia didn't argue but just held tightly to her mother's arm and turned her back towards Cumberland Street. In the house she led the dazed Janette to a chair and then put the kettle on. It was always on the hob and didn't take long to come to the boil.

'It might not be the works, mammy,' Virginia repeated. Janette didn't answer. She was just staring sightlessly ahead. Outside a back court entertainer had begun singing 'The Old Rugged Cross'. Virginia jerked open the kitchen window and flung out a coin, at the same time shouting, 'For God's sake, away you go. My mammy's not well.' Then she retreated back into the kitchen and shut the window. She put out a couple of cups. The milk and sugar were already on the table.

'Come on, mammy, drink this. I'll go and see if I can find out what's happened.'

She had to hold the cup to her mother's lips. 'Come on, mammy. Please. It'll make you feel better.'

Janette made an attempt to rally. She accepted the cup and held it between her palms.

'Thanks, hen. On you go.'

Outside in the close, Virginia stood for a moment to gather her courage. She was hardly aware of the briquette man as he passed by, whirling his wooden rattle and bawling, 'Coal briquettes, coal briquettes, ye'll all be cauld if ye forget, yer coal briquettes.'

Ian might be safe. And in any case, it wouldn't do any good if she went to pieces now. If anything had happened to Ian, her mother would need her. She had to be strong for her mother and father's sake. Duncan's too. He and their father would have been waiting as usual outside the wall of Dixons in the hope of getting work. They would have heard the explosion. Virginia's feet quickened through the narrow cobbled streets that were crowded with barefoot children and women standing in close mouths gossiping. Some had babies wrapped in their shawls.

Reaching Dixons Blazes, as the blast furnace was nicknamed, Virginia gazed anxiously at the crowd of men, some shuffling around the gates, some trudging back and forth alongside the high brick wall. Others were huddled together against the wall. All were dressed like Virginia's father in thin trousers tied with string beneath the knees, shabby jackets, white fringed mufflers and cloth caps pulled well down over their brows as if to hide the misery in their eyes.

Virginia spotted Duncan first because he was taller and heavier-built than the rest. Tougher looking too with his broken nose and dour aggressive look. Most of the younger men, like the older ones, were thin and emaciated, with lacklustre eyes.

'Duncan,' she called out. 'Have you heard anything about that explosion? Mammy's worried in case it's where Ian works.'

'Aye, it's in the factory, they say. Da's away there to see what he can find out. He told me to stay here in case I missed a job. But there's nothing doing. Even if I did get offered work I wouldn't be able to concentrate. I told Da.

He shouldn't be long if you want to wait.'

They stood in silence among the shuffling crowd of men for a few minutes. Then Duncan said, 'Here he comes.'

They knew as soon as they saw his tear-stained face that the worst had happened.

'Oh Christ,' Duncan said.

Virginia ran towards her father. He shook his head.

'It was his department. All killed. All killed...' He shook his head again as the tears streamed down his cheeks and gathered wetly on the edges of his moustache. 'He was such a cheery soul. Everybody liked him.'

Duncan reached him and grabbed hold of his arm. Virginia linked into Tam's other arm.

'Come on home, daddy,' she said.

'Had you no' better stay, son?' Tam's tragic gaze turned on Duncan. 'What if a job comes up?'

'Da,' Duncan said firmly, 'I'm coming home with you. We need to stick together at a time like this.' Then, 'Who's going to tell Ma?'

Virginia said, 'She'll know as soon as she sees us. I think she knows already. When we heard the explosion...' She couldn't continue. She was thinking 'Why couldn't it have been me instead of Ian. What have I got to live for?'

They made the journey home slowly, reluctantly, each dreading Janette's reaction to the dreadful news.

She was sitting exactly where Virginia had left her, still clutching at the tea cup. Virginia gently took the cup from her.

'I'll make some fresh, mammy.'

'It won't make me feel any better, hen. Nothing will. Not ever again.'

'Ma, Ian thought the world of you,' Duncan said. 'He wouldn't want you to be sad.'

'Aye,' Tam said. 'He was a good lad.'

'Did you go?' Janette asked Tam.

'Aye. They told me the whole department went up. Aw those good men. And for what? To line the bosses' pockets. Ian never complained, but he knew what the bosses were like. They were aw working longer and longer hours for less and less money. And this is their reward...'

'Daddy,' Virginia protested. 'This isn't the time for politics.'

'It's exactly the time,' her father said angrily. 'By God, it is. This bloody war that our Ian died for is a war for trade. Never mind all that King and Country nonsense!'

'All right, all right, Daddy.'

'No, it is not all right. I've just lost my son because of them. The rumour is that some of these firms are selling war material to neutrals. Knowing full well they're being resold to Germany. They don't care who they sell them to. As long as they make their bloody profits.'

Duncan touched his father's arm. 'I know you're angry, Da–'

'Of course I'm bloody angry. I've a right to be bloody angry.'

'I know. And so am I. But you're upsetting Ma.'

Tam sat down on the nearest chair.

'I'm sorry, hen. It's just...'

'I know, Tam,' Janette said.

Virginia poured out the tea.

'Have we any whisky?' she asked Duncan. 'A wee drop of whisky in the tea might help to steady us.'

Janette said, 'In the press.' She nodded towards the cupboard on the wall at right angles to the kitchen sink. Virginia found a half bottle that her mother kept for medical emergencies. She poured some into each cup.

They sipped from their cups in stunned silence. Soon there was a knock at the door. Virginia opened it and ushered in two of the upstairs neighbours – Mrs MacDougal and Mrs Friel.

'We've just heard.' Mrs Friel was a plump little woman with loose pouches of cheeks and a pink scalp shining through wispy grey hair. 'We're that sorry, hen. Is there anything we can do fur ye?'

'Aye, anything at aw, Mrs Watson.' Mrs MacDougal was thin and bent, with an unhealthily flushed face. Recently Janette had remarked, 'I think poor Mrs McDougal's got the consumption. She's just wasting away.'

'That's kind of you. Sit down and have a cup of tea. I'm sorry I haven't any scones or anything to offer you.'

'Don't be daft,' both the neighbours cried out. 'A cup of tea'll do us fine.'

Later in the day, they were both back, Mrs Friel with a plate of scones she had baked specially and Mrs McDougal with some homemade pancakes. A continuous stream of neighbours came and went during the next few days, all offering support and comfort.

Ian's body was brought home. The closed coffin was propped between two chairs in front of the room bed. Tam and Duncan slept in the bed, and Virginia shared the kitchen bed with Janette. The minister came the next day and gave the service and the coffin was carried out of the close and on to the hearse. Outside, strangers and neighbours alike took off their caps as a mark of respect, and stood silently as the hearse passed slowly along the street. And along the whole street every blind was drawn.

The women stayed behind in the house and prepared the formal tea for the men's return from the graveside. All the neighbours had contributed to the meal so that it could be the usual steak pie and peas, home-made scones and cakes. There were big pots of piping hot tea, as well as whisky, to warm the men up. It was a cold rainy day more like January than July.

The kitchen was packed with women all bustling and bumping into one another in the small space. They wouldn't allow Janette to do anything. One of them took the pulley down, removed all the washing that had been hanging from it and dangling over the table. She folded it, then stuffed it out of sight behind one of the bed curtains.

'Just you sit there and relax, hen,' they told Janette. 'We'll see to everything.' Janette allowed herself to be pushed into a chair. She sat with dull eyes and hands lying limp on her black-clad lap.

Virginia said, 'I'll see to the room.' She needed to be on her own for a few minutes. There she busied herself putting back the chairs that had held her brother's coffin. She rubbed the duster over them and the high chest of drawers and the window ledge. The room was in shadow because of the drawn blinds. It had an almost greenish tinge as if it was under water. There was the silent aura of death about it. Only then did the loss of her brother seem real. Before, it had been like a waking nightmare, now it was cold, dismal reality. She felt broken-hearted. Standing by herself in the centre of the gloom, she wept and sobbed until she was exhausted. Later, Mrs Friel came looking for her.

'Och, come on, hen. Here, use ma hanky.

You've got to be brave for your mammy. That's the men back. Come through and help dish their tea. Or just sit and keep your mammy company. We can manage fine, don't worry.'

Virginia nodded, then dried her face.

'You've all been awful kind.'

'Och, what are neighbours for? You'd have done the same for us. Your mammy's helped us many a time. Are you going tae be all right now, hen?'

Virginia nodded.

'Come on through then.'

The men had the first sitting but even then it was a terrible crush at the table. There was much talk, even laughter now. Eventually the men went through to the room for a glass of whisky and a smoke. Some sucked at clay pipes. Others enjoyed a comforting puff at a Woodbine. The women gathered round the table for their meal. They too chatted away in an attempt to be normal and cheerful. Even Janette made a brave effort. So did Virginia.

It wasn't until much later, when the last guest had said their goodbyes and Virginia, Janette, Tam and Duncan were in the house alone, that silence descended once more. There was no longer any excuse or even energy left to put on a brave face, to pretend to be cheerful.

Tam said, 'I'll just go on sharing the bed

with Duncan. It's not right that you sleep on the floor, Virginia.'

'Are you sure, daddy? I don't mind.'

'No, no, hen. You cuddle in with your mammy.'

None of them kissed each other good-night. They'd never been a demonstrative family. Except Ian. He had always been easy going, open and affectionate.

Virginia put out the gas, climbed into bed and lay stiffly beside the equally stiff form of her mother. They didn't speak. There was nothing left to say.

12

Virginia had to find work as quickly as possible. Her mother was no longer able to go out scrubbing, and nowadays she was barely able to creep about the house. Her skin had gone an unhealthy putty colour and she had begun to suffer from breathlessness. It was as much as she could do to make a pot of tea or peel a few potatoes. Neither Tam nor Duncan could find a job. They might have been able to find work at the munitions factory, but their socialist, anti-war principles made that an impossibility. Virginia didn't blame them, especially after what had happened to Ian. She couldn't face going back there herself, and the thought of any of them working there now would have been more than her mother could bear. But something had to be done as there was now absolutely no money coming into the house.

The money Mrs Cartwright had given her had been used up. For a time she managed to get a few hours work each week at what her mother had been doing – scrubbing out pubs. It sickened her beyond measure each time she went into the stale, stinking places. The air was thick with the previous night's tobacco smoke. The floors were covered with vomit, and stained with dried-up beer. Added to this was the never-ending struggle to keep their close in Cumberland Street clean. Sometimes Virginia would just stand and stare helplessly at the narrow entrance to the tenement, with its paved corridor and stone stairs leading up to one of the communal lavatories and think, 'Why bother trying to keep this place decent? What's the use?' Her only comfort was that she hadn't brought her baby to this stinking hell hole. At least her son wouldn't have to suffer the deprivation of living like this.

Over and over again, she'd scrub the few yards of the close out through to the back, hardly able to see what she was doing because during the day only a dim light managed to penetrate the close. At night there was a feeble yellow flicker from the tiny gas mantle on the wall above the stair foot. All the stone steps were broken with jagged edges where bits of tread had fallen away. Care had to be taken going up to the lavatory, and most people at some time or other had fallen and injured themselves. The lavatory in the back close had long since become totally unusable. The whole place deeply depressed Virginia. She was depressed enough as it was with missing her baby, without having to look at walls with plaster coming away from ceiling to floor every miserable day. In the yard, stray cats and rats furiously scavenged and scattered the rubbish all over the broken flagstones. At first she had tried to sweep the yard and keep it tidy, but it was a hopeless task. Just as it was hopeless to try to keep the close, the stairs and the landing decent. They all kept trying, all of the neighbours, but the landlord now refused to have the lavatory fixed and so it went on overflowing. The mixture of urine and faeces kept cascading down the stairs, sickening everyone with the stench of it. No repairs or maintenance of any kind was ever done to the building. Yet the tenants were forced to pay ever-increasing rents.

Yet despite her depression, there was emerging in Virginia a sense of outrage. Her stay in Helensburgh had shown her how people with money lived, and she was angered that decent working-class folk should have to put up with such conditions as these. She and her father and brother fuelled each other's anger, and she began going with them to John Maclean's meetings. At one meeting in Bath Street, he told the audience that four hundred shipwrights at Fairfields had stopped work in protest against the Munitions Act – better known as the Industrial Slavery Act. Maclean said it was meant to tighten the chains of economic slavery on the workers. Virginia stood with the huge crowd, transfixed by the man's passionate address.

'You have lost,' he declared, his arms stretched out as if longing to encompass every soul there, 'the right to organise, the right to strike and the right to move from workshop to workshop. In ordinary times, the capitalists would find themselves faced with the unanimous opposition of the working class if they attempted to interfere with workers' liberty to move from one firm to another. In fact they did not make the attempt.' His lips tightened with contempt. 'But the war, the glorious war, gives them the opportunity, the excuse, they desire... Comrades, capitalism is the right to rob you – you, the real creators of wealth. Capitalism must be killed, and it can be done in twelve solid months, starting any time, if the workers are ready. Emancipation of the working classes must be achieved by the working classes themselves.'

Soon after this, seventeen men from Fairfields were hauled before a Munitions Tribunal and each was fined £10 with an alternative of thirty days in prison.

Maclean exhorted the men not to pay the fine, promising that if they were sent to prison there would be an uproar and they'd have the support of all workers. Only three men followed his advice, but there was indeed an uproar and the Fairfields & Govan workers prepared for a strike. The union officials quickly took the matter into their own hands. The workers thought they were going to call a strike but instead they called for a government enquiry. That dragged on for so long that the union officials were discredited and lost their influence over the workforce. The real leaders, as Maclean always said, were to be found in the workshops.

By the end of October, Maclean was summonsed under the Defence of the Realm Act and his trial was fixed to take place a few weeks later. Both Tam and Duncan had now become active agitators and when yet another crippling rent rise was demanded they, and a great many others, refused to pay. This added worry was too much for Janette. She seemed to be shrinking before Virginia's eyes, bent like an old woman, her eyes staring and haunted.

'It's all right, mammy,' Virginia tried to reassure her. 'They can't evict you. We're all standing together and refusing to allow the factor even to get near any of the closes.'

'I'm not worried about that. I'm not worried about myself,' Janette said. 'It's Tam and Duncan. They're getting deeper and deeper into trouble. I'm worried about you as well, Virginia. I thought you were all pacifists, but there's nothing but anger and fighting all over Glasgow now and you're in the thick of it with the rest of them. Now we're all being sued at the Small Debt Court. I'm ashamed, Virginia. Me and all my good respectable neighbours getting sued for debt. I'd rather have paid the extra rent.'

'Mammy, you couldn't pay it. You haven't got the money. Anyway, nobody's going to pay it. We're going to collect John Maclean at his school and then gather in front of the court. The sheriff will have to back down.'

'I thought Maclean had been dismissed long since.'

'Oh, they're trying to dismiss him. It's a disgrace. It's because he's an atheist. He's refusing to fill all his pupils' heads with superstitious nonsense.'

'Virginia!' Janette trembled with distress. 'I don't want you to have anything to do with any atheists. You were brought up to be a good Christian girl.'

'Oh mammy!'

'He causes nothing but trouble, that John Maclean.'

'Yes, trouble for the capitalists and the bosses. Anyway, I've got to go now, mammy.'

Virginia rushed away to meet up with her father and Duncan at Lorne Street School in Govan. When she arrived there, they were talking to someone she hadn't met before. He was a sturdily built young man with short, tufty, brown hair, bushy brows and piercing eyes. He was introduced as James Mathieson, a teacher who worked with John Maclean and knew him well. When he shook hands with Virginia, she nearly cried out – he had such a strong grip her hand felt crushed. The mass of people who were now milling all around the school were shouting for Maclean. Virginia could see, in the way that he was lustily joining in the shouting with the others, that Mathieson shared much of Maclean's fervour.

Eventually the great man emerged from the school and Mathieson was one of those who rushed forward to carry him shoulder high through the streets until they reached the Sheriff Court. There, a crowd of over ten thousand people had gathered. Every street was packed and all traffic had been brought to a halt. Poster boards, picked up from newspaper shops, were improvised, placed on willing shoulders, and the speakers lifted onto them. Maclean was speaking directly in front of the court. Roars of rage kept erupting from the mass of listeners as they heard about the robbery and injustice of the factors. Inside the court, which was packed with a deputation from factories and yards, the Sheriff and his clerks sat ashen faced with anxiety. Eventually realising the situation was becoming dangerous, the panic-stricken Sheriff telephoned Lloyd George, who was then the Minister of Munitions. Lloyd George, looking to calm the situation, and no doubt influenced by the Sheriff's anxiety, told him to stop the case immediately and instructed him to announce that a Rent Restriction Act would be introduced as soon as possible.

When they heard this news, the crowd was elated and there was spontaneous dancing in the streets. Virginia found herself whisked off her feet by James Mathieson. Eventually everyone calmed down, and by the time the crowds dispersed Virginia was laughing and breathless.

'You don't know your own strength,' she told Mathieson. 'I'm so exhausted I can hardly stand.'

He locked her arm in his. 'Hang on to me and you'll be all right. Come on, we'll have a seat in the park for a wee while. Then I'll take you home.'

They found a seat in the park and although it was a cold November day, Virginia still felt flushed and hot.

Mathieson had begun talking about Maclean. 'His background is similar to mine, you know. His parents, like mine, were victims of the Highland Clearances. Like him, I've been brought up with tales of the suffering the landlords inflicted on our people. They forced our families – decent, hard-working folk – from their homes and farms and left them with nowhere to sleep, nothing to eat and no means of earning an honest living. Many of their friends had to take ships to America, husbands were parted forever from their wives, and parents never saw their children again.'

Mathieson's face darkened as he spoke, as if a heavy thundercloud was passing over it. 'My grandmother had to walk most of the way to Glasgow with my mother in tow and carrying her baby brother. My grandfather had walked the journey before her to find work and a roof over their heads. Much the same happened to John's parents and he hates the landowners as much as I do. The landowners and all the bloody capitalists.'

Virginia put her hand on his arm to comfort him, much as she'd once done with Nicholas. She felt the tremor of his distress and passion.

'I understand. Really I do. But it doesn't do any good to get so upset,' she told him gently. But he answered in a fury,

'Yes it does. It does! That has been the trouble. Nothing'll ever change unless people have the will to stand up and be counted. I suppose that makes me a revolutionary.'

'Are you not a pacifist?'

'I will not fight and kill any working class man – in France, Flanders or anywhere else. Like Maclean says, the only war worth waging is the class war. The rich are nothing more than murderers. You only have to look around you at the misery we endure every day, while they live in pampered luxury.'

Virginia shivered and Mathieson immediately looked concerned.

'Are you cold? Do you want to go home now?'

'Yes. I didn't realise how cold it was before,' she said. 'Thanks to all that dancing.'

They began making their way out of the park, their feet crackling the frosty grass. Once more she was surprised at the natural way Mathieson tucked her arm through his. To anyone else it must have looked as if they were sweethearts and had known each other for years, instead of barely a few hours. He did not seem in the least conscious of anything unusual in his behaviour. As they walked, he talked of Maclean again and the beliefs that he shared with him.

Virginia couldn't help thinking of Nicholas and remembering him in his khaki uniform, remembering his gallantry and patriotism.

He had gone to war with a heavy heart, yet believing that it was his duty to do so. She could not think of Nicholas as her enemy, just because he happened to belong to the class that Maclean and Mathieson so despised. Her depression returned. Thinking of Nicholas, her heart ached for him, and she suddenly felt utterly exhausted, not only by the events of the day but by James Mathieson's unrelenting bitterness.

'I'd better go in.' She said as they reached her close. 'I didn't realise how late it was. Mammy'll be worried.'

At last she managed to escape into the house. Janette, her shawl clutched tightly around her, was anxiously waiting.

'Where on earth have you been? Tam and Duncan are in their beds.'

Virginia flopped down onto a chair.

'With James Mathieson. What a talker that man is. I just couldn't get away from him. Did daddy tell you about what's happened with the rents?'

'Aye, but what's next? There's nothing but trouble nowadays. One thing after another.'

'That's not daddy's fault, mammy. It's the fault of the landlords.'

'Och, don't you start, I've had enough of that already the day. Fine words never fed anyone and all this talk isn't getting any food on the table is it? There isn't even a spoonful of tea left in the house.'

'I'll go out first thing tomorrow and look for a job.'

'Where? Surely not at the munitions works?'

'No. Not there. I'll find something else. I promise.'

Once she had undressed and climbed into bed, Virginia tried to think of some way, any way, to make money. Eventually she did think of something. There were the so-called 'old clothes' that Mrs Cartwright had given her. In fact they were good quality garments that might be worth quite a decent sum of money. If she could hire a wee barrow she could try to sell them. Barrows could be hired by the day, and there was always a whole line of them in Clyde Street alongside the river with traders selling everything from pins and needles to stags' heads. Although she was thankful she'd thought of a solution, albeit a temporary one, for her family's problems, at the same time she felt sad. The clothes, belonging to Nicholas's mother and the world he had belonged to, were her last link with him.

Then she remembered a few lines from one of the poems he had given her. It was called 'The Rocking Horse'.

I touch my ear to the soft stretch of skin
and hear the music of a new pulse.

Impending joy until
sharp fragments of memory
tear the gauze curtains of my past.

Runners dusty and cracked
supported hooves
that sparked on the golden trail
of my childhood.
Handles and stirrups
offered safe grip.

My father scolded,
thrust a tin soldier with gun
and hard eyes into my small
unwilling hands.

I touch my ear to the soft stretch of skin
And hear the music of a new pulse.

Its beat a balm to my past.

As she sobbed in silent grief, Virginia remembered also the words of James Mathieson – aggressive and filled with fury.

'I loathe and detest them. Every last one of the so-called upper classes. Come the revolution, you and I will see them stripped of everything they possess, ground into the dust by the righteous anger of the working class.'

Virginia could only be grateful that in his short life Nicholas had never been exposed to such hatred.

1916-17

13

'Squeeze yer barra in here, hen.' The woman grinned invitingly at Virginia before introducing herself. 'Ma name's Aggie – Aggie MacAllister.' She was a long, loose-bosomed woman in rolled-up shirt sleeves with a brown sacking apron tied round her waist.

'Mine's Virginia. Virginia Watson.'

'Virginia – sounds posh.'

'I come from Cumberland Street.'

'Ye even talk posh.'

Virginia laughed. 'Do I? I suppose that's with hearing folks talk in the big house. I used to be in service up there.'

'Fancy!' Aggie said. 'Is that where you pinched aw them fancy claes?'

'Oh no, I didn't steal them. The lady gave them to me.'

'Aye, like the King gave me aw them braces an' boots. Them are aw His Majesty's hats as well.'

'Honestly,' Virginia said. 'She told me they were her old clothes. She'd bought loads of new ones and didn't want these old ones any more.'

'They're bloody perfect.'

'I know. But that's how rich folk are. They

get fed up with things and just buy more. Money's no object for them.'

'Well, yer best bet, hen, is a shopkeeper. Or any kinda better-off folk. Some o' them wander alang here lookin' fur a bargain. They'll huv mair cash tae gie ye a decent price. Anyway, best o' luck.'

'Thanks.'

People had begun to crowd round all the barrows in Clyde Street facing the expansive River Clyde. Most women in the crowd wore shawls over their heads and shoulders but there were some potential customers in wide brimmed or high crowned hats and long coats. Likewise, most men were in cheap, tightly buttoned jackets, with the usual white mufflers at their throats and cloth caps sitting squarely on their heads. But quite a few men were to be seen in collars and ties, and bowler hats, and homburgs. Virginia noticed that many of them were most interested in a nearby book barrow. The thought flickered through her mind that she could also sell her books, but she immediately shrank from the idea. Her books were like much-loved friends. Some of the barrow renters were shouting out encouragement to shoppers.

A fruit barrow man with his broad Glasgow bawl of, 'Honey Perrs. Honey Perrs. Mooth watterin' honey perrs.'

A frowsy fish woman wearing a long black skirt, a sackcloth apron and her man's cloth

cap was crying out, 'Fresh finnan haddies–
Gie yer man a treat. Gie him wan fur his tea.
Go on, hen, he'll luv ye fur it.'

One of the book men was small and bandy
legged, and had to stand on a stool to reach
the books. Stiff-faced with cold, he kept
stomping around his barrow and rubbing his
hands in an effort to keep his circulation
going. The icy breeze from the river was obviously cutting through his thin jacket. Virginia
felt chilled to the bone herself, but at least
she was healthy and strong. There were too
many undersized, bandy-legged folk in the
poorer areas of Glasgow. This was usually the
result of rickets, a disease which stunted
children's normal development. Rickets was
caused, so Virginia had heard, by lack of
proper nourishment. She was thankful that,
despite her family's poverty, her mother had
always managed to keep her family well fed –
making nourishing pots of lentil or mutton
broth, shepherd's pies and rice puddings.
They seldom went hungry, especially when
her father was working. She had happy memories of slices of fresh new bread liberally
spread with pink-coloured Co-operative
apple jelly. It was a long time since there had
been such a mouth watering luxury in the
Watson house. Virginia resolved that if she
sold any of the clothes she'd buy a jar of apple
jelly in the Co-op on her way home. It would
be a treat and a nice surprise for her mother.

Before long, she had quite a crowd round her barrow, admiring the dresses, capes and coats. But most people could not afford to pay what Virginia was asking for each garment. Although they realised she was not overcharging, being well aware of what such clothes would have originally cost in the shops in Sauchiehall Street.

Virginia was just about to drop the prices when a respectably dressed woman bought a black velvet shoulder cape and a pair of long black gloves. Then her companion purchased a loose-fitting tailored day costume. Virginia was delighted – she now had enough money for a lot more than just a jar of Co-op apple jelly. Enough in fact to feed the family for several days.

She didn't manage to sell anything else that first day, and she was glad to give up eventually, trundle the barrow back to its owner, then make her way home, carrying the bundle of left-over clothes slung over her shoulder. Her feet were like blocks of ice, but she knew that her mother would have the fire on and she'd soon thaw out. There was still some coal in the bunker and now she'd be able to give her mother enough money to get another bag put in. Geordie the coalman was a regular sight in the street, ambling along beside his Clydesdale bawling out,

'Coo-ee! Coo-ee!'

There was no mistaking him – a muscly,

moustached man with a voice like all the foghorns on the Clyde put together.

His ringing call drowned out all the other noises of the street for a moment, even the rag man who passed by blasting energetically on his horn.

Janette was pleased with the apple jelly and the fish and chip suppers Virginia had brought. Tam and Duncan immediately dived into the food, not even waiting for Janette to bring out plates or to get cutlery on to the table. They ate with their fingers, relishing each morsel of fish, each chip, straight from the newspaper wrapping.

Afterwards, they smacked their lips and Tam said,

'God, that was good, hen. You're a wee miracle worker. It must be a year or more since we've had a fish supper.'

'Aye,' Duncan agreed, leaning his big frame back in his chair and patting his stomach. 'I enjoyed that.'

The small kitchen was warm and redolent with the aroma of fish and chips and the mouth-watering tang of vinegar which the chip-shop man had liberally sprinkled over each supper. The food had created a happiness and contentment which, although temporary, was nonetheless real and keenly appreciated. They all sensed it, and clung to the intense pleasure of it for as long as possible.

Tam took out an old Woodbine packet in which he used to collect tobacco from 'douts', cigarettes smoked down until they were too short to hold between the finger tips. He had picked away the bits of cigarette paper and teased out what was left of the tobacco. Now he had enough to rub between his palms and, using a piece of newspaper for wrapping and a bit of gummed paper from the flap of an old envelope, he made a new cigarette. It was bulky and lumpy in shape but he enjoyed taking a long slow draw on it, expanding his chest and holding in the smoke, until eventually blowing it out between narrowed lips.

'Aye,' he said. 'You did well, hen.'

'And no bosses either,' Duncan added. 'Good for you. By the way, James is coming round tonight.' He grinned. 'You made a big impression there, Virginia. It looks as if he wants to start courting you.'

'He never said anything to me. About coming round, I mean.'

'Maybe so. But what do you bet when he arrives, it won't be me or da he'll ask to go out with him?'

Virginia felt disturbed and slightly annoyed. She didn't want to start walking out with anyone, especially someone as sure of himself as James Mathieson. It wasn't that she didn't like, even admire, the man. She had always admired anyone with brains and an education. She even agreed with most of his political beliefs. The simple fact was that she could not forget her feelings for Nicholas Cartwright. But what was the use of that?

When Mathieson arrived, he had to squeeze into the kitchen. He stood against the coal bunker and refused Janette's offer of a chair at the table.

'I was hoping,' he addressed Virginia, 'that you'd accompany me to a show at the Pavilion. I've heard it's very good. And we should support that theatre as much as we can. They've allowed us to hold many a good meeting there.'

Virginia was embarrassed by the barely suppressed hilarity of her father and brother. To escape it she rose and said, 'Yes, all right. I'll fetch my coat.'

Then she felt embarrassed at appearing so eager when she wasn't eager at all. Later, however, as she walked arm in arm with James and felt the warmth of his body so near to hers, her pulse quickened. Nicholas had awakened her to the pleasures of the body and despite herself, she was awakening again.

They both enjoyed the show in the Pavilion, although Mathieson's laughter at some of the turns surprised her. It was loud and robust and up until that point, she had regarded him as far too serious and intense. She hadn't been able to imagine him relaxing and laughing so heartily. Later, as they chatted about the show and laughed over it again in the tramcar on the way back to the Gorbals, she was more relaxed herself than she'd been for a long time. Once in her close, Virginia was able to say truthfully,

'I've really enjoyed myself tonight. Thanks, James.'

'My pleasure. I hope this will be the first of many enjoyable evenings.'

She smiled. 'We'll see. I'd better go in now.'

'Am I not even going to get one wee kiss?'

She hesitated for one shy moment before giving him a peck on the cheek. But his arms went immediately around her and gripped her close. He gazed down at her and said softly,

'Is that what you call a kiss? Here, let me show you.'

His mouth fastened down over hers, hard and demanding. He held her body so tightly, her breasts were crushed against him and she felt the hardening of his penis against her groin. Panic mixed with arousal. She struggled and pushed at him in an effort to break free.

'For goodness' sake,' she gasped breathlessly. 'What do you think you're playing at? We're right outside mammy's door. She could open it at any minute.'

'Come on through to the back close then.'

A dark corner of the back close was the only place that Gorbals lovers, or lovers in any poor district, could expect to be left undisturbed. Most tenement flats were overcrowded and there was never any chance of privacy.

'No, I want to go in. Let go of me.'

'You're a bonny fechter as they say, and I admire you for it, Virginia. But you'll soon find out that I never take no for an answer.'

'Let me go at once.' Her voice was rising in panic.

He immediately lifted both hands in a gesture of capitulation.

'All right, all right. I only meant that I'm determined to see you again. You're the girl for me, Virginia. I knew it the moment I saw that beautiful blonde head of yours.'

'Goodnight, James.'

'Goodnight, sweetheart.'

Hastily she slammed the door behind her before he could touch her again. She felt angry and shaken but aroused nevertheless. That night, lying in the bed recess beside the quiet form of her mother, she imagined what it would be like to have sex with James Mathieson. Her imaginings made her body pulsate almost to the point of orgasm. She had to turn away and lie curled up on her side in case her mother would suspect anything. She felt ashamed of the desire that was taking possession of her. Yet in the cold light of day, she told herself that it was perfectly natural and nothing to be ashamed of. She was a healthy young woman and there was now no other man in her life. She had already decided to accept another invitation to go out with Mathieson before he'd even asked her.

On their second 'walking out' a week later, he made no attempt to get her into the back close, or even kiss her. This disturbed her even more. The next time his kiss was gentle, almost absent-minded. She discovered later that his widowed mother had taken ill. On subsequent meetings they attended John Maclean's classes together and his talks in Bath Street. On each occasion, Mathieson showed passion in his agreement with Maclean but with her he behaved with admirable restraint. She was beginning to wish that he would sweep her off her feet and into the back close. Or anywhere at all to have sex. She felt ashamed of lusting after him. Especially while he was so worried about his mother. For a time he didn't come to see her or meet her. When his mother eventually died of TB, it took him some time to get over her death. Yet although Virginia missed him, she knew she didn't love James Mathieson. At least, not in the way she'd loved Nicholas. Despite trying to erase the memories of Nicholas from her mind, his face would still return at unexpected moments to sadden her. She'd see his dark eyes, his blue-black hair, his tall, elegant figure. Then into her mind would come the memory of the baby he'd never seen and pain would tear at her heart. Her only escape from this pain was to keep as busy as possible. She did this not only by working at the market, but by going out scrubbing again after she'd sold all the clothes and some of her books. She also began helping James by distributing political pamphlets. Sometimes, she would even speak at meetings he'd organised. Like Maclean, James was a fervent champion of women's rights, arguing in favour of equal pay for equal work. Virginia was more than happy to support him in his work for this cause.

Virginia sometimes wondered how Mrs Cartwright was coping. She thought of her now without any bitterness. Mrs Cartwright was simply a product of her class, just as Virginia was a product of hers. Now she only remembered the older woman's human side, and the way she'd eventually succeeded in being a practical help at the birth, her excitement and her pride in having helped bring her grandson into the world. Virginia could imagine Mr Cartwright being proud too. Baby Richard was no doubt a comfort to them both, and Virginia tried to find solace in that thought.

'Get on with the rest of your life,' Mrs Cartwright had told her.

'All right,' Virginia thought. 'I will.'

14

On Sunday 6th February 1916, Maclean was speaking at the usual Bath Street meeting when he was suddenly seized by the police and taken to Edinburgh Castle as a prisoner of war. James Mathieson nearly got arrested for trying to stop the police arresting Maclean. Virginia had to drag him off before he made things worse than they already were. It was only because of widespread protests that the authorities agreed to release Maclean on bail. His trial was set for the 11th of April.

Mathieson became more and more incensed as socialist newspapers like *Forward* and *Vanguard* were banned. Late one night police raided the Socialist Labour Press in Renfield Street, seized the type and manuscripts of *The Worker* and closed the premises. The editor was arrested along with other socialist leaders.

With Maclean out of the way, Mathieson took the lead in speaking at Bath Street, at street corners and at factory gates. By this time, he and Virginia had been walking out regularly and he was a frequent visitor to her home in the Gorbals. Janette had come to regard him almost as one of the family and she was now worrying about him as well as Tam and Duncan.

'James, son,' she told him, 'can you not take a lesson from John Maclean and the rest of his crowd. They've all ended up in jail and so will you if you're not careful. You could lose your job.'

'One thing I've learned from John Maclean is to be honest and stand up for my socialist beliefs, Mrs Watson.' His eyes strained with sincerity. 'And I'll do that till the day I die – no matter what the cost. You see, it's not the individual that matters, it's the success of our collective struggle against the oppressors.'

Janette did not look convinced by James' bravado. Part of her concern was that Virginia was spending more and more time helping him. She now attended all his meetings, not only distributing pamphlets but helping to write them.

Virginia herself admired Mathieson's courage, his idealism and his talent as a public speaker. Maclean had taught him well, and in his public speaking he was showing much of Maclean's fire, dedication and ability to grip and hold an audience. He was also, with other comrades, trying to continue Maclean's work for the Scottish Labour College. Virginia could see, however, that he did not have Maclean's superhuman energy. Nor Maclean's calmness under pressure. James could lose his temper with hecklers.

Especially if one of them shouted, as they often did, 'You're no' even a bloody worker!'

She had often seen him almost collapsing with exhaustion after a difficult and rowdy meeting. Sometimes, in this over-tired state, he would snap at her. Afterwards he would nurse his head in his hands and say, 'I've had one hell of a day. It wasn't the easiest of days at the school and then there was all that aggravation at the meeting. It's those damned police infiltrators – they come in plain clothes and mix with the crowd and try to stir up as much trouble as they can.' He sighed. 'But I shouldn't take it out on you. I'm sorry, Virginia.'

Now, looking at his earnest face topped with hair that was sticking up in untidy tufts, she felt a tenderness towards him.

'It's all right, James. You're just doing too much. Mammy's quite right.'

'I thought you understood. I thought you believed in what we're fighting for.'

'I do. I do. But what good are you to the cause if you're in jail?' She hesitated, then added in a whisper because they were in the kitchen at the time and her mother was washing the dishes over at the sink, 'I'm fond of you, James. I care about you. I don't want anything bad to happen to you.'

He squeezed her hand and the passion glowing in his eyes told her he longed to do much more. Later that evening, after they'd

156

been to a meeting in the Pavilion Theatre, he tried to pull her into the back close but she refused to budge from her mother's doorstep.

'It's just...' She tried to think of a way to explain. 'It's not that I don't want to ... you know. But it's such a terrible place.' Her voice shook. 'Terrible. I hate it. I hate the whole stinking place. It's not even fit for animals.'

He nodded. 'You're quite right. I wish I was still living at home. We could have gone there. But after mother died, the bastard of a landlord put me out. The rent book was in her name although I always paid the rent.' His mouth twisted with bitterness. 'He would never allow my name to go on the rent book. The factor said it was because I was too much of a troublemaker. Now, in my digs, there's no privacy at all.' He gazed down at her very seriously.

'Virginia, it's time we were married. We should be looking for a place of our own. We can't go on like this.'

What he said made sense. He was a good man and she thought he loved her, although he'd never actually said the words. There was nothing unusual in that. Scotsmen were notoriously reticent in appearing to be what was regarded as 'soft' or 'soppy'. She certainly could not imagine her father ever being romantic towards her mother. Although she didn't doubt that he had always loved her.

Nicholas had been romantic. He had not

been afraid to show tenderness and to speak the soft words of love. Thinking of him made the usual weight of sadness descend on her.

'Virginia,' Mathieson repeated with some aggression. 'Didn't you hear what I said?'

She knew it wasn't fair to go on as they had been.

'All right,' she told him. 'I'll start looking for a place.'

Immediately he grabbed her and held her tightly against him as he kissed her deeply, his tongue prising open her mouth and searching inside. She experienced such a surge of lust, she could have allowed him to take her right there and then. However, the neighbour in the close opened her door to let her cat out.

'Hello therr,' she laughed. 'Sorry fur interruptin' yer winchin', but yer askin' fur it standin' therr. That's whit the back close's fur.'

Virginia pulled the door bell.

'It's all right, Mrs MacKechnie, I was just going in. Goodnight, James.'

She could see the anger and frustration in his face but her mother arrived at the door and he had no opportunity to say anything more than a brief goodnight.

She had long since realised that James Mathieson had a volatile and fiery temper and she suspected that one day it would get him into serious trouble. And it did. It was what happened to John Maclean at his trial that was the catalyst.

At the trial, the six counts of the indictment against Maclean were read out with all due solemnity. Each was connected with statements he was alleged to have made at different meetings.

1) That conscription was unnecessary, as the government had plenty of soldiers and munitions; that after the war, conscription would be used to secure cheap labour; that should the government enforce the Military Service Act and the Munitions Act, the workers should 'down tools'; that if the British soldiers laid down their arms, the Germans would do that same, as all were tired of the war.

2) That the workers should strike in order to attend a meeting.

3) That the workers 'down tools' and resist conscription.

4) That if conscription became law, the workers would become conscripts to industrial labour – the real aim of the government.

5) That the workers should strike and those who had guns should use them.

6) That the workers should sell or pawn their alarm clocks, sleep in in the mornings and not go to work.

Maclean pleaded not guilty and put up a very good defence. He dealt with every charge and especially ridiculed the charge that he'd asked the workers to use guns. 'That type of thing might be good enough for men in Dublin,' he pointed out, 'but it is no good whatever for the Clyde workers. Even if they had the inclination to use guns, they have not got them.'

In the end, he was found guilty on the first four charges. Not proven on the fifth and not guilty on the sixth. The packed court was stunned not so much by the guilty verdicts as by the judge delivering a sentence of three years penal servitude. That meant imprisonment with hard labour. Maclean however was unperturbed. As he was led away, he turned and waved his hat to his wife and friends. They in turn promptly stood up and sang 'The Red Flag' as they'd never sung it before.

Mathieson was consumed with fury at the sentence. Maclean had been branded a traitor to his country and an enemy of the people. James couldn't bear this slur and he immediately called a meeting outside the court. He actually stood in the entrance and addressed the crowd. Virginia tried to calm him and pull him away but it was no use. He told his audience that Maclean was absolutely right.

'Conscription means bringing all young men under the control of the military authorities. That includes men in the factories and workshops, as well as in the field of battle. All the workers would come under military discipline. Men, as a result, would be bound hand and foot to the bosses, to the factory owners. The only weapon we can use is to strike. That's the only weapon we have!'

By now a crowd of policemen had appeared, batons drawn.

'For God's sake, James,' Virginia shouted at him. 'Stop this.'

But ignoring her, he carried on, 'John Maclean is a revolutionary socialist and so am I, comrades! And we are Internationalists. We will not do anything to help the capitalists in their war against our fellow workers in Germany or anywhere else in the world!'

The police pushed through the crowd, jerked Virginia roughly aside and grabbed Mathieson. He struggled wildly and one policeman lashed out with his baton. Despite his powerful build, the force of the blow, quickly followed by a second and then a third from another policeman, felled Mathieson. As he lay there in a crumpled heap, there was a roar of rage from the crowd who stampeded forward, fists flying. The police lashed out viciously with their batons, and when further reinforcements arrived on the scene the unequal struggle came to an abrupt end and order was restored.

Virginia was shocked at what had happened to Mathieson. He was in a dreadful state, with blood pouring down his face from a wound on his head. She tried in vain to stem the flow with a ripped-off piece of her white petticoat.

'Don't worry,' he told her. 'It's not serious. I'll live.'

'Aye,' one of the policemen said, 'and it'll be in Calton Jail for a while, my lad.'

Sure enough, James wasn't even allowed bail, and he soon joined Maclean in Calton Jail in Edinburgh, a gloomy tomb-like building which was notorious as the worst prison in the country. No books, writing materials or cigarettes were allowed. The prisoners were not allowed their own food or clothes. Sanitary conditions were terrible and bunks were as hard as concrete. But worst of all was the 'separate and silence' system, where each prisoner was confined alone in a cell so tiny there was scarcely room to move about. Only half an hour of exercise in the sunless courtyard was allowed and even then, the silence was rigidly enforced. All of these things were torment enough for anyone, but for men like Maclean and Mathieson, it was torture to be without literature and newspapers and to suffer the terrible isolation and nerve-racking silence. But at least Mathieson caught glimpses of Maclean and other socialist friends who had also been incarcerated.

The prisoners were moved, and Mathieson was sent north to Peterhead prison, where he had to work outside in gangs in all sorts of weather. Even there the regime of silence was strictly observed, with severe punishments meted out to anyone who dared utter a word. And the warders were well qualified to enforce these punishments, having been specially chosen from the army, the police force and mental asylums for their harshness and brutality.

It was hell for James Mathieson, but it was also terrible for Virginia. Once more the war had torn her life apart. Still, at least James was alive...

It was not until June 1917 – a little more than a year after he had been locked up – that Mathieson was finally released.

Virginia was shocked at the change in him. He had lost a lot of weight. This, he told her, was inevitable because the food was so inadequate. He said no more about his time in prison, but Virginia guessed that he'd suffered much more than hunger. She had only been allowed to make a couple of visits while James had been in prison and she had seen that he didn't look well. But he had always put a brave face on things. He never wanted to talk about himself but was always anxious to know what was happening outside. Were the workers' economics classes still being held and were they still well attended? Were their comrades speaking regularly in the Pavilion and in Bath Street and at factory gates? He seemed to have lost interest in anything other than politics.

It wasn't until he had been released from prison that Virginia was able to tell him all her news. Duncan had got married – a shotgun affair – to a girl called Celia. He'd also been conscripted. Celia wouldn't hear of what she called the disgrace of him becoming a Conscientious Objector.

Tam said, 'That girl has got Duncan so much under her thumb he's gone like a lamb into the army. Proud as punch she was to see him in uniform. Stupid bitch. A good thrashing's what she needs to bring her to her senses.'

Tam was refusing to allow Celia over his doorstep.

'I'll never forgive that girl for ruining Duncan,' he told James angrily, 'He was always such a sensible boy before he met her.'

James had been dismissed from his teaching post and had been thrown out of his digs. Even if he had not lost his job, he would not have been fit to do any kind of work for a while yet. He needed plenty of rest and good food to build up his strength. Almost before Virginia realised what was happening, and certainly before she had time to think whether or not it was the right thing to do, it was agreed that she and James would have a quiet wedding. Then they would live with the Watsons until they could get a place of their own. Tam had already gone back to sharing the kitchen bed with Janette, and Virginia now had the room bed to herself.

Until the young couple were married, however, there was no question of them sharing the room bed. Neither Janette nor Tam would have countenanced such an impropriety. Indeed it was going to be embarrassing enough for all of them even after they were married. Meantime Mathieson had to share the room bed with Tam and Virginia moved back to the kitchen bed with her mother.

They wasted no time in arranging the registry office ceremony. Most wartime marriages took place at the registry office. There was seldom time to arrange a big church wedding, and weddings were often hurried affairs arranged during a soldier's brief leave. Janette was sad that James and Virginia weren't going to be blessed in the church, but she had long since resigned herself to the fact that they were both atheists.

Virginia had carried on with her job scrubbing, and now cleaned out halls as well as pubs. It was hard work and she hated it but at least it put food on the table and coal on the fire. Despite his frailty, James was desperate to find work.

He said, 'I'm no' going to allow my wife to keep me. It's not right.'

Tam overheard him and asked sarcastically, 'Oh aye? You're going into the munitions, are you? You're going to make guns to kill your fellow workers, are you?'

'I'm sorry, Tam,' James said. 'I wasn't sniping at you. I respect the way you've stuck to your principles. And I will too. I was thinking more of something in the teaching line. The Labour College pay a few of the tutors. I might have some luck there.'

'That's all very well,' Virginia told him, 'but in the meantime, I'm going to see that you get your health and strength back. You'll rest here and eat decent meals for another few days before you even think about working.'

Tam laughed.

'Here, you'd better be careful, son. Or you'll be under her thumb before you know it.'

'No chance,' Mathieson said without laughing. It occurred to Virginia then that he hadn't really much of a sense of humour. He was a very serious minded man. She sighed to herself. At the moment she not only didn't feel in love with him, she didn't even lust after him. It was true, however, what her mother said. He was a good, decent man. She should think herself lucky.

She tried to.

15

For the wedding James wore his homburg hat, a dark suit and stiff-collared shirt. Virginia perched a flowerpot hat over her long silky blonde hair which she'd wound into a chignon at the nape of her neck. White gloves matched the flowers on her hat. A blue coat, hobble skirt and long button boots with Louis heels completed the outfit. Duncan was home on leave before being sent to France and he looked enormous in his khaki uniform and Army boots. He and Celia were witnesses. Celia was a tiny girl with mousy, finger-waved hair peeping out from under a wide brimmed hat. She giggled all the time, even during the wedding ceremony itself, and kept fluttering her eyelashes at Duncan as she clung to his arm. Duncan seemed to enjoy all Celia's infantile attention, but James was distinctly unimpressed. Afterwards, he told Virginia 'That girl's a right pain in the arse. She'd drive me mad.'

Virginia agreed. 'I don't know what Duncan sees in her. She's not even all that pretty.'

'She must have something.'

They both silently wondered if Celia was

good in bed. That was the only thing they could think of that could explain Duncan's obvious infatuation. Virginia was anticipating her own coupling with James with mixed feelings. Despite the fact that it was nearly three years since her time with Nicholas, she had never been completely able to banish the memory of his love-making. Weeks, months would pass and it was as if he'd never existed. Then suddenly, without warning, she would be dancing naked with him in the misty beauty of the woods. Their bodies warm against each other, yet fresh and tingling with dew. She could feel his lips nuzzling her neck. She could hear his cultured voice intoning beautiful lines of poetry to her. His voice was a joy to listen to. It was so different from the broad Glasgow voices she was now used to, with their glottal stop and hard, often coarse, edge.

Thoughts of Nicholas would bring thoughts of her baby and she'd long for them both. The longing came to her on her wedding day and she felt ashamed to be standing beside James, taking solemn vows to love, cherish and obey him until death parted them, when she was thinking of how death had parted her from her love. Gazing up at James's serious face, she determined to put everything else out of her mind once and for all and to concentrate only on being a good and faithful wife to him.

After the ceremony they went to Miss Cranston's for high tea. Then they went to the Central Station to see Duncan off as he was due back with his unit that night. As usual, Central Station was crowded with folk seeing off their friends and relations in the forces. Duncan's train was packed solid with the boys and as many as possible were hanging out of doors and windows to wave a last goodbye. Wives and mothers were standing with tears streaming down their faces and singing 'Will ye no' come back again', and the station echoed to the mournful refrain.

After seeing Duncan off and saying goodnight to Celia, James and Virginia made their way back to the Gorbals and to the Watsons' room and kitchen. They had not yet found a place of their own and so would have to start their married life in Janette's front room.

Janette had said her goodbyes to Duncan earlier in the day. Her first words now as soon as Virginia and James showed their faces in the kitchen were,

'Did he get away all right then?'

'Yes, mammy,' Virginia said. 'Will I make a cup of tea?'

Her mother nodded.

'He didn't need to go. I wouldn't have minded him being a C.O.'

'It's that stupid lassie.' Tam had been sitting by the fire drawing on a Woodbine.

'She'll be the death of that lad yet.'

'Daddy!' Virginia cried out reprovingly. 'Be quiet. You're just upsetting mammy.'

Janette said, 'The telegram boy's never away from here.'

James took off his hat and coat and hung them on the peg in the lobby. Then he settled himself at the table. 'That doesn't mean anything's going to happen to Duncan, Mrs Watson. Thousands and thousands of men are out there and surviving. They've made it through Ypres and The Somme, so maybe the worst's behind them. Let's just hope sanity will prevail and the whole damned thing will soon be over.'

'Aye, I hope ye're right son,' nodded Tam in agreement.

'Celia's just a silly young girl,' Janette said. 'But if anything happens to Duncan, she'll feel as bad as any of us.'

'Huh!' Tam shouted derisively and tossed his cigarette dout into the fire. Immediately regretting this angry and thoughtless act, he shouted, 'Now look what she's made me do!'

Virginia shook her head at him, and in an obvious attempt to change the subject said to her mother, 'I thought it all went very well today. It was over a bit quick, right enough, but that's because there was a queue waiting. And the haddock and chips we had at Miss Cranston's was nice, wasn't it, James?'

'Very tasty,' James agreed. 'We all enjoyed it. Then we went to see Duncan off at the Central. The place was absolutely mobbed. We would hardly move along the platform.'

'Was he upset?' Janette asked.

'No, not a bit. He waved to us very cheerily.'

Janette sighed. 'He was never one to show his feelings.'

'Here, drink your tea, mammy.' Virginia poured everyone a cup and then took the tin biscuit barrel down from the mantelpiece. With her last wage packet she'd bought some digestives, her mother's favourite. 'And have a biscuit.'

'Thanks, hen. You're lucky you're a bit older than Duncan, son. You'll not be bothered with this terrible conscription.'

'Oh, it'll probably come to me yet. But I'll go to prison rather than have anything to do with this capitalist war.'

Virginia lingered over her tea. She suddenly had the feeling that James was a stranger. But, for now, embarrassment was the thing uppermost in her mind. It somehow didn't feel decent to go and share the room bed with a man. They would just be through the wall from her mother and father.

Eventually Tam said, 'Are you two going to sit there all night. I want to get to my bed.'

James immediately rose and bade Tam and Janette goodnight.

Virginia said, 'I'll just wash up these cups.'

Janette got up. 'No, no. I'll do that. Away you go, hen.'

Through in the room, Virginia whispered, 'The quicker we find a wee place of our own, the better. I feel embarrassed, don't you?'

James had begun to undress. He shrugged. 'A bit. But don't worry, we'll find somewhere.' Once naked, he folded his clothes neatly on to a chair. Then he climbed up on to the high set-in-the-wall bed. 'Hurry up,' he told Virginia. 'This room's like the North Pole.'

Virginia had been staring at his stocky frame. His muscly upper back made his shoulders look rounded. His chest was covered with a mat of hair that thinned to a line travelling down over his abdomen. Then it tufted out over his bulging genitals. It was gingery brown, not light brown like the hair on his head. She experienced a surge of distaste bordering on revulsion, yet at the same time lust came throbbing to life in her. As quickly as possible, she undressed and climbed into bed beside him. He immediately grabbed her against him and fastened his mouth over hers. In a few minutes he had mounted her and the bedsprings began to creak loudly.

'Shh, shh,' Virginia hissed jerkily. 'They'll hear us.'

But he just went on grunting with pleasure,

the sounds filling the room and, Virginia feared, passing through the wall of the kitchen, right into her mother and father's bed. Her body and mind split. She was physically excited. Her body opened to James, indulged him, indulged herself. Her mind squeezed shut, in an effort not to think of her father and mother listening. Afterwards she wished the immediate peace of sleep could black her out as it had with James. For hours she lay staring into the darkness feeling acutely embarrassed and ashamed. She knew that being married made love-making between husband and wife a perfectly natural and acceptable fact of life that neither her mother or father would object to. But it was embarrassing nevertheless. She determined to waste no time in finding a place where she and James could live in decent privacy. She must have dozed off eventually because she woke with James shaking her shoulders.

'Come on, Virginia. Time you were up. We've a lot to do.'

'Have we?' Virginia murmured sleepily while at the same time beginning to struggle out of bed.

'Lloyd George is coming to Glasgow today. They're giving him the "Freedom of the City", would you believe? There's going to be thousands on the streets, all demanding Maclean's release.'

'Oh yes, I forgot.' She pulled on some

clothes, tugged a brush through her long hair and started plaiting it as she followed James through to the kitchen.

'Hello, hen.' Her mother was standing at the fire, stirring a black iron pot filled with porridge. 'Did you have a good night?'

Tam chuckled. 'I don't think there's any doubt about that. It was her wedding night, Janette.'

Both Janette and Virginia flushed and Janette said, 'You know what I mean.'

It was what she usually asked first thing in the morning, and simply meant – did you sleep well.

James said to Tam, 'You'll be going out to welcome Lloyd George, Tam?'

Tam sat down at the table as Janette began dishing out the porridge.

'He'll get a welcome here that he'll not forget in a hurry!'

'We'd better get out early. I was just saying to Virginia, there'll be thousands. And all demanding John's release.'

'Aye, don't worry, I'll be there all right.'

Janette sighed. 'For goodness' sake, try not to get yourself arrested. You especially, James. Remember you're a married man now with Virginia to think about.'

'Virginia's coming as well.'

Virginia would have preferred it if he'd asked her first, but she'd always gone to the demonstrations before so it was natural for

James to take it for granted she'd be at this one as well.

'I thought,' she said, 'you were going to ask about work at the Labour College first.'

James nodded. 'Yes, there's time to do that. I'll go as soon as I've finished this. You wait here. I'll come back for you.'

He washed his face and neck at the jawbox – as the sink in Glasgow tenements was called. He plastered Brylcreem on his hair, but it was too short to smooth down, and always stood up in tufts. He put on his homburg, gave it a pat and said, 'Right, I'll see you later. Wish me luck.'

'Good luck, son,' Janette said.

Virginia was still drinking her tea but she raised a hand in goodbye to him as he strode purposefully out of the house. Virginia prayed that he would get a teaching job. She couldn't imagine him hanging about the house doing nothing. She could imagine how restless, angry and frustrated he would become. He would be very hard to live with.

She washed up the breakfast dishes and replaced them in the press beside the sink. Then she went through to the room and made the bed. After that she went back to the kitchen and asked her father to go through to the room while she had a wash.

While she was at the sink there was a knock on the outside door. Virginia hurried to finish her ablutions. She could hear her father going to the door and saying,

'Oh, it's you, Mrs McKechnie. Come away in, hen.'

Virginia just managed to throw on her clothes in time before the kitchen door opened and her father and the neighbour came in.

'Hello hen,' Mrs McKechnie greeted Virginia. 'Ah jist brought ye this wee mindin'.' She produced a teapot and a teapot cover. 'Ah know ye said it was jist a quiet affair wi' yer brother goin' away tae the army and aw that, but here's a wee teapot anyway.'

'Oh thanks, Mrs McKechnie. It's lovely and I'll need one when we get a place of our own. I'm going to start looking tomorrow. Today there's a big demonstration...'

'Aye, they're gatherin' in the streets already. I'll be there masel. Ah'd better away back in and get ready. Ah'm takin' the weans as well.' She laughed. 'Ah've telt them they've tae shout as loud as they can – Free John Maclean. They're aw excited already.' She gave a wave to Virginia. 'Aw the best, hen.'

'Thanks, Mrs McKechnie.'

Janette saw her neighbour to the door. When she came back she said to Virginia, 'Fancy her taking her weans. They could get hurt in all that crowd. I'm worried enough about you and James and Tam.'

'It's a friendly crowd, mammy.'

'Friendly? With all that shouting?'

'We'll all be shouting at Lloyd George, not at each other. Do you want me to give this floor a wee scrub while I'm waiting for James?'

'No, just leave it for today, hen. It's more the floorboards to scrub than the lino now with all these holes.'

'If I make enough in the next week or two, mammy, I'll buy you some new lino. There's a man down at Clyde Street sells it really cheap.'

'You'll do no such thing,' Janette said. 'You're a married woman, don't forget. You'll need all you have for your own wee place when you get it. And if James gets work, he won't let you go out scrubbing.'

Virginia couldn't deny this but she insisted on black-leading the range and energetically rubbed all the steel bits at the front with emery paper. She was barely finished when there was a loud rapping at the door.

'That'll be James,' said Virginia, washing her hands at the sink. She took the towel from the hook inside the press door and went to answer the knock as she rubbed her hands dry. Already she could recognise James's impatient, aggressive knock. As soon as she opened the door, James pushed past her into the kitchen. He was rubbing his hands with glee.

'I got it,' he said. 'The teaching job. It's not much money but still it's better than nothing and I can feel I'm doing something useful.'

'Aye, you're right, son,' Tam agreed. 'If there's one thing the working class need it's education. Good for you, son. Congratulations.'

'Thanks, Tam. Come on, Virginia, get your coat on and we'll be away. Are you coming, Tam?'

'I've some pals coming for me. They'll be here in a few minutes. On you go with Virginia, son.'

'Cheerio, mammy,' Virginia called once she'd grabbed her coat and struggled into it.

'For pity's sake, be careful,' Janette pleaded. 'Yes, yes.'

And off they went into the streets that were already heaving and seething with people. All over Glasgow, there was a buzz of excitement – but anger and hatred were also in the air. It was the calm before the storm.

16

'I can't help worrying about the McKechnie children,' Virginia said. 'They could be trampled to death in a crowd like this.'

The workers had come out on to the streets in their thousands, and everywhere yells of 'Release Maclean' tore through the air.

Everyone surged in the direction of St Andrew's Hall where Lloyd George was to be speaking. All along the route onlookers struggled to get near his car – which had been slowed to a snail's pace – but he was surrounded all the way by soldiers and policemen. When he finally appeared at St Andrew's Hall, he was met by a huge, threatening mass of men and women, many waving the red flag. An enormous red flag was flying from an adjacent building.

'Release John Maclean!' The chant grew to thunderous, ear-splitting proportions. Then word was given that Maclean would be released next day and the chants gave way to riotous cheering. The whole crowd immediately made for Duke Street prison where they raised lusty cheers in the hope that Maclean – who was inside – would hear them.

Next day, James and Virginia were in the crowd who welcomed Maclean on his release and went to hear him speak at what they both agreed was the most inspiring meeting they'd ever been to. Many had feared that Maclean would have lost much of his intensity after his suffering in prison. But all the old passion, enthusiasm and devotion to the socialist cause was still there.

'Comrades!' he had greeted them as the cheering subsided 'Glad as I am to be back with you once more, let us not forget those I have left behind. Those brave souls still suffering, whose only crime is to stand up and speak out for what they believe!' He ended on a rousing note by declaring that the workers' movement must stand firm in both its opposition to the war and the continuing struggle to overthrow capitalism. Fists were then raised in salute as a stirring rendition of 'The Red Flag' rocked the hall.

'Wasn't that bloody marvellous?' James said to Virginia on the way home in the tram car. He had to raise his voice to be heard over the rattling and clattering of the tram.

She knew what he meant. The audience had been euphoric and this feeling still clung to her.

'Marvellous,' she agreed.

James continued, 'He's the catalyst that makes everything happen. He rouses indignation, sweeps aside doubts and hesitations, inspires courage and confidence.' He folded his arms at the back of his head and relaxed against them. 'He's such a brilliant educator as well – there's already hundreds enrolling in his new classes – he's so clear-headed about society and about the war. The energy of the man!' James heaved a sigh of admiration. Virginia hugged his arm in enthusiastic agreement.

When they arrived home it was getting late, but the house was empty. Tam was still out on the streets and Janette had left a note to say that she was visiting one of the upstairs neighbours. Their euphoric excitement was immediately channelled into sex and they couldn't get into the room and on top of the bed quickly enough. Rejoicing in the fact that they didn't need to care about making a noise, even Virginia let herself go and her moans and squeals rivalled Mathieson's groans and shouts in loudness and abandon. Afterwards they were both exhausted. Mathieson collapsed back off her.

Virginia suddenly felt depressed.

'We'd better get up before mammy and daddy come back.'

'Right.' Mathieson jerked into a sitting position then swung his feet out of the bed. 'I'll away upstairs to the lavatory.'

Virginia went through to the kitchen and hastily, furtively, washed between her legs. She hoped Mathieson would wash himself before her parents returned. She didn't want them to smell sex on him. However, he actually arrived back at the same time as her mother and father and so didn't get the opportunity.

Tam had barely set foot in the kitchen when he announced in an absolute fury, 'Do you know what I've just found out?' His face was flushed and his moustache looked wildly untidy as if he'd been tugging and rubbing at it.

'What?' Mathieson asked.

'Who do you think owns that death-trap

where our Ian worked?'

'I've no idea, Tam.'

'That bastard that Virginia worked for.'

Virginia's legs gave way and she groped for the nearest chair.

'Mr Cartwright?'

'Aye, George murdering Cartwright!'

'Are you sure, daddy?'

'Of course I'm sure. It's all round the place. I got it from a union man. The union's been fighting for better and safer conditions and this bastard appeared and talked them down. Spouting all about patriotism and the war effort and how his son had been killed doing his duty without a word of complaint. Holding up his son as an example to the men. Trying to shame them back to work to pile up more profit for him and to hell with how many of them get killed.'

Now James was flushed with rage. 'Bastard! For him to be blown up in his own bloody factory would be too good, too easy for him. He needs to suffer something much worse! Something–'

'James, for pity's sake!' Virginia interrupted, distressed by the mad gleam in his eyes, the tightness of his mouth and the scarlet blotches of colour firing his cheeks. 'Control yourself, or you'll be taking a fit or a heart attack.'

'I've no pity for the likes of him and neither should you. He's responsible for what happened to your brother – and many other women's brothers as well. Many other women's sons. He deserves no pity and no working man will give him any. We'll organise a march to his house, drag him out if necessary and– '

'No, James, you mustn't,' Virginia cried out in panic. 'You'll only be flung back in prison again. For goodness' sake, have a bit of common sense and self control for once. For my sake if not for your own.'

Janette spoke up then. 'Virginia's right, son. I don't want you to go either. It won't bring our Ian back. It'll only mean we'll lose you as well. So sit down and try and calm yourself. Have a wee drop of whisky in your tea.'

He sat down at the table but Virginia could see a pulse beating furiously in his neck.

'I know how you feel, son,' Tam said. 'I feel the same. But we'd better think what we're doing here. Let's try to simmer down and have a think about a better way to deal with this.'

James nodded. Then, 'To think my wife slaved after him.'

'Not him,' Virginia said. 'I mean, I just worked in the kitchen. He was hardly ever in the house. I didn't even see much of Mrs Cartwright until that time at her holiday house.'

'It's the same thing. You were helping to keep the wheels of capitalism running smoothly. I'll make sure you never have to do anything like that again.'

Virginia was becoming irritated. 'What do you mean? Anything like what?'

'Working for any other rich bastards like the Cartwrights.'

'Don't worry. I've no intention of ever going back into service. I didn't enjoy it, you know. I was just trying to make a living and help mammy with the rent. And none of us knew what business he was in.'

Janette patted her hand. 'It's all right, hen. You did your best. You didn't mean any harm.'

'What do you bet,' James said, 'we'll find out he owns not only his bloody factories and hundreds of acres around his house, but half the Highlands as well!'

'Not all that again!' Virginia said. 'You and your obsession with the Clearances. It happened long ago, James, and whatever you may think, it had nothing to do with Mr Cartwright.'

James ignored her and carried on, 'I'm telling you. It's people like him who own half of Scotland. People like him who made my family suffer. Homelessness, humiliation and death.'

'You don't know that he or any of his ancestors or his friends ever had anything to do with land in the Highlands.'

'Who's side are you on?' James demanded.

'I thought you were supposed to be a socialist.'

'I am. You know perfectly well I am. But you're just being ridiculous.'

James's eyes bulged with fury. 'Ridiculous, am I? Ridiculous to remember what happened to my mother and father and grandmother and grandfather? Ridiculous to care, is it?'

Janette leaned over the table and patted James's hand. 'Now, now, son. Drink up your tea. She didn't mean that. You're a good loyal son to your folks. I can see you care about them and their memory. But I'm sure they wouldn't want you to get into serious trouble because of them, son.'

Tam was carefully rolling a Woodbine. 'Anyway, no harm in organising a wee protest.'

'Have you no sense either? Virginia said impatiently. 'Can you not see the state James is in. You've done enough to stir him up already.'

'Huh?' her father gasped indignantly. 'Do you hear that, James? What did she expect me to do? Not tell you about who owned the factory where my son was killed?'

'Now *you're* being ridiculous,' Virginia said.

'That's enough,' James growled. 'Don't speak to your father like that. Go through to the room.'

'What?' Virginia gasped, half laughing.

'Go through to the room. I'll be there in a minute.'

'You've a nerve. I'm not your servant to order about. Some socialist! And after all I've heard you saying about women's rights!'

Janette was becoming agitated. 'Now, Virginia, James's your man and he's upset. We all are. Away you go through, the pair of you. Tam and me want to get to our bed.'

Without another word Virginia got up and walked out of the kitchen. She was furious and had developed a thumping headache. As James followed her she turned on him, 'Don't you ever order me about like that again, do you hear?'

James sat down and nursed his head in his hands. 'I'm sorry. I got carried away. It's just that bastards like Cartwright shouldn't be allowed to get away with it. All the misery and suffering they cause.'

Virginia's anger melted away at this. She put an arm around Mathieson's shoulders. 'Come on to bed.'

He nodded and began tugging at his tie. Once in bed, he lay stiff and tense.

'I remember my grandmother, you know. A lovely old lady she was. She didn't deserve to suffer as she did. And my grandfather was a real gentleman. When I think of what they were made to go through. Thrown out of their home in the middle of the night, left to walk about cold and hungry, and with young children. Can you imagine it? And despite it all, they retained their decency and their integrity to the last.'

'Shh, shh,' she soothed. 'Try to get some sleep, James. You've your job to think about, remember. You'll be doing something really worthwhile at the college.'

'Yes, you're right. It's important that workers are educated and ready for the revolution. Then the Cartwrights of this world won't know what's hit them. When I think of young men, like your brother, with everything to live for, ending their days in that factory, while Cartwright in that grand house of his hasn't a care in the world.'

'Shh, shh.'

'I want to kill the bastard...'

17

Since October 1917, when the first shattering news of the Russian Revolution reached the west, the British government had been acutely concerned about the worsening situation on the Clyde. The authorities began to refuse permission for any socialist or workers' meetings to be held in any of their halls. Only the Pavilion Theatre continued to allow meetings and workers congregated there whenever possible. However, this did not affect the hastily-arranged protest meeting in connection with Cartwright's factory, as it was to be held in the open outside the factory gates.

Despite Virginia's pleadings and angry remonstrations, the meeting had hardly begun before James jumped on to the soap-box and tried to rouse the workers to march to Cartwright's home. Fortunately, other speakers argued against this rash action. James, however, persevered, and there was a point when the crowd seemed to be swayed by his arguments. In desperation, Virginia got up on the soap box and told the crowd that she had lost a brother in one of the accidents in this factory, but she didn't believe that any safety regulations or improvements would be won by attacking Cartwright's home. Quite the reverse. 'We have to make our situation and our protests known in calm and logical arguments by letter, and by organised, lawful representations to the police and to the government.' Many nodded their approval of Virginia's arguments, she received a round of applause and her recommendations were adopted. James was furious.

'Why do you keep sticking up for the Cartwrights?'

Virginia rolled her eyes heavenwards.

'I wasn't "sticking up for the Cartwrights",

as you put it. You've missed the point of what I said. It would have done nothing but harm to the cause if they'd followed you. It wouldn't have been a peaceful demonstration, James, and you know it. You're no John Maclean. You can't keep your temper. He can.'

However, once the meeting was over, James' anger was soon diffused. He was hard put to it to keep up with his work – all his time was taken up with tutorial duties at the college and travelling around teaching classes of workers all over the country. Meanwhile, Maclean had gone down to England where he'd been invited to address a variety of meetings. As James told Virginia, after he'd arrived home utterly exhausted one night, 'The work Maclean's doing this winter has never been and never could be equalled by anyone. I just don't know where he gets the energy.'

Apart from his educational work, Maclean was carrying on terrific propaganda and agitational campaigns, devoting every waking moment to the revolutionary struggle. Above all else, his message was that the workers should have faith only in themselves. They must, with boldness and confidence, take matters into their own hands and seize both the land and the means of production.

Virginia and James normally went together to Maclean's meetings, but her mother took a dose of 'flu, and so Virginia was kept busy nursing her back to health.

No-one cheered on Maclean or supported him more eagerly and enthusiastically than James Mathieson. He agreed with Maclean on everything, including his prophecy that the war, far from being the war to end all wars, would be followed by another war within twenty years. And one day there would be a war with America.

Virginia ridiculed this idea. 'A war between Britain and America? That's crazy, James. I don't believe for one moment that will ever happen.'

'It'll be an economic war with them,' James said. 'You should have heard John explain how he believes it will happen. I wish you'd been there, Virginia. It always comes down to money, you know – the ruthless pursuit of profit regardless of human suffering.'

Virginia had also been looking for a place of their own, and went with James to see a 'single end', a one apartment house in the Calton district. The district was on the opposite side of the river from the Gorbals. It was bounded by the Saltmarket on the west and the River Clyde between Albert and Rutherglen bridges in the south. Main Street, Bridgeton was part of the eastern boundary, and Gallowgate the northern. Of the five streets which converged on Glasgow Cross, three were associated with the Calton ward – Gallowgate, Saltmarket and London Road.

On their way to view the single end in Bankier Street, James and Virginia walked through Glasgow Green.

'There used to be fairs here in the last century,' James said. 'Opposite the court house. But there was so much trouble it was decreed that boothkeepers must keep beside them a halbert, jack and steel bonnet. They must have been turbulent times.'

Virginia couldn't resist remarking with a touch of sarcasm, 'Not like now.'

James didn't seem to notice the sarcasm and continued with his lecture. 'Calton used to be famous for its weaving industry. All the weavers lived here in Bankier Street.'

'I've heard of the Calton weavers, right enough, but I didn't realise they came from Bankier Street.'

'Yes, it was called Thomson's Lane then. They were paid such a wretched pittance that they went on strike for a decent wage. The employers refused to give them a penny. They demonstrated and the military were called out, the Riot Act was read and then the guns were turned on the weavers. There's a tombstone in the local graveyard. It says on it, "They were martyred by the military".'

They had reached the close of one of the gloomy four storey tenements. Mathieson looked around.

'What a dump!'

Before coming to live in the Gorbals, James had lived in his mother's more respectable room and kitchen in Shawlands. His digs had also been in a comparatively comfortable and respectable area.

'There's nothing else. At least at a rent we can afford,' Virginia told him. 'There's no use in turning up your nose at it.'

'I wasn't turning up my nose at it. Not in the way you mean. I was just thinking what a disgrace it is that landlords expect human beings to live in overcrowded conditions in places like this.'

'Right enough. But it won't do any harm to have a look anyway.' Virginia linked arms with him. 'It's upstairs. One up.'

They passed the lavatory on the first landing. The usual smell followed them as James put the key in the door and pushed it open. A dingy shoe box of a lobby led directly into the kitchen which was also to act as living room, dining room and bedroom. There was the usual hole-in-the-wall bed with space underneath to store belongings, including the zinc bath. A black range and a press took up most of the wall. Opposite was the built-in bunker and dresser, high above which were two long shelves. Lastly, over at the window, was the black sink and swan tap.

They surveyed it all in silence. Then Virginia said, 'At least it faces the front.' From the window the only view was of the equally gloomy tenements across the narrow road.

Then Virginia rallied. 'Don't worry, I'll soon have it cleaned up and cosy looking. There's our wedding presents, and I'll get a few things cheap from my friends at the Clyde Street barrows.'

James said, 'I know an unemployed cabinet-maker. He'll make me a table and chairs.'

'Great. That's all we need really. Mammy's knitted a blanket with all the odd bits of wool she's collected.'

'Like Joseph's coat of many colours.' James smiled.

'She knitted squares and then sewed them all together. She crocheted the squares for the blanket on her own bed. It's nicer than any ordinary blanket you could buy in the shops.'

'I'm sure. It's very kind of your mother to go to all that trouble.'

'And there's the teapot from Mrs Mc-Kechnie, and a big iron soup pot from Mrs Friel, and a kettle from Mrs MacDougal– '

'All right, all right. You don't have to go through the lot. I suppose we've no choice but to take it.'

'Come on, let's go to the factor's office,' Virginia said, 'We can get the rent book. Then I can start getting this place cleaned up.'

They couldn't afford linoleum to begin with, so after Virginia scrubbed the floorboards, she polished them. She scrubbed the space under the bed very thoroughly before packing it with as many of their belongings as possible, including James' books and her own. The shelves above the coal bunker and dresser had to hold dishes and a couple of 'wally' or china dogs they'd been given by one of Virginia's barrow friends. Another friend who sold odd dishes and pieces of cutlery from her barrow had given her five big dinner plates and a tureen. Virginia had also bought a piece of red and cream checked oilcloth to cover the table. She was pleased with that as it made the tiny room look more cheerful and homely. A glass cover for the gas mantle was decorated with red poppies and the bright, multi-coloured blanket brightened the bed recess area. Although she hadn't been able to afford bed curtains or a valance to hide all the articles stuffed under the bed, she looked forward to getting some nice cream-coloured material eventually and making her own curtains. Once that was done, the place would look very nice, she told herself proudly. With the range sparkling and the fire glowing and everything spotlessly clean, it would be a cosy little place with all anyone could need for their comfort. James, however, simply reminded her of the lack of hot water and the lavatory out on the downstairs landing.

'But all the same,' he conceded, 'you've done a grand job.'

She was sweating and exhausted with all her hard work and would have loved a luxurious hot bath. But by this time she hadn't enough energy left to pull out the zinc bath and start filling kettles of water. She just fell into bed. Mathieson immediately got on top of her.

'No, James. Not tonight.'

'I've been looking forward to this all day. It's all that's kept me going. Coming home to you.'

She was barely able to whisper, 'All right.'

She felt sore now as a result of his desperate passion. And he was a heavy man. At times unable to lift her chest to breathe, she thought she was going to die. Then it was over, his passion spent, and he rolled off her and within minutes he was sound asleep. She felt exhausted but lay wide awake and feeling sad. She told herself that she was lucky to have a good man who would work for her and give her housekeeping money and never abuse her. Yet the sadness remained. She reminded herself how many women she knew were beaten by their men. Others never received a penny from theirs. Most of the men were unemployed but often they gambled or drank what little money there was. James neither drank nor smoked. He was totally devoted to the betterment of his fellow beings. She admired and respected him for that. But still the sadness weighed heavy on her soul.

Next day she was up early seeing to her husband's breakfast. Then after he left for one of his classes, she washed the dishes and tidied up and went out for something for his dinner. Bankier Street had shops underneath all of its bleak tenements and she first went to the grocer's and bought bread and potatoes. She could make a lot of economical dishes with potatoes. She was just passing the paper shop clutching her messages in one hand and her purse in the other when her eyes caught sight of something in bold, black type on one of the billboards outside the shop.

It was the name 'Cartwright.'

She stopped and read, hardly daring to believe her own eyes – 'Nicholas Cartwright found alive.'

Her legs gave way. She dropped on to her knees. Her purse and her message bag tumbled on to the ground. She crumpled forward. The last thing she remembered was seeing potatoes rolling away down the street.

18

When she came to, she was being propped up on a chair inside the paper shop.

'Are ye aw right, hen?' A small woman with bandy legs and a frizz of uncombed hair was bending close to her face. She reeked of whisky. 'Ye gi'ed us a hell o' a fright. Here's yer purse and yer message bag. Ah gathered up aw yer tatties.'

'Thanks very much.' Virginia took a determined grip of the purse and the bag. 'I'm fine now. I'll just buy a paper and then I'll get off home.'

'Wid ye like me tae come wi' ye, hen?' The woman looked none too steady on her feet.

'No, no,' Virginia hastily assured her. 'I'll be perfectly all right. But thanks all the same.'

'Ta, ta, then.'

'Cheerio and thanks again.'

As soon as the woman had disappeared outside and the shop assistant had finished serving a customer, Virginia struggled up and with shaking hands took a copper from her purse and asked for a newspaper. As soon as she got back to the single end, she collapsed into a chair and started reading the article about the Cartwrights. Mr and Mrs Cartwright had been contacted by the War Office and told that their son, Lieutenant Nicholas Cartwright, had been found in a military hospital in the South of England. He had been suffering from shell-shock and loss of memory as a result of a head wound. The confusion over Lieutenant Cartwright's fate had arisen because his watch and other personal effects had been found near another, otherwise unrecognisable corpse in the same area of the front-line where he had been posted as 'missing in action'. Naturally enough, this corpse had been presumed to be that of Cartwright and his family had been duly informed of their son's tragic death. Lieutenant Cartwright was not yet fit enough to travel but in a few weeks time, his parents would be allowed to take him home for a further period of convalescence. Needless to say, the article concluded, Mr and Mrs Cartwright were overjoyed at the wonderful news.

Virginia felt absolutely shattered. For a few minutes she became hysterical, laughing and weeping at the same time. After she managed to control the mad sounds she was making, she still went on trembling. She hadn't the strength to get up from her chair. She didn't know what to think, or what to do. A loud knocking forced her to try and control herself, and like a drunk woman she staggered towards the door.

'Hello then, hen,' Standing on the doorstep was a long leek of a woman in a fusty black dress. She had a red nose on a face like a sad bloodhound. Her grey hair was pinned severely back. 'Ah'm Mrs Finniston, wan o' yer neighbours.' With a sniff, she jerked her head to indicate across the landing. 'Ah wis speakin' tae Mrs McGann and she telt me ye wisnae well.'

'Come in.' Virginia stood back to allow Mrs Finniston to sail into the kitchen. 'How did she know where...'

'Och, she saw ye goin' up the close and knew ye must be the wan that's jist moved in tae this hoose. Ah meant tae come and see ye anyroads. Here's a wee mindin' for ye.' She handed Virginia a glass butter dish with 'Welcome to Scarborough' emblazoned on it.

'Thanks very much,' Virginia said. 'I haven't got a butter dish.'

'There ye go then.'

'A cup of tea?'

'Aye, ah might as weel.' Mrs Finniston sniffed again. She obviously had a problem with her nose. She sniffed quite a lot. 'Ye've done a lot o' work on this place. Ye'll no' get any thanks fur it.'

'From the landlord, you mean?'

'The rents keep goin' up. Ma Jeannie's gettin' merrit on Saturday an' the other day she an' Danny got a single end across the road. The very same as oors but that crook o' a landlord's askin' mair rent fur it. The exact same as oors.'

'Fancy!' Virginia tried to sound sympathetic but her mind and her emotions were still bound up with what she'd just read in the newspaper. The kettle had been simmering on the hob and she made a pot of tea while Mrs Finniston went into some detail about her daughter's forthcoming wedding. It was to be in the registry office, and then a sit-down tea of steak pie, peas and potatoes, followed by Scotch trifle, was to be served in The Coffin.

'The Coffin,' Virginia echoed in honor.

'It's shaped like wan. The hall.'

Afterwards there was to be dancing to Jocky Scott's band which consisted of a piano accordion and a set of drums. The whole thing, according to Mrs Finniston, was costing her 'a fortune'.

'You an' yer man huv tae come alang.'

'Oh, I don't think... I mean, I don't know your daughter. I don't know anybody yet.'

'A good chance tae get tae know everybody at wance. Aye, you an' yer man come alang tae The Coffin. Ah might as well be killed fur a sheep as a lamb. It's the Co-op caterin'.'

'Oh, very nice.'

'That's settled, then.'

'Well...'

'If ye huvnae any biscuits, ah'll bring some in frae next door.'

'Oh, no. I mean, yes.'

Virginia hurried over to the press and brought out a packet of tea biscuits.

'Nae biscuit barrel, hen?' Mrs Finniston helped herself to a biscuit. 'Ma Jeannie's got three fur presents. Ah'll ask her tae gie ye wan.'

'Oh no, please. My mother's got one for me,' Virginia lied.

'She goat two fireside sets.' She glanced at the range. 'Ah see ye've got a set. It's no' as nice as the wans Jeannie's got though. So whit's up wi' ye? Are ye gonnae huv a wean? There's twenty up this close.'

'Oh no. No. I just felt a bit faint. I had forgotten to eat anything. I've been so busy with the house.'

'Ye'll no' get any thanks fur it. Mrs Taylor in the close killed hersel' trying to keep the place clean. Fightin' wi' the rats when wan o' them killed her.'

'A rat killed her?' Virginia was momentarily distracted from her thoughts of the Cartwrights.

'The bite went septic. She died in agony.'

'That's awful!'

'Dinnae think ye'll be safe wan up. They can climb like naebuddy's business. Up the stairs, up the walls. In the doors, in the windies–'

'Yes, well,' Virginia interrupted in desperation. 'It's time I was getting on with my husband's dinner.'

Mrs Finniston heaved a deep sigh. 'Aye, right.' She rose. 'Ah ken when Ah'm no' wanted.'

'Oh, I didn't mean... You're very welcome. But I've not been married very long and I worry about cooking. I'm not used to it yet. It takes me ages.' She followed Mrs Finniston's tall straight figure to the door. 'Thanks for coming.'

'Aye, right,' Mrs Finniston sniffed. 'On ye go, then. Ah'll see ye an' yer man at The Coffin the back o' six.'

'Lovely.' Virginia managed a grateful smile. 'Thanks very much, Mrs Finniston. I'll look forward to it.'

She shut the door and leaned against it for a minute before returning to the kitchen. There, she picked up the paper again. She couldn't believe it. Her mind couldn't take it in. She forced herself to begin peeling potatoes at the sink. Down in the back yard a man in the usual shabby uniform of the unemployed was singing a Catholic song. Most of the Calton area was populated by Catholics, a fact which livened up the annual Orange walk. They made a point of marching down every Catholic road and banging their drums as loudly and provocatively as possible, especially when they passed a chapel. James was very much against this. It was another thing they had in common. He was always going on about how the working class would never make any worthwhile progress if they fostered differences and fought among themselves. She put sausages into the frying pan and watched them sizzle. She added chopped onion, and the pungent smell quickly filled the small room.

The paper was lying open on the chair and she kept glancing over at it as if she might have dreamed the whole incident. But it was always there.

James didn't notice it at first when he came in. He went straight over to the sink, washed his hands, then stood drying them on the towel hanging inside the press door.

'You'll have to remember to buy candles for when we go to the lavatory. Even during the day, once you shut the door, it's pitch black in there.'

'I'll get some this afternoon.' She dished his meal. 'Sit in at the table and take this while it's hot.'

He sat at the table with his back to the chair and the paper. Virginia wondered if she could surreptitiously remove it, hide it under the pillow in the bed perhaps. Anything to do with the Cartwrights – even the mere mention of their name – could ignite one of James' dreadful rages.

'Aren't you having anything?' he asked as he cut up the sausages.

'Yes, I'm just dishing it.'

She put her plate on to the table but hesitated about sitting down.

'Is something wrong?' Mathieson asked. How could she hide it from him? If he didn't see it on the billboards, somebody was bound to tell him.

'It's just something in the paper.'

'What was it? Have you got it there?'

He turned and saw the paper. He stretched out and picked it up.

'Good God,' he shouted. 'Could you beat that? So much for his patriotic sacrifice speeches to the workers. Thousands of ordinary men are dying in the trenches and this rich bastard, who's always enjoyed a privileged life, he survives. Can you beat it?' he repeated. 'How lucky can you get?'

Virginia didn't say anything.

'I hope he dies before the Cartwrights see him.'

'James!' Virginia cried out. 'What a thing to say. You don't even know him.'

'He's had more than his fair share of the good life. Why should I care about him?'

'He's a human being who must have suffered in the trenches. He's been seriously injured.'

'He'll get the best of attention. Once he's home he'll be spoiled and cossetted and have everything that money can buy. While thousands of other men will face nothing but misery, unemployment and homelessness when they get home. I don't understand why you keep sympathising with the Cartwrights.'

'I don't keep sympathising with them. I just don't like to see you getting so angry and bitter. I worry about you making yourself ill.'

'He'll come home and after he's been petted and pampered he'll marry into some other rich family and so capitalism will be strengthened and perpetuated. Just you wait and see. And George Cartwright will no doubt get a knighthood for his services to the war effort. It makes me sick, just thinking about it.'

Virginia pushed her food absently around her plate. Maybe James was right. That's exactly what would happen. In sudden panic she realised she was in imminent danger of weeping. She got up and went over to the range.

'I forgot to make the tea.' She kept her back to the table, her chest heaving jerkily, her lips desperately pressed together in an effort to suppress her sobs.

James took no notice and continued reading the article. 'It is wonderful news, Cartwright is quoted as saying. The injustice of it! Here's a man who wouldn't even spend one penny on safety measures in his factory to save good working men from being blown to pieces! So why should his son be spared?'

But Virginia didn't hear a word James said. All she could do was think of Nicholas and thank God he was safe.

19

'Where's yer man, hen?' Wee Mrs McGann staggered towards Virginia not because she was drunk but because her legs were so badly deformed with the rickets.

'He had a class to go to.'

'A class? Hiv ye merrit a wean or whit?'

'He's a teacher.'

'Aw, a shame. He'll miss a good feed.'

Long wooden tables covered with white sheets stretched the full length of The Coffin and were set with cutlery, salt and pepper pots, bottles of HP sauce and saucers of butter. There were also plates heaped with slices of the Co-op's 'plain bread', as opposed to 'pan bread' which was more expensive and not nearly so popular.

They were joined by a fat Buddha of a woman with a fluff of dark facial hair around her mouth and chin.

'We're jist waitin' fur the bride.'

Mrs McGann confided in Virginia, 'Her Aunty Lizzie made the dress. She's a wizard wi' a needle is Lizzie. Lives across the road frae us. She's here somewhere.' She tried to stand on tiptoe to gaze around but failed and staggered back. 'Anyway, ye're sure tae meet her. An' if ye want anything made up, she's yer man.'

'Aye,' the Buddha agreed. 'Lizzie's a great wee seamstress. She made a rerr shirt fur ma man tae wear at his funeral.'

'Oh, you're a widow?' Virginia murmured sympathetically.

'Naw, Ah like tae be prepared but.'

Mrs McGann gave a screech of laughter. 'Be prepared! Ye should be in the Boy Scouts, Annie.'

The band suddenly burst into a rendition of 'Here Comes the Bride', and The Coffin was soon filled with heartfelt cries of 'Och she's lovely, so she is,' and 'She looks a real treat, so she does.'

Jeannie Finniston had obviously become Mrs Chapman in the nick of time. Despite the crafty width of her white crinoline wedding dress, Virginia recognised the wide-legged, leaning back, carrying everything before her walk of a heavily pregnant woman. Danny Chapman, a cocky youth with a Glasgow swagger and a wide grin, followed his waddling wife up to the top table. Then there was a loud scraping of chairs as everyone got seated. No sooner, however, had the Co-op waitresses bustled in with the first plates of steaming steak pie than the bride gave a sudden howl of anguish.

'Mammy, daddy!' she bawled at Mr and Mrs Finniston, 'Get me tae Rottenrow.'

Rottenrow was the maternity hospital.

Her new husband looked pained. 'For Christ's sake, Jeannie, can ye no' wait till after oor tea.'

'Naw Ah cannae, ye stupit wee bastard!'

Jeannie was being helped up by her mother who was saying to Mr Finniston, 'Are ye gonnae sit there an' listen tae that selfish wee nyaff tryin' tae stoap oor Jeannie gettin' tae the hospital?'

Mr Finniston rose and pointed a finger at Danny. 'See you, if ye dinnae shut yer stupit mooth, ah'll shut it fur ye. Ye think mair aboot yer tea than ma lassie.'

'She's actin' the goat,' Danny said. 'Ah never came up the Clyde in a banana boat. She's been hunky dory aw day. Things cannae happen aw of a sudden like that.' He turned to his wife who was now on her feet and clinging to her mother. 'Sit doon an' stop yer carryin' on. Ye're gi'en us a showin' up.'

'Mammy, daddy!' the bride screeched.

Her daddy pushed his wife and daughter aside, grabbed the groom by the lapels and hoisted him up. Then he gave him what was commonly known as a 'Glasgow kiss' – he head-butted him, and blood immediately spurted from the young man's nose. The best man jumped to the rescue.

'Here, hang on then! Ah'm no' huvin' this.' And he landed such a punch, it knocked the older man on to his back. In a matter of seconds, all was in uproar, with the bride's guests versus the groom's guests. Even the women laid about each other with their handbags. In the midst of the chaos, a hysterical Jeannie was bustled out of the hall. Virginia later learned that the baby had arrived within minutes of Jeannie's arrival at the hospital. Meantime, Virginia slipped away unnoticed and thankfully returned home.

Thoughts of Jeannie's baby brought back thoughts of her own. Richard must be nearly three by now. He'd be talking and running around. She tried to imagine him with black glossy hair and deep dark eyes and a beautiful cultured voice like Nicholas's. She longed to catch a glimpse of him. She longed for a glimpse of Nicholas too. Once Nicholas had returned to Hilltop House, maybe she might somehow find a way to see him.

The thought only lasted a moment. She knew it was neither possible nor wise for her to venture anywhere near Hilltop House. Nicholas had his own life to lead and she had hers. They had both known right from the beginning that it was impossible for them to have any lasting relationship. A chasm of class and background separated them and always would. And now she was a married woman. She determined to be glad for Nicholas, to be thankful that he was alive and to wish with all her heart that he would have a happy, fulfilling and peaceful life from now on.

She went over to sit at the window to watch for James. Several women on both sides of the street were having what was called a 'hing'. The window would be opened, a cushion placed on the window sill, and then the woman of the house would rest her folded arms on the cushion and gaze out at the panorama of life going on outside. She could also call out to others having a hing and exchange a bit of gossip.

Virginia couldn't bring herself to have a hing at the window. She felt the need of a certain amount of privacy. Although she did open the window a little so she could get a breath of air. She sat in the shadows of the room and gazed out. The street was packed even though it was becoming dark and the lamplighter was tramping along with his pole. She could hear the clatter when the gas flap went up and let the end of the pole through. Then there was the plop when the light came up and the tinkle of the flap when it went down again. It reminded her of a poem she'd learned at school.

My tea is nearly ready,
And the sun has left the sky.
It's time to take the windie,
To see the Leerie going by.

She watched as the yellowish pools of light surrounded each lamp post, and the eerie glimmer came to each dark close. Groups of women stood laughing and talking in the road. Some were wrapped in tartan plaids, some had babies slung securely in the inner fold and held close like a papoose. Barefoot boys were running about kicking a home-made ball. Girls played peevers with boot polish tins. Others were skipping with bits of clothes rope and singing in time.

Eventually Virginia saw the stocky figure of James coming along. He looked tired. There was a droop to his shoulders and he was walking slowly. He smiled at some children who dribbled a ball past him. Virginia went to the door to give him an affectionate hug of welcome.

'What did I do to deserve that?' he said, peeling off his coat and hanging it on one of the hooks in the lobby.

'Just being you,' Virginia said. 'Are you ready for a cup of tea.'

He nodded. 'I'm surprised you're home. Weddings usually go on later than this.'

'I know but it turned out a right shambles. Everybody started fighting one another.'

'No!' He went over to hold his palms in front of the fire, then rub them together. 'What went wrong?'

'It's a long story and you look tired. I'll tell you all about it later. Drink your tea and then get some sleep. You've been on the go all day.'

'John's been invited down to England for a lecture tour. He'll be a lot more tired than me before he's done.'

'You know what he's like. You said yourself he's got superhuman energy.'

'Aye,' he sighed, 'right enough. I wish I could match it.'

'You do more than your fair share, James. I'm proud of you.'

He looked up in surprise. 'Are you?'

'Of course I am. You're a marvellous worker for the cause. Everybody knows that.'

Pleasure brightened his face. 'Aye well, I do my best.'

Virginia poked the fire into crackling life. The warm light from it and from the gas mantle which hissed above it gave the small room a cosiness which prompted Virginia to remark,

'This isn't so bad, is it? It'll do us for a while anyway. And the neighbours are all very nice and friendly.'

'I suppose,' Mathieson said. 'As long as you can stand it.'

'I'm all right.'

'It's not all right that you should have to live in a place like this, Virginia. Not you, not anyone.'

'You know what I mean. It'll do us just now.'

'It'll have to, won't it?'

Thumping and banging sounds started to come from upstairs, accompanied by screams and oaths. James added ruefully, 'Sounds as if your wedding fight is continuing above us. We'll be lucky if we get any sleep at all.'

He undressed and heaved himself into the bed. Virginia followed him after giving the fire some more attention, and turning out the gas. Once in bed, she put her arms around him. She wanted to be held and loved and reassured.

But James said, 'Sorry, I'm absolutely all in.'

'That's all right,' she said, giving him a peck on the cheek before turning away. As she lay, as usual, listening to his heavy breathing punctuated by the occasional jerking snore, tears filled her eyes and spilled down her cheeks. She had never felt so isolated, so alone.

'I'm going to have to work extra hard while John's down in England,' James said the next day. 'There's nearly two thousand enrolled in the classes already.'

'Well, just try not to overdo it. Nobody can be expected to go on working night and day.'

He shook his head. 'You're an awful worrier.'

After he had left the house, Virginia went to the library to read the newspaper there and see if there was anything else about Nicholas. There was the usual propaganda about the war, and the usual attacks on C.O.s and on John Maclean and what were referred to as the 'Red Clydesiders'. Never before in living memory had there been such vitriolic attacks by the newspaper writers on their fellow citizens. There were several sensational features about 'The man who came back from the dead', as they were now calling Nicholas. Eventually, she found an article, a well-written piece, about him. It spoke of his courage, his leadership as a young officer, and even his talent as a writer.

Virginia wished she could show the article to James.

'See,' she wanted to say. 'How can you hate such a man. Especially after what he has suffered.'

But she knew she could not do it. She would have to make sure she never mentioned Nicholas Cartwright ever again. To James, Nicholas must remain no more than a forgotten story in a yellowing, discarded newspaper.

1918

20

'The thing is,' James explained, 'there's a large body of people in the country now who want the war to stop immediately. But the powers that be are determined to crush Germany completely so that she'll never rise again to threaten the British Empire. They know,' he continued grimly, 'that this rising anti-war tide must be stemmed. They also know that the Clyde is the danger spot and John Maclean's the centre of the movement. So he must be silenced.' James had just told Virginia of Maclean's arrest.

'When did it happen?' she asked.

'As soon as he returned from England. He's been charged with sedition and refused bail. We're organising a demonstration on May Day to show our solidarity. The press is trying every trick in the book to stop us, but they won't succeed.'

And they did not. Over a hundred thousand workers took the day off to march in the procession, and thousands more, Virginia included, lined the streets as they passed by. Glasgow was afire with red banners, red ribbons and red rosettes. The air was alive with revolutionary songs and with the stirring sound of massed bands. Virginia felt excited, uplifted and proud. She hurried along to Glasgow Green where orators spoke from twenty-two different platforms, and every platform commanded a crowd. Virginia pushed her way to the front of the crowd who were listening to Mathieson speak and at the end of his oration, she cheered him along with the rest.

The extraordinary events of the day ended with the enormous crowd marching to Duke Street prison where three times a tremendous shout arose from thousands of lusty throats,

'John Maclean! John Maclean! John Maclean!'

Eventually Maclean was taken to Edinburgh to face trial in the High Court. Virginia and James were there to support him. In an impassioned speech to the jury lasting seventy-five minutes, he stripped the war of all its glamour, and made clear its real meaning. He also made plain his darkest forebodings of another war to come. The newspapers called this the ravings of an unbalanced fanatic. But Maclean had been called insane before. As he said to the court, 'No human being on the face of the earth, no government, is going to take from me my right to speak, my right to protest against wrong, my right to do everything that is for the benefit of mankind. I am not here then,' he continued, 'as the accused. I am here as the accuser of capitalism dripping with blood from head to foot.'

Despite Maclean's powerful oratory, the sentence of the court was penal servitude for a period of five years. Maclean looked taken aback by the severity of the sentence but as he was being led to the cells, he turned to the gallery where Mathieson and the rest of his comrades were sitting and cried out,

'Keep it going, boys. Keep it going!'

At first James was deeply shocked, then shock was swiftly replaced by righteous anger.

'Bastards! Bastards, the lot of them! Cartwright and his capitalist cronies will be rubbing their hands in glee at this. They'll think that getting rid of John Maclean will finish us off, but it won't. I'll see that it won't.'

Virginia was angry too. There was no justice in such an outrageously severe sentence. Five years! For simply expressing the views he'd held all his life. She caught a glimpse of Mrs Maclean's distressed face and felt keenly sorry for her. How on earth were she and her daughters going to survive while John was locked away for so long?

Virginia and James discussed the trial and the sentence all the way home. They had never before been so much in agreement with one another. On reflection though,

Virginia worried about how much and how deeply it seemed to have affected James. He would be going insane if he wasn't careful.

He couldn't stop talking about it. He couldn't make love for brooding about it. He only ate absent-mindedly. His talks to his classes and his street corner oratory became more and more wild, as he put himself at the forefront of the many mass demonstrations to free Maclean. The whole movement was involved in the fight on Maclean's behalf.

'The authorities are beginning to think John's about as dangerous in jail as at liberty. They're dead against the July demonstration we've got planned. But it's going ahead all right.'

When the time came for the demonstration, Virginia went with James to George Square. The police were out in full force and she couldn't help but feel apprehensive. However, nothing happened there and the crowd, led by a band playing 'The Red Flag', set off in the direction of Jail Square. The police followed. Once Jail Square had been reached, Virginia's anxiety increased when she now saw that the crowd of demonstrators were surrounded by a force of hundreds of policemen. Suddenly, without any provocation whatsoever, the policemen drew their batons and the wildest scene ever witnessed in Glasgow began. Hundreds of unarmed men and women were struck down with sickening violence. Almost immediately, James was felled at Virginia's feet and she knelt beside him, trying desperately to stem the blood pouring from a wound above his eye.

Somehow she managed to drag him away from the crowd and get him to safety. Later, as his wound was being dressed, he was white-faced but still defiant.

'We'll have our revenge yet,' he told her. 'And what a revenge it'll be!'

'I wish you wouldn't talk like that, James,' Virginia said wearily.

'Why not? It's the truth.'

'It won't do us any good. It won't do John Maclean or his poor wife and family any good either.'

'Don't be so selfish and small minded.'

She sighed but didn't say any more. She supposed leaders like Maclean and Mathieson always suffered for their causes. As their families always suffered as well. She supposed it was inevitable and she didn't know what the rights and wrongs were in such a situation. Good men like Maclean had to devote themselves totally to great causes, and he had accomplished a great deal for the working man. Perhaps it was too much to expect that he should accomplish any more than he did for his wife and daughters. They obviously loved him and were totally loyal to him. That surely said something.

James was out as usual at his classes and meetings the next day as if nothing had happened. Yet he was obviously in pain from his head-wound, and she could see the strain in his face and the haunted look in his eyes. Virginia had arranged to visit her mother and so after breakfast, she set off for the Gorbals.

'There's a letter for you,' her mother greeted her and took down an envelope that was propped up against the tea caddy on the mantelpiece.

'Thanks, mammy.'

'It must be somebody that doesn't know your new address.'

Virginia opened the envelope. Inside was one sheet of paper with the Hilltop House address at the top. The letter couldn't have been briefer, yet she could hardly believe what it contained. It just said to meet at their usual place the next afternoon and it was signed 'Nicholas'.

Virginia hastily stuffed the letter into her pocket and sat down on the nearest chair. For now, she would just have to stay calm and try not to think about what this could mean. Her mother had her back to her and didn't notice her distress.

'I won't be a minute, hen. The kettle's on the boil.'

'I've brought a packet of biscuits.'

'Och, you didn't need to, hen. But I'll enjoy them just the same.'

'Have you heard anything from Duncan recently?'

'I had a wee letter not long ago. He's fine, he says, but he wouldn't tell me if he wasn't fine. He wouldn't want to worry me so I don't really know. He asked me to look after Celia until he gets back.' She smiled. 'You can imagine what your daddy said about that.'

'You can't blame him.'

'Och, I know. But she's just a silly wee lassie.'

Virginia stayed for an hour or two chatting until her mother said, 'You'd better away home and make your man's tea now, hen.'

'Yes.' Virginia rose. 'Take care of yourself now, mammy.'

'I'm all right. Your daddy's got a few days' work and it's fair cheered us up.'

Out in the street, Virginia gave her mother a wave. As the older woman turned away from the window and Virginia began walking down the street, she noticed the now familiar figure of the telegram boy on his red-painted cycle. As usual he looked bursting with importance in his fitted blue jacket and high, round collar. There was a red stripe down the side of his blue trousers and around the band of his hat. As Virginia crossed the road, she was horrified to see the boy stop at her mother's close. Virginia, in sudden panic, raced back and got to her mother's door while the telegram boy was still standing waiting for her mother to open it.

'Telegram for Mrs Watson,' he called. Her mother opened the door. Virginia said to the telegram boy, 'I'll take it.'

'It's addressed to–'

'I know.' She snatched it from the boy, got inside the house and closed the door.

'Oh, mammy,' she said to the stricken figure of her mother. 'Come on into the kitchen and sit down. I'll open it.'

'We regret to inform you,' she read out loud, 'that Duncan Watson has been reported missing in action, believed killed...' Her mother groaned and slumped to one side. Virginia threw down the telegram and rushed to support her.

'Oh mammy, mammy,' was all she could say. What use were words at a time like this?

Slowly her mother recovered herself and the first words she said were, 'That poor wee lassie will have had one as well. I'll have to go and see her. Will you come with me, Virginia?'

'Of course but you're not really fit enough, mammy. I can go on my own.'

'No, it's my boy and her man. We need to be together, Celia and me. You help me to get there. And then come back and tell your daddy. He'll be home from work in about an hour.'

As an afterthought, her mother said,

'What about your man?'

'Oh, never mind about him just now.'

Janette gazed at her.

'You shouldn't talk like that about your James. You must treasure him.'

Virginia stared at her mother's tragic face and marvelled at her courage as she rose with dignity from the chair.

'Treasure him, Virginia.'

21

Celia was a pathetic, dazed creature. They had found her wandering about the street in her slippers and without a coat or hat or even a shawl around her. She hadn't recognised them at first.

'Come on back to your house.' Janette had put a comforting arm around the girl's shoulders. 'I'll stay with you.'

In a way it was a good thing that Celia was so helpless. It gave Janette something positive to do and kept her own mind from being overcome with grief. Tam had taken refuge in rage.

'What did he die for? What did my son die for? Cannon fodder. That's all he was to these bastards pushing pins about on a map. Thousands are being slaughtered for a few yards of mud. Why did he have to go? It was against all he believed in to fight against his fellow workers. It was that bloody girl. He did it to please her. And now he's dead.'

'Och daddy, don't blame Celia.'

'You've changed your tune. Well, I never will. That girl is as responsible for my son's death as the bastards that pulled the trigger.'

'I've seen her. She's distraught. He was her man.'

'Guilt,' Tam said bitterly. 'Don't you ever let that girl come near me again or I won't be responsible for my actions.'

'She was barely seventeen when she married Duncan. Lots of girls haven't any sense at that age. They've all sorts of romantic, silly ideas. They don't think...'

'Aye, well, she'll have plenty to think about now. Where's your mammy?'

'She's staying at Celia's place tonight. She's had to get the doctor for her.'

'Janette's far too soft for her own good. You tell her from me that she'd better not stay there for much longer or I'll go over there and haul her out.'

'No you won't, daddy.'

Tam never had been violent to Janette or any woman in his life.

'Have a wee dram.' Virginia put what little money she had on the table. 'Go to the pub and talk to your pals for a while. Will I ask James to come over? Mammy might have to

226

stay a few days. Celia hasn't got anybody else.'

He suddenly looked deflated. Clearly he was devastated by the death of his one remaining son. She was worried about him.

'Aye, if you like, hen.'

James was even more enraged than Tam at the news, when Virginia got back to Bankier Street and told him. But his anger was not aimed at Celia. It was directed at the government, the generals, the munitions makers. 'Men of wealth and influence,' he said bitterly, 'who continue making huge profits at the expense of men's lives – good men like Duncan.'

'Could you go over and stay with daddy for a couple of days, James? Mammy's with Celia and I don't think he should be alone. I could go but I think he'd appreciate your company better.'

'Yes, of course,' James agreed. 'I'll have to keep going to my classes but I'll arrange it so that if I'm not with him, someone else will be there. Is he on his own just now?'

'I told him to go out and have a dram with his friends. He'll be in the pub.'

'I'll go and meet him there so that he doesn't need to go home to an empty house.'

'That's kind of you, James. I know he'll appreciate it.'

She packed a clean shirt and a few other things he'd need into a small case while he put on his coat and hat. He looked tired and more in need of going to his bed than trailing away across the river to the Gorbals and then having to cope with her father who was probably drunk by now.

'I really appreciate what you're doing,' she repeated. 'You're a good man, James.'

'Give me the case,' he said impatiently, 'and stop blethering or I'll miss the last tram.'

This was an exaggeration. There would be plenty of trams rattling and clattering about for a while yet. But she could see he was embarrassed. He didn't know how to cope with compliments.

'I'll see you in a couple of days or so,' he told her. 'And don't worry. Tam'll be all right. He comes from good tough working-class stock. Like the rest of his class he's had to weather many a bad storm.'

The door banged shut and left Virginia standing in the tiny windowless lobby. A couple of steps took her into the kitchen. She looked out the window and watched James make his way along the street. He didn't look up to wave to her.

Her own mind and her emotions were in turmoil. She grieved for her brother. But she couldn't put Nicholas out of her mind. She felt ashamed and guilty to be thinking of her lover at a time like this. There was no way that she could have a secret tryst with him. It would be wicked at any time to deceive her husband – even if it was only an innocent meeting. But to take advantage of the tragedy of her brother's death and James' absence because of his kindness would be totally unforgivable. Especially when the meeting was with one of the hated Cartwrights. She dreaded to think what James might do if he found out.

Yet, how she longed to see Nicholas, to be held by him, to comfort him and be comforted by him. She visualised him going to their secret place in the woods and waiting for her. Waiting and waiting. He obviously didn't know that she was married. He wouldn't understand when she didn't appear. He would be hurt and disappointed and sad. He would think she no longer loved him.

But then another thought came to her. He must have come through a great deal of pain and suffering – how could she add to that pain now? The more she thought about it, the more she became convinced that she had to go. She *would* go.

By the next day, she was collapsing inside with fear and apprehension thinking of the dangers of what she was about to do, and the amount of nerve it would take. But then, there had always been danger in her relationship with Nicholas. She thanked God that she hadn't given her father her last penny. She still had some money in her purse to pay for the bus that would take her to the nearest point to Hilltop House and the woods. She would have to walk the rest of the way, but she'd walked further than that before.

The woods were just as she remembered them. Greenery dappled by shafts of light and the heady, sweet, pine-scented air. Despite her trembling excitement, she noticed the new autumn tints on birch and bracken. She remembered dancing with Nicholas on this soft, mossy earth. Oh, how they'd danced. His tall, lean, broad-shouldered figure came to vivid life in her mind, his smooth black hair, his dark deep-set eyes, and how they'd fixed on her. He'd looked long and seriously as if imprinting her every feature forever in his mind.

Then suddenly he was there before her. Her first reaction was one of shock. He looked haggard. His handsome face seemed as if it had been hollowed out, flesh had been pared away and only the bone structure remained – a skull covered with skin from which haunted dark eyes stared out.

'Oh Nicholas, my love.' She ran to him, her arms outstretched, to pull him close to her. His arms caught and held her. He kissed her hair, her brow, her eyes, her throat, her lips.

'Virginia, how I've longed for this moment. Ever since I regained my memory.'

He told her how things had slowly come

back to him. Scenes from his childhood. The trenches... He paused for a moment. Then continued, 'I suffered everything all over again. But then gradually, another memory kept recurring. I kept seeing these woods and feeling the peace of them. I saw you. I heard your voice. That's when I knew I was going to get better. I had a reason to recover. I wanted to get well. I had to get well enough to get back here and to you. Oh Virginia, I love you. I've never stopped loving you.'

She kissed him and stroked his hair. 'And I love you, Nicholas. Nothing has changed as far as our love is concerned. But so many other things have happened.'

His eyes suddenly shone with happiness.

'Yes, our son. What a beautiful child. Virginia, you have made me the happiest man on earth. My only sadness and regret is that my mother did not keep her promise to me.'

'She did look after me and helped me at the birth.'

'Yes, but she'd already put you out of the house. And she abandoned you again after the birth.'

'We agreed it would be best for your son.'

'*Our* son. If you had been from Campsie Castle, or any other upper-class home, would she have taken your baby and sent you away, Virginia?'

'Of course not. But I was a kitchen maid from the Gorbals.'

'Virginia,' Nicholas said, 'listen to me. This war has changed many things and one of them is this rigid adherence to class. You are a beautiful, intelligent, loving person and I love you. I don't care about you being a kitchen maid. I never did. I don't care where you come from. I want you to be my wife.'

He put up a palm in a gesture to stop her astonished protests. 'And I don't care what my father or mother, or your father or mother, or anyone else in the whole universe says or thinks.'

She knew she should tell him that she was now a married woman. But the sight of him, his closeness, brought up such strong feelings of desire that all other thoughts were driven from her mind. 'Oh Nicholas, make love to me, please. Just the way you used to.'

They undressed each other and he kissed every part of her, gently reaching down to each foot and each toe. Gradually his passion increased and she began to moan with pleasure and love. They came to a wonderful climax and he held her afterwards and whispered how much he loved her and would always love her. At last they dressed and Nicholas said,

'You must come back to the house with me now and we'll tell my parents that we are going to be married.'

'No, Nicholas,' Virginia told him sadly. 'I can't do that.'

'Darling, have faith in yourself. I know it will be an ordeal, but they'll come round in the end.'

'It's not that, Nicholas. I wish that was all it was. I wouldn't think twice about facing your parents now as long as you were by my side.'

'Well then...'

'I told you so much had happened. I didn't just mean the birth of Richard. Afterwards I became involved in politics. And there was this man who used to come to meetings with my father and brothers. We all went together and then gradually ... eventually he asked me to marry him. I thought you were dead, Nicholas. I never forgot you. Never stopped loving you. But I thought...'

Nicholas looked stunned. Then he took a deep breath and said, 'I understand, darling. It was foolish and self-centred of me not to think of that possibility.'

'Oh Nicholas, I'm so sorry. I feel I could die of sadness. I don't know how I'll go on living without you.'

Nicholas put his arm around her.

'Now that I have found you again, do you actually think I'm going to let you go?'

22

'It's impossible,' Virginia kept insisting.

Nicholas shook his head. 'I keep telling you, Virginia, I don't care about class. I don't even want to talk about it.'

'Nicholas, you don't understand. My husband and all the people I know talk of nothing else. They've suffered because of it, you see. It's not so easy for them just to forget. Especially James. Nicholas, he's so full of hate, he frightens me sometimes. I daren't think what he'd do if he found out about us.'

'Nevertheless, he'll have to know, Virginia. You'll have to get a divorce. I'll talk to him. I'll explain that we knew each other and loved each other long before you met him.'

'Oh no, Nicholas, please. He'd kill you, I know him. Oh please, promise you won't go near him.'

'Virginia,' Nicholas said gently. 'You're obviously afraid of him. All the more reason to end the marriage.'

'I'm afraid for you because I love you. I can't bear anything to happen to you. I couldn't go through all that suffering again.'

'I'm not afraid of him, Virginia.'

'That might be so but it wouldn't make

any difference. He not only hates your class, he hates your family. My brother Ian was killed in an accident at your father's munitions factory.'

'Oh God!' Nicholas closed his eyes. 'I'm so sorry.'

'It wasn't your fault. It had nothing to do with you, Nicholas. But you're a Cartwright. That's more than enough reason for James to hate you – without knowing anything about us.'

'But he'll have to know sooner or later.'

'Leave things as they are just now. Until I've had time to think. Until I can work something out. Please, Nicholas. Let's just go on meeting here as we used to.'

He hesitated. 'All right, we'll do as you say for now. But whether you agree or not, Virginia, the time must come when all this will have to come out in the open.'

'Yes, I know. But not right now. It's too soon. Especially after Duncan's death. My family have enough to cope with at the moment.'

'Of course.' He shook his head. 'What am I thinking of? Of course you must have time, darling. Take all the time you need. But promise you'll meet me here as often as you can. Until we can be together for good.'

They arranged when she would come again before reluctantly parting. Her whole body still throbbed with the passion of his lovemaking. Her skin tingled. Her mind was racing in confusion and fear. Her love affair must never be brought out into the open. Never. But how to prevent it? She had a temporary reprieve but that wouldn't last for ever. If she did not keep meeting Nicholas in secret, he would come after her. Then James would find out and all hell would break loose. If it had been anybody else but Nicholas Cartwright. If it had been anybody else but James Mathieson...

When she arrived back home she flopped into a chair, mentally, emotionally and physically exhausted. She hadn't even the energy to make herself a cup of tea. But a few moments later, she was roused by a knocking at the door. With a supreme effort she dragged herself up and went to open it.

There on the doorstep stood two women – wee bandy-legged Mrs McGann and big Annie. Virginia had not yet learned Annie's second name. Everyone just referred to her as big Annie.

'We heard about yer brother, hen,' Annie said in a low, suitably sympathetic voice. 'We're that sorry, but.'

'Aye,' Mrs McGann echoed. 'That sorry, so we are.'

'Come in,' Virginia said listlessly. They followed her into the kitchen.

'Ye look fair done in, hen. Sit there and Ah'll make us aw a cup o' tea.'

Virginia obediently sat down. Her mind was still gripped by the awful dilemma she was in, while at the same time she was suddenly overwhelmed with grief for her brother. It was all too much.

'It's yer poor mammy who'll be the worst but,' Annie said.

'Aye,' Mrs McGann echoed, 'the poor soul.'

In a daze, Virginia offered them biscuits from the box on the mantelpiece.

'Och, we aw need tae stick thegither when there's trouble, sure we do, Annie.'

'Och aye, aw the time. Here, gypsy creams. You're well off, hen.' Then suddenly realising her good cheer was tactless in the tragic circumstances, her face quivered with regret. 'Eh, Ah meant... Ah didnae mean...'

'It's all right.' Virginia forced a smile. 'Enjoy them. You're very welcome. No, I won't have one just now. But thank goodness for a cup of tea. It's putting some life back into me already.'

'Where's yer man. Is he hiding frae me, or somethin'?' Mrs McGann gave a whoop of laughter, then smothered it behind a hasty palm. 'It's just Ah seem tae always be askin' ye that,' she said in a small voice.

'I don't blame you. He's out first thing in the morning and sometimes doesn't get back until late. But he's with my daddy just now. My mammy's helping my sister-in-law.

My husband and my daddy have been good friends for a long time. We thought he'd be better comfort for daddy than me.'

'Aye, well, don't you worry, hen, we'll see tae you, so we will.' Mrs McGann staggered over to refill Virginia's cup.

'I'll be all right.' Virginia smiled. 'I'm a lot tougher than I look.'

Annie shook her head. 'There's no' a pick o' flesh on ye, but.'

'I've always been like this. I'm really very strong and healthy.'

'Fancy. An' you wi' such fair hair an' such a peely-wally face,' Mrs McGann said. 'Mair like a candidate for TB.'

'No, honestly. I worked for a while out in the country. I suppose the country air helped. My sister never saw outside the Gorbals. She died of TB.'

'There ye go, then.' Annie's voice had become doom laden. But she perked up a bit at the sound of the door bell ringing. 'That'll be Mrs Dolan. She said she might call round.'

'Ah'll go, hen.' Mrs McGann tottered towards the door and returned almost immediately with three women wrapped in tartan plaids. Virginia had seen them in the street but had never actually spoken to any of them. The kitchen was now packed.

'We're awfu' sorry, hen,' they said in unison.

'Thank you,' Virginia said. 'There's a cup of tea, I think. Is there enough left, Mrs McGann?'

'Dinnae worry, hen. I'll soon fill the pot up again.'

'There's gypsy creams,' Annie confided in a respectfully serious voice. After a while, Virginia was surprised but relieved to hear James' key in the door. He looked taken aback at the sight of the crowded kitchen. The ladies immediately rose.

'We're just goin', Mr Mathieson,' Mrs McGann informed him. 'We've jist come in tae give ye our condolences.'

'Oh, thank you very much.' He squeezed back against the coal bunker to allow the ladies to pass. After they'd gone, Virginia said,

'I thought you were staying at daddy's tonight.'

'I am. I'm on my way there. I just came to collect some papers I'll need for tomorrow. Have you heard the latest?'

'No. What?'

'They're force-feeding John. Twice a day, they shove an india rubber tube down his gullet or up his nose. He's being tortured. It's a bloody disgrace. I've called a special meeting about it.' He flopped into a chair. 'I tried to get permission to visit him but they wouldn't hear of it.'

'How did you find out?'

'From Mrs Maclean. She's taking it very

badly. John suspected that his food was drugged last time he was in prison and this time he was sure of it. He tried to refuse the food. Then he did his best to fight them off when they tried to force-feed him. But he was outnumbered and it was hopeless.'

James shook his head. 'Those bloody maniacs of guards. They hate him at the best of times. You can imagine how they made him suffer!'

'You look tired, James. Maybe I'd better go over to daddy's and let you get to your bed.'

Mathieson pulled himself to his feet and went over to drag a case from under the bed.

'No, your father's expecting me. I can tell him all the latest about John. It'll take his mind off things.'

He selected some papers and notebooks from the case and stuffed them into his coat pocket. 'I'll away. I'll stay with him until your mother gets back.'

Virginia nodded.

He turned at the door. 'There's going to be demonstrations all over Scotland and England. They won't get away with this. They'll have to release him.'

'I hope you're right,' Virginia said.

Then he was gone.

She looked bleakly round the small room. For a short time she'd been proud of what she'd accomplished here. The way she'd whitewashed the walls and polished the floor and displayed her dishes up on the shelf and spread out her pretty knitted blanket over the bed.

Now she gazed at it in the knowledge that it was just the same as thousands of other tenement kitchens with its ugly black sink and range and the coal bunker from which black dust billowed over everything every time the coalman called. And in every tenement was the same suffocating six-by-four hole-in-the-wall bed.

The room pressed in on her. Panic swelled up to her throat. Her breath quickened. She had to grip the arms of her chair and force herself not to get up. Not to try to escape.

23

The newspapers kept up their vitriolic attacks on John Maclean. The *Glasgow Herald* produced a special two-column article on the menace of Bolshevism in Scotland, arguing that in any other country Maclean would have been put to death.

'Bolshevism, or to call it by its old familiar name, anarchy, is not only a disease, it is a crime which, like any other form of morbid and unnatural offences, immediately brings a host of weak-minded and degenerate imitators in its train.'

But by this time the working men and women of Glasgow had learned to think for themselves. Even if some didn't understand or believe in all of Maclean's ideas, he remained their friend and their hero. They continued to fight for him and were united in the battle to get him out of prison.

Meanwhile, events were taking place in Germany that were striking terror into the hearts of the British government. The German fleet had mutinied. Its bases were in the hands of the elected workers. By 8th November 1918, revolution had triumphed all over Germany and a German Republic was proclaimed.

'Now,' James told Virginia jubilantly, 'Remember what John Maclean said at the trial – the working class, when they rise, are more dangerous to capitalism than even the German enemies at your gates.'

All the Cabinet agreed that the real danger now was not the Boches, but Bolshevism.

The Armistice was signed on 11th November. James did not share the country's wild jubilation at this news. He refused to join the street party and the neighbours – adults and children – as they danced for joy and relief in the streets.

'Maclean is still lying in Peterhead prison

being force-fed twice a day. It's a disgrace. He'll be lucky to survive all that he's suffered.'

Virginia had no heart for celebration either. She kept thinking of her brother – buried in an unmarked grave, somewhere in a foreign land.

'They'll surely release him now that the war's over,' Virginia said. 'And especially after all the demonstrations in London. It must be obvious to the government that it's not just Glasgow people who are outraged at his treatment.'

James nodded. She could see that his mind was far away from her. He was already planning his next letter to the government, his next street corner meeting, his next demonstration.

She felt both guilty and glad of all his many distractions. It made it so easy for her to be with Nicholas without James knowing anything, suspecting anything, or even noticing that she had been away. He had come back unexpectedly one afternoon to an empty house, but when she returned, still floating on a wave of love and passion, he hadn't even asked her where she'd been. His lack of interest, his blindness, made her more and more daring. She was meeting Nicholas twice, sometimes three times a week now. A couple of times he'd taken her for a run in his open-topped car. She thought he looked

243

wonderful in his long leather coat, leather cap and goggles. It was only afterwards that she experienced a pang of fear. What if someone had seen her? But she knew no-one from the Calton or the Gorbals would be anywhere near country roads on a cold November day.

The only trouble was, Nicholas had begun to say, 'Don't you think it's time now for us to speak to your husband and parents? And to my parents. I'll see my lawyers as well. I want us to be together, Virginia.'

He had wanted to bring Richard with him on one of their secret meetings but she had panicked and said no, not yet. She'd made all sorts of excuses. The truth was that she knew once she'd seen the little boy, once she'd held him in her arms, she wouldn't be able to let him go. Then of course all hell would break loose. Mathieson must never find out. Nicholas had no idea what he was like. There was no way that she and Nicholas could be together as a family. No way that they could get married. She couldn't risk what would happen.

But Nicholas was showing a determination that she hadn't realised he was capable of. He had begun insisting that she must make up her mind. She must settle a date. Next week, next month, but no later. They had to decide on an exact date now, and keep to it... She opted for the end of the following month to give her time to think and gather enough courage to tell Nicholas, not James, that they would have to part. It was the only way.

She didn't know how she was going to do it. She loved him so much, so tenderly, so passionately. They were like one flesh together. Sometimes it felt like a dream being with him. She wanted it to go on forever. She dreaded having to hurt him by saying goodbye. Her life and happiness would end that day. But if she didn't go through with it the consequences for all of them would be too terrible to contemplate.

Meanwhile, James and his comrades were planning a welcome for John Maclean, whose release was imminent. Maclean had told his wife to keep the exact date a secret. He wanted her alone to meet him at the station, because he did not feel fit to cope with a crowd. The good news, however, could not be kept a secret, and all Glasgow knew and was ready.

On 3rd December, thousands of Glasgow men downed tools, left their places of work and came out onto the streets to welcome Maclean. He was to arrive at Buchanan Street Station and by the time his train was due, the crowd had swelled so much that the traffic was brought to a standstill. The whole city was agog with excitement and joy. When Maclean eventually appeared, cheers roared up from thousands of fervent throats, immediately followed by a vigorous rendition of 'The Red Flag'.

'I'll never forget this day as long as I live,' James told Virginia afterwards. She too had found it unforgettably impressive, the sight of Maclean's carriage being dragged through the thronged streets by a score of men who had willingly taken the place of horses was a remarkable sight. The exultant mass of people, the incessant cheering and joyful singing were amazing. But most moving of all was the sight of John Maclean, standing upright in the carriage, supported by friends and waving a huge red banner with an air of triumph and defiance. Yet it was obvious that the man had suffered. Despite his defiance, he looked haggard and ill. The procession halted at Calton Place and short speeches were made, although Maclean himself did not speak. It was said that his throat was so badly affected by the brutal force feeding he'd suffered that it was likely to give him trouble for the rest of his life.

After it was all over, Virginia and James left arm in arm. We must seem, Virginia thought ruefully, an ideal, happily married couple. For all she knew, James was happily married. He certainly never complained. Perhaps if she had never known Nicholas, she might have felt happily married too. As it was, she felt more and more alone when she was with James. In her mind and in her heart, she was always with Nicholas.

On the way home, they decided to call in to see her mother and father. Virginia had been worried about her mother's heath for a long time, but especially since Duncan's death.

'The only thing that keeps me going,' Janette would say, 'is the thought that I might have a wee grandson yet. I want to live to see him. It's such a comfort to me,' she always added, 'that you're comfortably settled with a good man, Virginia.'

This was another reason why she couldn't break up her marriage. It would kill her mother.

'Oh, come away in.' Her mother's face lit up with pleasure. 'Hello, James. Nice to see you, son.'

She led them into the kitchen and went straight to the range to make a pot of tea. 'Sit ye down.'

'I'll make the tea, mammy,' Virginia said.

'No, no, hen. I'm fine.'

She didn't look fine with her thin face and dark skin hanging loose under her eyes.

'Is daddy not back yet from the welcome?'

'No, but he shouldn't be long. How was it?'

'Marvellous. Wasn't it, James?'

James had taken to smoking a pipe and he was intent on filling it. 'Indeed it was, Mrs Watson. I wish you'd seen it. I don't think Glasgow will ever witness the likes again.'

'They took the horses from the carriage and a crowd of men pulled it instead.'

'Goodness me, that must have been a sight worth seeing, right enough. You can fetch the cups out the press, hen.'

'Right. He didn't look well though. And he couldn't speak.'

Mathieson paused in his efforts to light the pipe. 'Is it any wonder? After all he's been through. He's always had such a powerful voice. They found a way of silencing it. But give him time. He'll be speaking again. He won't allow them to defeat him.'

Just then Tam burst into the kitchen. 'What did you think of that then?' He addressed Virginia and James.

'We were just telling mammy.'

'The workers,' James said in between puffs, 'recognise a great man who's totally sincere and devoted to them. That's what today was all about.'

'Aye,' Tam said, 'and what a turn-out! I've got a half bottle here. Would you like a wee drop in your tea, Janette? You too Virginia? James and me can have ours neat.'

Janette passed over her cup. 'It'll maybe put a wee bit strength into me.'

James lifted his glass. 'Here's to John Maclean and the revolution!'

Tam echoed grandly, 'John Maclean and the revolution!'

Janette shook her head. 'All this talk about

revolution. As if there wasn't enough trouble in the world. I'm just thankful the war's over. So many good lads killed.' Helplessly, she shook her head again. 'Our Duncan...'

'Drink up your tea, mammy. It won't do any good getting upset.'

'No, you're right, hen. I was always that proud of him. He was such a fine looking lad, wasn't he?'

'Yes, he was, mammy. And he thought the world of you.'

Janette nodded and began sipping at her tea. 'War is such a waste,' she said eventually.

'Indeed it is, Mrs Watson,' James said. 'As I've said many a time, the only war worth fighting is the class war.'

'Which reminds me,' said Tam, 'have you seen today's paper?'

'No,' James replied. 'Why?'

'There's an article about the Cartwrights. They're going to buy a whole lot of land up north. It says George Cartwright thinks it'll be the best kind of life for his son and that wee boy they're bringing up. Easy for some, eh?'

Mathieson's fist clenched round the stem of his pipe until his knuckle whitened.

'Next thing they'll be flinging out the crofters and everyone else who's trying to make a living on the land. That's what people like them always do – get rid of anyone who gets in the way of their hunting, shooting and fishing. If I had my way, it'd be the Cartwrights who'd be shot, not a load of defenceless animals.'

Janette and Virginia exchanged worried glances but neither of them spoke.

24

A wee unshaven man in a flat cap was singing drunkenly in Bankier Street and doing a soft shoe shuffle on the cobbles.

If you were the only girl in the world,
And Ah wis the only boy,
Nothin' else wid ma-er in the wurid the day,
Ah wid go on lovin' in the same auld way...

Virginia hurried past, forcing a path through the crowd of giggling barefoot children who surrounded the man. She caught a tram and then a bus and then ran almost all the rest of the way. She was breathless by the time she reached their meeting place. Nicholas was waiting and immediately caught her up in his arms and whirled her around as he'd so often done before. This time she didn't throw back her head and laugh with joy.

250

'Darling, what's wrong?' Nicholas was concerned.

'Why didn't you tell me, Nicholas?'

His deep set eyes creased with puzzlement. 'Tell you what?'

'About your father buying an estate up north and all of you going to move there. It's in the papers.'

'Oh that! Nothing's settled yet. I only found out myself the other day and I was going to tell you. My father is a strong-willed man used to getting his own way. He isn't in the habit of consulting anyone. If he wants to do something, he just goes ahead and does it.

'But will you all be going up to the Highlands?'

'My father has decided to retire and live up there. And he expects me to go with him. But I wanted to discuss it with you. It might be a good idea – not to live with my parents but perhaps for us to have a cottage on the estate.' He sighed. 'I've come to realise I'm never going to be much of a poet, Virginia, but I do feel I've something worth saying – perhaps in a novel. But to write a novel I need time to concentrate. A cottage away from it all in the Highlands might–'

'I think your poetry is wonderful,' Virginia interrupted in protest.

He smiled and kissed the tip of her nose. 'I think you're prejudiced, darling. But I know my limitations. Anyway, I've been scribbling away, and I mentioned it to a friend who's a literary critic. He persuaded me to show him what I'd done, and the other day he came to see me. I must say, I was actually rather embarrassed at the strength of his enthusiasm. He seemed very impressed, to put it mildly. Far more impressed than he's ever been about my poetry.'

'Well, I don't care what he thinks about your poetry. I think–'

'Never mind that. What do you think about us going to live up north, that's the important question at the moment. One of the alternatives is going through to Edinburgh. Or, we could always go down to London. What do you think? We'd have to consider what would be best for Richard as well.'

She wouldn't have cared where they lived as long as they could be together as a family.

'I'll think about it, Nicholas, and let you know.'

'Virginia, you really must make up your mind soon. About everything. What good can it do to keep postponing the decisions we have to make? It doesn't make them become any easier.'

'I know.' Worriedly she bit her lip.

'I've told you,' he said, 'I'll come with you to tell your parents and your husband. I'll be there by your side to support you. You don't need to say anything if you don't want to. I can do all the talking. But this is something that has to be done, Virginia.'

'I know.'

'Well then?'

'We agreed the end of January.'

He sighed. 'Very well. But not one day after that, Virginia. By then we must decide how we tell everyone and where we go. But whatever we do and wherever we go, we'll be together as a family. That's the important thing.'

She nodded and he continued, 'You must know that apart from anything else you can't keep trailing away out here in all weathers. It's ridiculous. If you'd even allow me to meet you in town nearer where you live...'

'No, no. Someone would be bound to see us.'

'Anyway, enough's enough. A few more weeks, Virginia. Then, whether you like it or not, I'll turn up on your doorstep and insist on speaking to your husband.'

'I promise, Nicholas. We'll discuss everything and settle everything at the end of January. The armistice and all the celebrations have stirred everything up for my mother. It's made me think of Duncan too and wish...' Her voice broke.

'I know, darling.' He took her in his arms and stroked her hair. 'But try to think of the future, for our son's sake. Think of us being together. Think how wonderful it will be. Hopefully, we'll have time to organise a place to live before then. I have some money of my own. Enough to buy a small place in Edinburgh, or London.'

She clung to him, her eyes closed, imagining how wonderful it would be. For the first time she began to consider the possibility of running away with Nicholas and Richard. Not telling anyone. Just disappearing. The thought of such an action raised her spirits and gave her an immediate surge of passion. She began to passionately caress Nicholas until they were both breathless and urgent to come together and reach a climax.

Afterwards Nicholas laughed. 'Do you think we'll be able to enjoy this as much indoors on a soft bed with no danger to excite us? I know there's not all that much chance of being discovered. This is private land. Nevertheless there is the possibility of a gamekeeper, or poachers, or ramblers or trespassers—'

'Stop it!' Virginia scolded. 'Thinking like that is more liable to put me off than excite me.'

'That's your story,' he said. 'You know you revel in a bit of danger.'

'I do not!'

Suddenly he burst from their shady hideaway and stretched out his arms, shouting, 'Here we are. Two lovers. Nicholas Cartwright and Virginia Mathieson and we don't care a damn who knows it.'

'Nicholas!' Virginia clawed at his arm. 'Have you gone mad?' She was trembling with shock.

'Mad with happiness. Happy that the terrible carnage of war is over. Happy to be alive, to be in love, and to have lived to see my beautiful son. I can't bear any more of this secrecy, Virginia.'

'You promised. Please, try to be patient for just a little while longer.' She hesitated. 'A thought has just occurred to me, Nicholas. There is another option.'

'What do you mean?'

'We could just go. Disappear. That way we would avoid all the trouble this will cause. James has such a violent temper and I'm scared of what he might do.'

'That might be easier perhaps. Cowardly definitely. I have no intention of taking that option, Virginia, and neither should you. Is this what it's really all about? Not consideration of your mother or anybody else? Just fear of your husband?'

'It was only a passing thought.'

'Well, let it pass right out of your head. We're going to face everyone together. We're going to tell them the truth.' He looked thoughtful. Then he burst out, 'For goodness sake, Virginia, think what that would do to your mother. Not knowing what's happened to you. And what it would do to my mother not knowing what's happened to Richard.'

'Forget what I said. I'm sorry. Just forget it.'

He didn't say any more but the atmosphere between them had changed. When the time came to say goodbye she tried to recapture their closeness and warmth. She twined her arms around his neck and kissed him and told him she loved him. He melted at that and smiled down at her.

'I love you, darling. I've always loved you and I always will. You know that.'

'Yes.' She kissed him again. 'I can't come here at Christmas, remember. James will be on holiday from the College. But I'll write to you.'

Always when they didn't manage to meet, she sent him a love letter, but warned him never to write to her. James received a great deal of mail and was always first to greet the postman each morning.

Nicholas sighed. 'You don't know how glad I'll be when all this secrecy is over, Virginia. I really hate it.'

'You don't hate seeing me, I hope.'

'I hate seeing you for such brief, furtive moments. It's got to stop.'

'I know.' Hastily she kissed him again. 'Soon, I promise. Now I'll have to run.'

He was right, she knew. It was cruel of her to keep him waiting like this. She tried to summon the courage to speak to James. Perhaps she could speak to her mother and father on her own. And then she could protect Nicholas by speaking to James herself. But first she had to make up her mind what was possible as far as the future was concerned. How would her mother react if she decided to go ahead and end her marriage? How would her father feel and what would he think of her for becoming part of the Cartwright family? He'd probably disown her... She could live with that. But could she destroy James? He trusted her completely. If she decided to leave him, she daren't think what the knowledge of her betrayal would do to him.

Most of all though, she worried about what he would do to Nicholas. Nicholas had fought in the trenches. If it came to blows, as Virginia feared it might, Nicholas would stand his ground. But Nicholas was a *gentleman*. He would not be prepared for the sort of violence James was capable of. Her stomach caved in with fear and horror every time she imagined Nicholas's tall, slim, elegant figure standing before James' stocky, pugnacious build. She heard Nicholas's quiet cultured voice explaining to James that he and James' wife had been lovers for years and that they had a child. She imagined James' rage. He had always been aggressive and with such provocation he would be more than capable of murder.

But perhaps if she told him herself? She couldn't imagine him being violent to her.

He had always condemned men who physically abused women. He might still rush to seek Nicholas out but at least she could get a message to Hilltop House to warn Nicholas. And she could call the police.

Even while these thoughts raced through her mind, she felt a great sadness for James. She had always admired his many good qualities and still did. She was fond of him. Their marriage was better than most she'd seen or heard about. If he asked her 'What have I done to deserve this?', she would have to say 'Nothing.'

It was a dreadful thought to have to face him with the truth about her and Nicholas. She couldn't sleep for going over and over it in her mind. Sometimes she even felt like running away on her own. Too easy and too cowardly, Nicholas has said, and he was right.

She began rehearsing what she would say to James, and to her mother and father. It might soften the blow to her mother if she learned the truth about the grandson she had always longed for.

How to begin?

'James, there's something I must tell you...'

'Mammy, sit down and try to keep calm, please. A long time ago...'

Once upon a time. Sometimes it felt like that, just a story. A story that could never come true. A story that would end tragically.

1919

25

Virginia planned to speak out as soon as Christmas was over. But before she got the chance, James became involved in yet another crisis.

The Clyde Workers Committee had held a conference of shop stewards in the ship-building and engineering industries, and decided to support the miners and strike for a forty-hour week.

'You see,' James explained to Virginia, 'demobilisation has created terrible un-employment and this way, if the employed work less hours, ex-soldiers will be able to find work and make a decent living.'

James helped draw up a manifesto and copies of it were sent out to all the industrial centres throughout Britain. A general strike was to take place on Monday 27th January. James had never been more intense. He was working and speaking as he'd never done before. Virginia simply didn't have the heart to undermine him at this important time.

On the 27th, he told her triumphantly, 'The shipbuilding yards and engineering shops are empty and the strike's spreading rapidly all over the country. There's a huge rally being held in St Andrew's Hall in a couple of days. We're going to march from there to the City Chambers. A deputation is going to speak with the Lord Provost. We're going to tell the Council to force employers to agree to the forty-hour week.'

James and his comrades saw the Provost and put their case, and he asked them to return on the 31st for his answer.

'I think it's going to be all right, Virginia. It means that all those unemployed ex-soldiers will get work – and all thanks to their fellow working men.'

Virginia asked what was going to happen at the rally on the 31st.

'It'll be a huge celebration of the power of the working class. Everybody will be there. It'll be a great day. You must come along and share it with us, Virginia.'

'Of course I'll be there.'

The truth was she was sick of mass demonstrations and rallies. She was sick of politics altogether, but she recognised that the action taken in this case was needed. She knew she was being selfish in just wanting to get on with her own life. She had never felt like this before. She still believed in the rightness of the socialist cause, but now all she longed for was to be able to go away with Nicholas and Richard and live a happy, peaceful and secure life. Now she wanted something for herself more, far more, than for other people, fellow socialists or not. She realised, not for the first time, that she did not have James' passionate dedication. Despite all this, to please him, she agreed to join the huge gathering in George Square.

When the day finally came, thousands of strikers poured in to the square from all directions. Virginia had arrived early with James, who had left her at the front of the City Chambers while he went in with the deputation to hear the Council's decision. The deputation were confident and expected no trouble – although they were somewhat taken aback to see the square lined with hundreds of policemen, both mounted and on foot. After the deputation went inside the building, the crowd waited peacefully and listened to speeches from William Gallacher and others.

The frost was still sharp in the air, causing breath to steam in gentle waves above the demonstrators. There was a palpable air of excitement and anticipation as the buzz of animated talk rose and fell in the square.

The police horses, skittish because of the ice under foot, snorted and stamped, making occasional sparks as hoof struck cobbles. One huge black horse lunged and pranced, its eyes rolling nervously, its nostrils flaring. As it champed and chewed at its heavy steel bit, flecks of saliva sprayed steaming on to its powerful neck. The constable tugged and strained on both reins and stirrups to control the nervous beast as it surged forward. The arrogant head was pulled back and the animal retreated, high stepping, to its line. But suddenly its back legs slid from under it and it clattered and collapsed onto the cobbles, causing horses on either side to whinny and spring sideways in panic.

Across the square, other mounted officers and constables on foot saw a surge in the crowd, heard a roar of voices and the sound of a horse in distress. They witnessed the sudden swirling and circling of horses and, nerves already stretched to breaking point by fear and apprehension, they broke ranks, drew their batons and charged. Horses pressed forward, constables ran swinging their batons, lashing out wildly in all directions. Virginia found herself screaming along with other women and children in the crowd.

Blows fell indiscriminately on strikers, bystanders and those who had simply been drawn to the scene through curiosity. Men and women, surprised and unarmed, went down like ninepins. In a few minutes, the whole square was in uproar. The strikers quickly recovered their wits and began fighting back with their fists. The deputation inside the City Chambers, hearing the noise, came rushing out to restore order.

One of them, David Kirkwood, was immediately felled by a policeman and carried away unconscious. James was yelling frantically for everyone to leave the square and go to Glasgow Green until a mounted policeman struck him a glancing blow that knocked him to his knees.

Virginia ran to him. But before she could get him to the shelter of the City Chambers entrance, they were engulfed by a sea of violence. Outraged strikers had now ripped up iron railings and engaged in brutal hand to hand combat with the police. A lorry full of lemonade bottles parked in a nearby street was commandeered and the bottles used as weapons. In the face of such stubborn resistance, the police were forced out of the square.

But eventually the Riot Act was read by the Sheriff of Lanarkshire. In a loud voice he commanded silence before bawling out, 'Our sovereign lord the King chargeth and commandeth all persons, being assembled, immediately to disperse themselves, and peaceably to depart to their habitations or to their lawful business, upon the pains contained in the Act, made in the first year of King George for preventing tumults and riotous assemblies. God save the King!'

The strikers knew only too well that to remain assembled for an hour after the Riot Act was read constituted a felony. At one time the penalty was death. Now it could mean penal servitude for life. However, the strike leaders, including James, were quickly rounded up and arrested and soon after the Act was read, the crowd began to disperse.

Virginia could do nothing more for James that day, so she went to the Gorbals in case her father had been involved and her mother was alone. But her father had arrived in the house before her.

'Wasn't that a bloody disgrace?' he said. 'It was a perfectly peaceful crowd waiting for the Council's answer. Well, they got the answer all right. Bloody violence.'

'James has been arrested.'

'Oh no,' Janette groaned. 'He wasn't hurt again was he?'

'No, they just dragged him off with the others.'

'What'll happen to him, hen?'

'I don't know. I just hope they don't put him in prison again.'

'Most of them will be charged with incitement to riot,' Tam said. 'But not James. He was inside the Chambers, wasn't he? He didn't do any inciting either that day or before it. No, don't worry, hen. He'll get off. You'll see.'

'Will they let him out on bail, do you think?'

Tam shrugged. 'Couldn't say. They might do but I doubt it. Not tonight anyway.'

'I was wondering about staying here tonight but maybe I'd better go home just in case.'

'Well, hen,' her mother said, 'you know you're always welcome here but your place is with your man, especially at a time like this.'

'Anyway, I'd better go,' Virginia said.

'Are you not going to have a wee cup of tea first?' Janette rose to fetch the teapot.

'No, mammy. I'll have a cup of tea when I get home. I'll maybe see you tomorrow or the next day – as soon as I find out what's happening to James.'

'Aye, all right, hen.' Janette saw her daughter to the door.

'Cheerio, daddy,' Virginia called before leaving. Her mother gave her a wave from the window and Virginia smiled and waved back. She didn't feel like smiling. She was concerned about James but angry at him too. She felt as if he was purposely doing everything he could to prevent her from speaking to him about ending their marriage. She wanted to discuss things calmly and logically, to tell him that her original association with Nicholas had nothing to do with him. And it was only because she'd thought Nicholas was dead that she had turned to someone else. She'd tried to be a good wife, but when Nicholas came back... That was going to be the really difficult part.

There was no escaping the fact that she had been unfaithful and betrayed James. But it was so difficult to talk to him about anything except politics. It was his only interest, the be all and end all of his life.

He'd taken her for granted. She felt angry at that too, remembering times he had been insensitive to her needs, or never really listened to her. By the time she got back to the Calton and Bankier Street, she had worked herself up to a fury of resentment against him. He cared more for all his so-called comrades than he'd ever done for her. She was ready to blurt out the whole story about herself and Nicholas as soon as she entered the house. But James wasn't there. He couldn't have got bail after all.

The place was silent and empty.

Once again she felt oppressed by the small, one-roomed house. It was becoming unbearably claustrophobic. She couldn't stand it. On an impulse, she ran out of the house, down the street and away to the nearest telephone box. The operator put her through to Hilltop House. If Mr or Mrs Cartwright answered, she would just hang up. But it would likely be the butler or the housekeeper. She put a handkerchief over the receiver when Mrs Smithers answered.

'I'd like to speak to Mr Nicholas Cartwright.'

'One moment, please.'

Then there was Nicholas's voice. 'Yes?'

'Nicholas, it's me. Can I see you. Can you meet me at Kirkintilloch at the bus stop?'

'Of course. When?'

'I'm on my way to catch the bus now.'

'I'll wait across the road in the car.'

'All right.' She hung up.

She couldn't bear to lie alone in the poky little room just longing for Nicholas. She had to be with him. Her mind and her body were desperately crying out for him. As promised, he was sitting in his open-topped car waiting for her. Not caring who saw her, she ran across the road, got in beside him and, for a few seconds, clung round his neck.

'Darling, what on earth's happened?'

'Can we go somewhere we can be alone?'

'Yes, of course.'

He started the car and they headed out of the city. Soon they found a small inn beside the canal. Before they entered, Nicholas said, 'Can you stay the night?'

'Yes.'

So he booked them in as man and wife. She didn't hear nor care what name he used. He got his room key and put an arm around her.

'Come on, we can talk upstairs. It'll be more private.' They could see the bar from where they stood in the small dark oak-beamed foyer. The bar was also low ceilinged, with ancient-looking beams and panelled walls. It was crowded with men and hazy with tobacco smoke. They passed it and climbed the narrow stairs in silence. Once in their room, Nicholas took her in his arms and said,

'Now, what's all this about? Why the sudden panic?'

'You know, Nicholas, I get just as frustrated as you. I long to be with you and Richard...'

'Well then, why don't we talk to my parents tomorrow and then we can drive into Glasgow and talk to your husband. Or talk to him first if you like.'

'I want to. I want to. Believe me.'

'All right, we'll do it.'

'You don't understand. It's not as easy as that.'

'I've never said it would be easy, Virginia.'

She went over and sat on a basket chair near the window. From there she could see the gleam of the canal through the trees.

'I'm not thinking of how it will be for us. It's James. He's in trouble again. We were both in George Square for the demonstration. And when it all went wrong and turned violent... It wasn't his fault, but he's been arrested. Daddy thinks he'll get off all right. But would it really be right for me to tell him at a time like this. I mean, honestly, Nicholas?'

Nicholas flopped down on to the bed.

'Damn!'

'Exactly.'

'I suppose we'll have to wait until his trial's over and hope he does get off. But on one condition, Virginia.'

'What?'

'Now that at least we've finally taken the plunge and come to a hotel, promise me we'll continue meeting here. Let's face it, darling – in the woods, in the winter...' He grinned. 'It's enough to cool anyone's ardour.'

'I haven't noticed it cooling yours.'

'But this is much more civilised, don't you think?'

She gazed appreciatively around the cosy half-panelled room with its Axminster carpet and comfortable bed.

'Yes.' She smiled back at him.

26

Lying in the steaming hot bath in the hotel bathroom the following morning, Virginia savoured the wonderful luxury of it. She felt totally removed from the difficulties and discomforts of a lifetime of bathing in a zinc bath, or trying to keep clean by washing at the kitchen sink. Or, as a very young child, being taken down to the back-yard wash-house to be bathed in the left-over water of somebody else's washing.

But she still felt bitter. So many people like herself, like her mother and father and brothers, like everyone they knew and had ever known, had to suffer a thousand indignities like that every day. Why should that be? It was intolerable. Suddenly she thanked God for men like her husband and John Maclean. They were the ones who were devoting their lives to changing the system that kept the vast majority of people living in desperate and dreadful conditions. What would happen without men who fought tirelessly to improve the conditions of the poor, the helpless and the unemployed? She supposed the rich would go on getting richer and the poor poorer, just as they always had done. Children would go on dying unnecessarily in the slums. Or if by some miracle they survived, they'd suffer all the ills that poverty, bad housing and under-nourishment so often led to – tuberculosis, rickets, whooping cough, measles, diphtheria, scarlet fever and meningitis. The fever van was never away from the streets, and the sanitary men were always coming round to disinfect the houses.

Virginia remembered how the men had come to the house when her sister Rose took ill. Everybody had to get out while the men burned rock sulphur on a shovel heated over the fire, and walked around wafting the acrid fumes about the place. She thought of the overflowing lavatory and bins, and rats, and bed bugs, and beetles. Long ago they should have knocked the whole building down and built something fit for human beings to live in.

Never before had she realised so clearly and strongly how right James was. Never before had she so admired what he was trying to do. Lying in the hotel bathroom, every pore of her body greedily appreciating the warm soapy water, she forgave James all his faults. He could get angry, he could fly into rages, but his anger was justified. He was entitled to be angry.

But she couldn't feel angry at Nicholas – even though he was a part of the system James was trying to overthrow. She had been awakened during the night by his sudden shout, as he jerked up in bed, eyes staring, sweat pouring off him. She had put her arms around him and tried to soothe and comfort him. He had told her about the nightmares he still suffered – terrible visions of horrors he had witnessed in the trenches.

A knock at the bathroom door brought her back to reality. She'd locked it because she treasured these brief moments of private luxury. Bath time would have no special meaning to Nicholas. It was something he would always have taken for granted.

'It's quite a nice day,' Nicholas called through the door. 'Would you like to go for a spin?'

'Yes, I won't be long.'

A drive in an expensive motor car, yes. Why not savour the comfort and luxury of it all, savour the sweet side of life for as long as possible. It couldn't last. But she would remember all this. Every single moment of it.

She laughed as they raced through the countryside, her scarf flying out behind her in the wind. Her normally pale cheeks became rosy, her eyes sparkled with excitement. Eventually Nicholas stopped the car and turned to her. 'I've never seen you look happier or more beautiful, Virginia. This is how it's going to be all the time. We'll be so happy together. When will I see you again?'

She felt suddenly deflated.

'It depends.' She shrugged. 'I just don't know what's going to happen. And what if you go up to the Highlands...?'

'Don't be silly. I'm not going anywhere without you. Do you know, I don't know which is worse – the way my mother and father never seemed to have the slightest interest in me when I was a child, or now when they both seem to have gone to the opposite extreme.' He shook his head. 'One of the things they can't understand is how

I've no interest in Fiona. They've done everything possible since I've come back to encourage me to take up with her again. But now I think they've come to the conclusion that I haven't sufficiently recovered my wits yet, and a change of scene will do the trick.' He laughed. 'I bet they're hoping to get the Forbes-Lintons up there as long-term guests. I've no doubt that right now they'll be planning a really jolly summer for Fiona and me.'

'Maybe that would be for the best.'

Nicholas suddenly grabbed her shoulders and shook her. His eyes suddenly seemed like dark pools that frightened her. For a moment he seemed unhinged, out of control.

'Don't you dare talk like that. Don't even think like that. You belong with me and if I go away you'll be the one who will spend the summer with me. The one who will be with me for the rest of my life, do you hear?'

'Yes, darling,' she said helplessly. 'It's just there are so many things against it. So many difficulties to overcome.'

'We'll overcome them together. We have a child to think of, remember. He deserves to be brought up in a proper family with his mother as well as his father.'

She nodded. 'I'll have to go now. It's time I was catching the bus at Kirkintilloch.'

Once in the small town, as she was getting

out of the car, Nicholas said, 'Promise you'll telephone me as soon as possible.'

'I promise.'

He looked so strained at times despite his cheerful bravado. She worried about him. Once she'd given him her promise, however, his expression changed and he gave her one of his beautiful smiles. Beautiful was the only appropriate word she could think of to describe him to herself. He would have been embarrassed and laughed at her if she'd told him. But he'd always been beautiful to her.

She waved him off and in a matter of minutes she was sitting in the bus en route for Glasgow. Soon she was walking reluctantly along the crowded Bankier Street. One of the group of shawl-wrapped women called to her.

'Hello then, hen. Been stayin' wi' yer mammy?' It was the ample bosomed Mrs Gilhooly from the top flat.

'Yes.' Virginia smiled. 'How's your husband?' Mr Gilhooly suffered a lot with his chest.

'Och, hawkin' an' spittin' wi' the best o' them. Ah hud tae get out though. I wis beginnin' tae boak.'

Virginia tried to look suitably sympathetic.

'I'd better go and get something ready for the dinner.'

'Aye, they're sayin' most o' the boys will be oot the day – yer man'll be hame fur his tea

Ah'm sure. Och well, make the most o' yer wee bit peace, hen. Ah wish they'd lock ma Charlie up and gie me a bit peace.'

Once in the house she realised there was no food in the cupboard and only half a loaf in the bread bin. She didn't feel like going out to the shops. It meant running the gauntlet of the crowd of women in the street. She didn't mind stopping to chat to them. It wasn't usually a problem. Today, however, she needed time to think. Not that thinking did much good. It never resolved anything. Conflicting thoughts kept chasing one another round and round in her head. One minute she'd be thinking she couldn't leave James. The next minute she was thinking she couldn't finish with Nicholas. That would be too cruel. He needed her. Sometimes she detected such a haunted look about his eyes, and she knew that dark horrors still clung to him, things he'd seen that could never be spoken of and never forgotten.

She was sitting beside the unlit fire staring into space when James opened the front door and came into the room. Virginia got up.

'James, what happened? I'm so glad they've let you out.'

He rubbed his broad hands together. Nicholas had slim hands. His fingers were long compared with James' short stubby ones.

'The Workers Committee kept their word and came up with the bail money. Any tea on the go?'

'Oh, I'm sorry. I just couldn't get going today. I've been so worried. I haven't even lit the fire.'

She hastily began raking it out. 'It won't take long to get started.'

James took the empty coal scuttle over to the bunker and energetically shovelled coal into it.

'They've still got Shinwell, Murray, Gallacher, Kirkwood, MacArtney and Bremner. You should just see what it's like out there today, Virginia. Glasgow's been turned into an armed camp. They've sent soldiers from England overnight – the city's full of them. There's even tanks on the streets. Tanks and machine guns everywhere! Can you believe it? And all we did was have a peaceful gathering in the square. I mean...' He shook his head in disbelief. 'It was like a gala day outing, wasn't it? So what on earth are they going to do with all these soldiers? It's probably just to intimidate us. They know we can't take on the army, even if we wanted to.'

The fire crackled and sparked into life. The heat, took the chill off the room. She put the kettle on.

'I haven't even been for any messages. After I make a pot of tea, I'll run down to the shops.'

'Get me a paper, will you?'

'Would you like a bit of bacon and maybe an egg and some fried potato scones?' She knew he enjoyed that.

'Have you enough?'

She went for her purse and studied its contents. 'Yes, I'll manage.' It occurred to her though that if James ended up in prison, she'd be forced to go out scrubbing again. Remembering the stinking pub lavatories made her shudder.

'What's up?' James asked.

'Somebody walked over my grave.' It was a common enough saying but today it somehow had an ominous ring. She struggled into her coat and clutching her purse and her message bag, she left the house.

'I won't be long,' she called back over her shoulder. She could hear James jabbing at the fire. Already his thoughts would be far away from her. They'd be with his comrades in cold police cells.

'Ah saw yer man goin' in.' Mrs Gilhooly was leaning against the wall talking to Mrs McGann in the close. Her bosom, supported by her folded arms, heaved with laughter. 'Ye didnae get much peace after aw, did ye hen?'

Virginia squeezed between the women in order to get past.

'I'm just glad he's all right.'

Mrs Gilhooly gave another roar of laughter. 'Aye, ye can say that again. A nice lookin' wee fella. Ah'd be glad he wis aw right if he wis mine as well.'

Virginia supposed that he was a nice looking man – compared with other grey-faced undernourished men in the neighbourhood. He looked fit, tough even, with his broad face, deep cleft chin and cropped hair that stuck up like a wire mat. He was different in the way he dressed too. He always wore a respectable shirt and tie and a homburg hat.

If only she loved him as he deserved to be loved. But she couldn't. No amount of thinking about it was ever going to make that happen. When she returned to the house, he was sitting at the table writing in a notebook. He had taken to wearing glasses when writing or reading – cheap-looking, steel-framed things. He cleared his papers away when she dished his meal. Then she sat pretending to eat a piece of bread and jam and watched him wolf down his fry-up. Eventually he noticed.

'Aren't you having any?'

'I'm not hungry. I had something not long before you came in.'

'How's your mammy?'

Virginia felt suddenly wary. 'Oh, struggling along the same as usual.'

'Mrs Gilhooly was saying you'd just got back from there.'

'Yes, I thought I might as well stay the night. It didn't look as if you would be getting home.'

'Quite right. You were best with your mammy. She's had a hard time of it with one thing and another.'

'I know. I worry about her.'

'I'm glad Tam didn't get hurt or pulled in by the police. It was terrible, wasn't it, the way the police laid into innocent people. Glasgow folk won't forget or forgive them for it in a hurry.'

'I suppose they were acting under orders,' Virginia said.

'Oh, I've no doubt about that. There's a rumour going around that most of them had to get drunk first. They couldn't bring themselves to do it otherwise. But I don't know how much truth there is in that.'

'Oh well,' Virginia sighed. 'Thank goodness it's all over.'

'Over?' James gave a mirthless laugh. 'Don't fool yourself. The trouble's just started.' His words made Virginia think about the trouble that would arise if he found out she hadn't been sleeping at her mother's. The only way to avoid this that she could think of was to get to her mother before James did.

But what could she say? Unless, of course, she admitted the truth.

27

She decided not to say anything. James was going to be busy every minute of most days and nights helping Maclean and others to raise money for the defence of those who had been arrested. Maclean had been away speaking in England and so had not been in George Square on what was becoming known as 'Bloody Friday'. The chances were that James would not be visiting her mother during the couple of months before the trial and by that time the night she was supposed to stay at her mother's place would have been forgotten.

During the next two months, more and more often, she met Nicholas at the small hotel, sometimes during the day. Sometimes during the evenings when James had a class to teach, and she made sure that she was always in just before he arrived home. She would bank up the fire with dross and briquettes before she left so that all she needed to do when she returned was poke it into life and put a few pieces of coal on top. She also left the kettle on the hob and set cups and plates out on the table and a sandwich ready for Mathieson's late snack.

She was becoming very well organised. More daring too.

Nicholas had begun meeting her in town. She had been adamant that he mustn't do this. It was too risky. In Glasgow she was well known as James Mathieson's wife. Nobody knew her in Kirkintilloch where Nicholas normally picked her up. But one day she had been standing in the bus station at her usual time when suddenly Nicholas's tall figure appeared in front of her.

'Come on,' he said, 'the car's round the corner.'

She went with him to avoid creating any fuss and even more attention than his handsome, expensively-dressed figure had already caused. But she hissed at him,

'Why have you done this?'

'Because I can't put up with this one moment longer. I'm not going to allow you to wait about in the cold and travel in buses when I'm sitting comfortably in a car. I'm going to drive you back as well.'

'Oh, Nicholas, I don't mind.'

'But I do. I mind very much.'

'What if someone sees me and recognises me?'

'We'll just have to cope with that the best we can if it happens.'

Her heart was racing with fear as she sat in the car and they set off down the road, and not because of Nicholas's slightly reckless, overconfident driving. All she feared was that she would be found out. But she soon began to feel exhilarated as they left the city and began to race along country roads.

'We could always book into a hotel in town,' Nicholas said.

'No!' she shouted at him in panic. 'Definitely not, Nicholas.'

He laughed. 'We only live once. Why not live dangerously?'

'Because I hate living dangerously.'

'What do you think you've been doing all this time?'

She leaned back and closed her eyes in despair. 'I suppose you're right.'

They had become well known to the inn-keeper by now, but he was a discreet man and never questioned their regular bookings. Not even when they spent only an afternoon in their room. During the winter, the only trade that kept his business going was the small bar – and even that was only full at weekends – so he was glad of their regular custom. He became quite an ally, often slipping them the key of their usual room with a conspiratorial lowering of his voice and a promise of afternoon tea brought up to them before they left. Virginia suspected that what helped to oil the wheels was Nicholas's generous tipping.

The afternoon tea always added to Virginia's enjoyment. On a silver cake-stand, there were sandwiches and home-baked scones, and an apple tart or a Victoria sponge. A maid, dressed much the same as the maids at Hilltop House, brought in the trolley. Virginia loved acting the lady. She'd once said this to Nicholas and he'd impatiently replied,

'You *are* a lady.'

She loved him for that. And for the way he had gone on to unfasten her fair hair and stroke it and kiss it and say, 'And a very beautiful lady. I'm a very lucky man.' She felt lucky too as she lay naked in his arms, flesh against familiar flesh, feeling so much a part of him it was as if they were one person. Often they'd suddenly say the same thing at the same time. Then they'd laugh at the wonder and the surprise of it.

Then one day, Nicholas said, 'My father's pleading with me now to at least go up and look at this estate he's buying. He says he wants my advice. He wants to know what I think of it and what I feel needs to be done with it. It's all a ploy. My mother and father will stop at nothing to get me to settle on the estate.'

'There wouldn't be any harm in going and having a look.'

He shrugged. 'I suppose not. I could use the visit to look around and see what property there is on the land. If I saw a really nice cottage that I thought you'd like...'

'It's what you'd like and what you'd want to do that matters, Nicholas.'

'No, it is not. All that matters to me is your well-being and happiness. But I'll go and have a look at the place. At least it'll placate my parents for a while. It'll mean I'll be away for a few days. A week perhaps.'

She gazed at him wistfully. 'I'll miss you.'

'And I'll miss you, darling. I won't go if you don't want me to.'

'No, it's all right. Honestly, you go. I'll look forward to hearing all about it when you get back.'

They made tender love. He licked every inch of her skin, even between her toes, until suddenly she felt unbearably passionate. She wanted to clutch him tightly inside her and never let go.

Afterwards Nicholas sighed, 'Oh Virginia, if only you'd stay in my arms the whole night through. Remember that night you did stay – how wonderful it was?'

She remembered. 'No, I'll have to go. James will be home tonight.'

'If you must, you must, but I'm driving you back to Glasgow.'

'I wish you wouldn't. I'd be perfectly all right on the bus.'

'I'm not going to argue. I'm driving you back to Glasgow.'

To add to her anxiety, he did not stop at the bus station but carried on towards the

Calton. 'Nicholas, for God's sake, you're surely not going to go right to Bankier Street?'

'I'll drop you a few streets away.'

'No nearer then. Any cars draw attention round here.'

'Are you sure you'll be all right? It looks a very rough area.'

'Nicholas, I've been brought up in a much rougher area than this. Just let me out of the car. Please,' she added, struggling not to spoil their time together by being impatient with him.

He stopped the car and she hastily got out. He raised a hand in goodbye, before speeding away. She felt sick with apprehension. There were people jostling out of nearby pubs. Some were arguing noisily. Others were swaying about and singing.

Swanee,
How ah love ya, how ah love ya,
My dear auld Swanee...

Two men, arms around each others' shoulders, were giving a rousing rendition of

Ye'll tak the high road
An' Ah'll tak the low road,
An' Ah'll be in Scotland afore ye...

Knots of women were gossiping in closes but Virginia didn't recognise any of them. As she hurried past, a man shouted after her, 'Hello therr, hen!'

She realised he was just trying to pick her up. He didn't know who she was. Still, she felt agitated and on edge, even when she was safely in the house and had lit the gas mantle and poked the fire into a good blaze. Undressing quickly, she put on her white cotton nightie and the blue cardigan her mother had knitted for her. It had to seem as if she'd been relaxing at the fireside for hours. Looking around the room, she thought, 'This is the full extent of my home in which James and I sleep and eat and try to keep ourselves clean. One poky room only half the size of the hotel bedroom I've just left. The kitchen alone at Hilltop House is three or four times the size of this place.'

She hated it.

Suddenly she was startled by a knock at the door. James had his key so it wasn't him. For a dreadful moment, a crazy idea came into her head that it was Nicholas. She could hardly gather enough strength to get to the door. Clutching her cardigan around her with one hand, she opened the door a crack.

'Ur ye aw right, hen?' It was Mrs Mc-Gann.

'Yes, fine. Come in.' It wasn't the done

thing to keep a neighbour standing on the doorstep.

Mrs McGann stumped from one bandy leg to the other into the kitchen.

'Oh my, ye're rerr an' cosy in here. Ye've goat it like a wee palace, so ye have.'

'Sit down, Mrs McGann. A cup of tea? I've just made a pot.'

'Is yer man at wan o' his classes, hen?'

'Yes, but he'll be in any minute.'

Mrs McGann pulled herself to her feet. 'Oh, Ah'd better make masel' scarce then. Ah jist came to check ye wisnae ill in bed or lyin' deed on the flair. Ah hidnae seen hint nor hair o' ye fur a while an' Ah've been chappin' at yer door mair than wance.'

'Oh, no, I'm fine. It's just I've to go out a lot too. I help my husband when I can. He's trying to raise money for the defence just now as well as attending to his other work.'

'Aw, the soul! He's a good lad, isn't he? He's in the same mould as oor Johnnie.'

'Johnnie? Oh, you mean John Maclean?'

'Aye. Know whit he did the ither day? A poor widow buddy in his street whose wean wis ill hudnae a penny tae pay the doctor. He went tae her hoose, and gave her aw he had tae pay the doctor and get the wean an' hersel' some nourishment. An' she'd never even asked. There's many a buddy begs for charity though an' if John has it, he gies it.'

Mrs McGann was making for the door as

she spoke. 'That's the kind o' man oor Johnny is. He looks as if he needs aw the nourishment he can get hissel' at the minute. The poor man disnae look right.'

'I know,' Virginia agreed. 'James was just saying that the other day.'

'Well, cheerio the noo, hen.'

'Cheerio, Mrs McGann.'

Mrs McGann was only away a few minutes when James arrived. He went straight over to the fire, bent forward and rubbed his hands near to the warmth. He did this every time he came in and it had begun to irritate Virginia, although she knew it was unfair of her to feel as she did. Why shouldn't her husband seek warmth as soon as he entered his own house? He'd probably been standing talking at street corners for hours. Even the rooms in which he taught his evening classes were pretty cold and comfortless.

'The tea's made,' she told him. 'And there's a nice sandwich.'

'Thanks, Virginia.' He took off his coat and hat and hung them on one of the hooks in the lobby. He came back in, rubbing his hands together again. 'You'll be glad to hear we've managed to raise quite a sum. If it goes on like this, it looks as if there's going to be plenty to cover everybody's defence.'

'That's good news.'

She poured out the tea.

'I bumped into Mrs McGann there.'

'She was in here having a chat for a wee while.'

'She told me she'd been worried about you.'

'I don't know why.'

'She thought you'd been ill, apparently.'

'I don't know why,' Virginia repeated.

'She'd knocked on your door a few times and got no answer.'

Virginia rolled her eyes. 'It's worse than the Gorbals here. You can't move without somebody checking up on you.'

He gave her an odd look. 'Don't you think that's a good thing? It's a sign of caring. Of good neighbours.'

'Yes, I suppose it is. It's just... I've been trying to have a peaceful read and there's always someone coming to the door. And sometimes I go for a walk in Glasgow Green. Just to think in peace.'

There was some truth in this. Nicholas had given her several books and she'd been trying to read them in secret. She had also gone for the occasional walk in Glasgow Green to try to think things out.

In between bites of his sandwich, James laughed. 'Like James Watt.'

'What?'

'James Watt was walking in Glasgow Green having a quiet think when he invented the steam engine.'

'Oh yes.' She managed to laugh as well,

291

'I'd forgotten about that. Mrs McGann was telling me about John giving his last penny to that widow woman.'

James was immediately filled with interest and enthusiasm, and the conversation was safely deflected into more normal channels. It occurred to Virginia, however, that she was skating on ice that was becoming dangerously thin.

28

It was fortunate that Nicholas was away and she didn't need to disappear from the street for at least a week. That gave Mrs McGann and anyone else time to forget her disappearances.

The week also taught her that she couldn't live without Nicholas. She had made up her mind. She needed to be with him and their child. If James was found not guilty and avoided a prison sentence, then she'd tell him the truth. She might speak to her mother and father first and then to James. But one way or the other, she'd tell him. It would be better to face him on her own, rather than have Nicholas suddenly appear. The more she thought about being with Nicholas and Richard, the more enchanted she became with the idea. She had never stopped longing to be with her baby. Yet there was always an underlying sadness at having to hurt James. But it had to be done.

If he was found guilty and sent to prison, that would complicate things. She wasn't sure what she would do then. Wait until he came out? But that might take years. She would just have to wait and see what happened at the trial. Meantime she could only hope and pray that he would be acquitted. Occasionally the thought struck her that it would be better if he were jailed. Then she could tell him without worrying about the consequences. That way Nicholas would be safe too. But she chided herself for even contemplating such a cowardly course of action. If James was flung in prison again, that would be more than enough for him to suffer.

Sometimes she even persuaded herself that perhaps James wouldn't be all that upset at losing her. After all, he spent so little time in her company. Even at mealtimes or in bed before an energetic but brief coupling, he'd seldom talked of anything to do with their personal lives. At the moment his main interest, apart from raising funds, was the fate of the Scottish Labour College. This was something that Maclean was particularly keen on and, as usual, James followed suit.

Virginia realised that it wouldn't be losing

her that would enrage James. It would be her relationship with Nicholas. In his eyes, her greatest sin would not be the betrayal of her husband, but of her class.

As soon as Nicholas returned, Virginia was able to tell him about the latest conferences James would be attending and how that would mean they would have plenty of opportunity to see each other before the trial. After the trial, if all went well, they could be together for good. Now that her decision had been made, a general mood of recklessness took possession of Virginia. No longer did she object to Nicholas meeting her in the Calton and bringing her back there afterwards. No longer did she worry about staying out overnight. If James was away overnight, then she stayed with Nicholas at the hotel. Let the neighbours think what they liked.

Then one day, one beautiful, never-to-be-forgotten day, Nicholas said he had a surprise for her. They weren't going to the hotel because he had something even better planned. He drove her to a large mansion house surrounded by a garden and trees. He stopped and got out of the car but told her to wait where she was, he would only be a few minutes. He returned holding the hand of a small boy in a school uniform. He was a slim, finely featured child with dark hair and brown eyes. There was a look of

Nicholas about him but she also saw a resemblance to herself as well. She could have fainted with joy, she felt so ecstatic.

'Virginia,' Nicholas said. 'I'd like you to meet Richard.'

The little boy politely put out a hand. 'How do you do?'

Virginia held the small hand in hers. Eventually she managed, 'I'm very pleased to meet you, Richard.'

'I thought we'd take Richard for a spin today. How about the seaside, Richard?'

Richard instantly abandoned his concentrated politeness. He jumped up and down, and with a huge grin on his face he clambered into the car.

'That's right. You sit in the back seat. And you, Virginia, sit in beside Richard. All right?'

Virginia was too happy to speak. She wanted to hug the wee boy. She wanted to keep touching him and hugging him but she knew that young children, boys especially, didn't like being overwhelmed and babied. She sat beside him. They smiled at each other. As the car started off, she said, 'I wonder if daddy will buy us ice cream at the seaside. Do you like ice cream?'

'Oh yes.' He bounced up and down on the seat. 'Very much indeed!'

Soon they were all laughing together. And by the time they'd reached Helensburgh,

Virginia and Richard were firm friends. It was lunch time and they were hungry so they made straight for a restaurant.

'You've made quite an impression,' Nicholas said while Richard was skipping ahead. 'I thought it best to introduce you as Virginia, not mummy at the moment. That can come later. Was that all right?'

'Yes, yes. Everything's just perfect, Nicholas. Thank you for bringing him. I know I wouldn't allow you to bring him before, but now that I know that we're going to be together it seems like the time is right.'

'That's what I thought. And I thought it would be a good idea for him to get to know you by stages.'

She was completely enchanted by Richard and enjoyed making him laugh at the beach after the meal. They bought a beach ball and the three of them played a riotous game of football. Richard laughed so much at her efforts to kick the ball that at one stage he collapsed on to the sand and rolled about in helpless hilarity.

Later she showed him how to build a sand castle, while Nicholas went to buy ice cream. When he returned with the cones, Virginia said, 'Do you know what we called these when I was your age? What they are still called where I live?'

Richard shook his head. His mouth and cheeks were white with ice cream. There was even a blob on the end of his nose. Virginia thought she'd never seen such a lovable looking child.

'What?' he asked with interest.

'Pokey hats.'

'Pokey hats?' he echoed, nearly choking with laughter. Nicholas laughed too.

'Honestly,' Virginia said. 'Pokey hats.'

Eventually they'd made their way back to Glasgow, this time with Richard asleep in her arms. While he slept, the tears ran down her cheeks. Nicholas caught sight of her.

'Darling,' he said, 'everything's going to be all right.'

'I know,' she told him. 'I'm so happy.'

Nicholas dropped her off at the hotel. But first she had to release herself from Richard's embrace. It was then he woke up. 'Where are you going, Virginia?' he asked sleepily.

Nicholas said, 'This is where Virginia's living just now.'

Richard gazed up at the hotel's sign creaking in the wind and read, 'The Canal Inn. Where's the canal?'

Nicholas said, 'Come on, we'll show you and then we'll have to get back to Hilltop House.'

Nicholas and Richard returned to the car and she waved them off. When Nicholas came back to the hotel, they lay in each other's arms and spoke about Richard and their plans for him and their plans for each other. She would have to try to get a divorce from Mathieson as soon as possible. But the law usually moved at a snail's pace in these matters and so they would just set up house together right away and get married as soon as Virginia was free.

They had decided not to live on Nicholas's father's Highland estate. 'I think it will be best if I'm completely independent,' Nicholas said. 'How about if we make a fresh start in Edinburgh? There are good schools there for Richard and I could start looking for a flat. There are some lovely New Town properties I think you'd like.'

'That would be wonderful, Nicholas.'

'We could drive through to Edinburgh soon and look at a few places together.'

And so it was arranged. Virginia could hardly wait. She cleaned the single end automatically. She took her turn at washing the stairs. She made James' meals. She allowed him to have sex with her. But all the time, day and night, only an empty shell of herself was functioning in the Calton. Her real living vibrant self was with Nicholas and Richard.

Then one day James announced he was going to the last of the conferences before the now imminent trial. It was to be held in Aberdeen and he would be staying overnight.

Impatiently she watched his stocky figure topped by his shabby homburg stride purposefully away down Bankier Street and disappear. As soon as he was gone, she flung on her coat and rushed to the telephone box. As usual, Mrs Smithers answered.

'Master Nicholas is not at home, madam,' she said.

'When will he be back?'

'He is expected shortly.'

'Could you give him a message?'

'Certainly, madam.'

'Just say usual time, usual place today.'

The housekeeper repeated the words, 'Usual time, usual place, today. And who shall I say called?'

'He'll know who it is.'

Abruptly she hung up and hurried away to catch the bus. It was a bright April day. There had been an early morning shower but now the sun was shining and glistening on the bushes and trees beside the road that led to the hotel. From the bus stop she headed down a side road to the hotel. Through the trees the canal glimmered and she could smell the brown earthy towpath. From the room she always shared with Richard, they would be able to see the canal snaking along, smooth and dark and quiet. Her feet quickened as she thought of Nicholas waiting for her. Into the small cool foyer now, with its floor ambered by the light filtering through the glass panels in the door. Up the narrow staircase, dark oak bannister, red turkey carpet. Bursting into the room, her face alight with love. She froze. Sitting over on the basket chair was Mrs Cartwright.

'How did you...?' Virginia began.

'I overheard the housekeeper.'

'But...'

'And the rest I already knew from Richard.' Mrs Cartwright's face was contorted with disgust. 'You had an innocent child brought to this hotel where you were having your illicit rendezvous. You involved my grandson in your sordid–'

'My son. And there is nothing sordid about my feelings for Nicholas. He is the father of my child and we love each other. I–'

'You are a married woman. And you must know that it is quite common for women of your class working in domestic service to tempt the man of the house. In your case, you were fortunate. Instead of having some back street abortion, as most of these women do, your child was given a wonderful chance in life.' Mrs Cartwright was sitting straight-backed, her gloved hands clutching tightly at the purse in her lap. 'I have kept my side of the bargain; I have given Richard everything including my love and attention. You have betrayed your promise. You have gone back on your word.'

'I'm sorry. But that promise was made when we both believed Nicholas was dead. Everything changed when he returned.'

'You have taken advantage of Nicholas's situation. I will never forgive you for that.'

'I don't know what you mean.'

'My son has not recovered from all that he suffered in the war. He puts on a brave face but I have heard him cry out in the night. I have seen the distress, the haunted look, in his eyes.'

'I know. And I want to help him. He needs me.'

'No, he does not need you, Virginia. He is still in a vulnerable and confused state. What he needs is quiet and stability so that he can get back to normality. He cannot be exposed to the scandal of a liaison with a married woman – especially one who's husband and friends are all Bolsheviks and revolutionaries.' She heaved a shuddering sigh. 'How can you say that you love my son when you obviously think nothing about putting him in such a dangerous position?'

'My husband's a teacher. He's not a Bolshevik, or a violent man.'

Mrs Cartwright flicked a withering glance in Virginia's direction. 'Don't lie to me. I can see that you are lying. And I read the news-papers. Your husband has been in prison and he's likely to be in prison again. The last time he was arrested, he and his friends were causing a riot – attacking the police with iron bars and bottles – and you say he's not a violent man!'

'He was trying to stop the violence. But all this has nothing to do with you, Mrs Cartwright. Nicholas and I are going to work everything out together.'

Mrs Cartwright shook her head in disbelief. 'It has always been Nicholas's destiny to marry Fiona Forbes-Linton, to unite our two families. This was what we all wanted, the fulfilment of everything our family has worked for.'

Her face darkened as she went on. 'How dare you try to ruin his life, destroy his future, by plunging him into your disgusting, immoral world, your world of instability and violence. You say you love him, but how can you, when you are so willing and eager to drag him down to your level?'

'For goodness' sake,' Virginia tried to sound angry even though she was beginning to see a grain of truth in some of what Mrs Cartwright was saying. 'You're being ridiculous, suggesting that I would do anything to harm your son, that in some way I'm going to ruin his life.'

'But you are, you and the whole sordid world that you are part of. What do you think your husband will do when he finds out about Nicholas?'

Virginia could not answer. Although she

knew the answer only too well.

'You know in your heart that I am right, Virginia,' the older woman said. 'I love my son and I love my grandson. I want to see them live happy, peaceful and secure lives. As I've already reminded you, I have kept my promise.' She flushed and turned her head as if she was gazing in a dignified manner at the view from the window. 'I am imploring you, Virginia, to keep yours. It's not too late. Please think this through. Think of the future and what it would mean for Nicholas and Richard. If you really, truly love them as I do, please think of what is best for them.' Her voice broke and she pressed her lips tightly together.

There was a long drawn-out silence. Then Virginia whispered miserably, 'I'll try.'

29

If she could find some way of avoiding the inevitable conflict, if she could get away from James before he knew anything about Nicholas. That was what she kept trying to think of. She could not risk Nicholas turning up on her doorstep. Not for any reason.

But if only they could be left in peace to bring up their son and be happy. They loved each other and that was all that mattered. Mrs Cartwright didn't understand, but she did have a point concerning the trouble James could cause. Something had to be done about that. She telephoned Nicholas and said she couldn't get away until after the trial, which was now due to start in a couple of days.

Virginia was in the public gallery of the High Court for the duration of the trial. The jury eventually returned a fourteen-to-one majority verdict that Gallacher and Shinwell were guilty of incitement to riot, and Gallacher, Murray and MacArtney were guilty of rioting. All the others defendants, including James, were acquitted. As he left the court, James talked heatedly about the unfairness of the verdicts.

'Even the Lord Justice Clerk thought it was a farce! Did you see his face?'

The newspapers were full of accounts of how the jury had reached their decision.

'Can you imagine it?' Mathieson said. 'Bremner only got off because some of the jury men thought he had a nice open face – and because they thought he had saved a policeman from being thrown into the Clyde.'

'Was that not Kirkwood?'

'Of course it was Kirkwood who saved the policeman. They didn't know what they were about, that bunch of idiots!' James' anger was fuelled by the fact that Shinwell was sentenced to five months' imprisonment and Gallacher to three.

'But surely that was quite lenient?' Virginia interrupted, 'considering some previous sentences. If John Maclean had been there, he would probably have got five years.'

'Oh, I know, but it still makes me mad,' he added bitterly.

'It's obvious they're afraid of a Bolshevik revolution, like the one in Russia, happening here,' Virginia said, 'and because of that I think it was a mistake to raise the Red Flag in the square. Especially such a huge one.'

'Och, that wasn't official. It was just one of the strikers letting his good spirits and enthusiasm run away with him. He didn't mean any harm. He just climbed on to the plinth to wave the flag.'

It was while they were discussing the sentences that Tam came to the door.

'Come in, daddy. We were just going to have our tea. Sit down and have something to eat with us.'

'No hen,' he said, 'I just came to tell you that your mammy's not at all well. She hasn't been able to get up these past two or three days and she takes awful breathless turns. She'll not admit she's in pain. You know what she's like, but I think you'd better come and see her.'

Virginia felt a rush of panic.

'I'll get my coat.' She snatched it from the peg and struggled into it.

James said, 'I'll come over as soon as I've finished at the college.'

She didn't care what James did. All she cared about at that moment was her mother. She was shocked at the sight that greeted her when she arrived in the Gorbals kitchen. Janette was lying on her back on the high bed. Her sunken eyes were closed, her hollow cheeks sagged allowing her mouth to hang open. Virginia thought she was already dead.

'Mammy,' she screamed and ran to her.

Janette's eyes opened and she made an attempt to smile.

'Oh, it's you, hen. You gave me a fright there.'

'I'm sorry, mammy. I'm just upset to see you like this. Have you sent for the doctor?'

'Och, what can they do, hen? It's a waste of Tam's hard-earned money. Anyway, he's spent all he has buying me tasty wee bites to try and tempt me to eat. He's been that good to me. He brought me a nice wee bit of haddock the other day, didn't you Tam?' Her voice had faded to barely a whisper.

Tam looked anxious.

'Maybe I shouldn't have got that haddock. Now I haven't enough for the doctor. But she wasn't eating anything and I thought...'

'You did your best, daddy,' Virginia said.

'Come on, we'll see how much we have between us.' She went over to the table and emptied her purse onto it. Her father dug deep into his pockets but could only find a few coppers.

'We need at least two and six for a visit,' Tam said.

Virginia was carefully counting out the coins that she had. 'We've just enough,' she said. It would leave her without even her tram fare back home. But that didn't matter, the priority at the moment was to get a doctor to her mother.

They carefully put the coins into an old envelope and Tam hurried off to the nearest doctor's surgery. Virginia turned back to the bed to gently smooth back her mother's hair.

'You're going to be all right, mammy.'

Her mother opened her eyes and gazed sadly at Virginia. 'Och, hen, you know that's not true. I didn't want to worry your daddy but I've an awful pain in my chest. It'll be my heart. It's what killed my mother. But I'm not worried. I'm just glad to be united with my boys. Oh, it'll be that good to see them again.'

'Please mammy, you mustn't talk like that. What about daddy and me?'

'You've got your good man and Tam's got all his pals and his politics.'

'Politics!' Virginia scoffed. 'What are they

to him compared with you?'

Her mother smiled faintly. 'Oh, I've never pretended that I could compete with the cause, hen. It's that strong, you see. My life's always been him and my weans. His life has always been his socialism.'

It occurred to Virginia that this was also true of James. And of John Maclean as well. Maclean was seldom at home with his wife and daughters. He was so often touring around England and Ireland now, as well as Scotland, speaking, sometimes two or three times a day. He'd be killing himself if he didn't slow down. He was still dressed like James in a suit and collar and tie and homburg, but his collar was frayed and his suit was paper thin. He'd saved up five pounds to buy a new and much needed suit, but James had told her he'd ended up giving the money to the striking miners.

'I'll make you a nice cup of tea,' Virginia told Janette.

'I don't think I've the strength to sit up to drink it, hen. I'll tell you what I'd rather you did.'

'What?'

'Hurry and clean up the kitchen as much as you can before the doctor comes. I'm that ashamed for anybody to see it like this. I've not been able to keep it tidy these last few days.'

'Don't worry. I'll soon have it like you

used to.'

Virginia rolled up her sleeves and grabbed her mother's apron that was hanging behind the press door. She filled a pail of hot water from the kettle, filled the kettle again and put it on the fire. As rapidly as she could, she washed all the surfaces, the mantelpiece, the fender, the coal bunker, the dresser. Then she got down on her hands and knees and began energetically scrubbing the floor. She was nearly finished doing this, her face wet with perspiration, when she heard her mother gasp for breath.

Virginia struggled to her feet and rushed across to the bed. Janette was clawing the air, fighting to get up, frantic to draw breath.

'Mammy!' Virginia wailed, not knowing what to do. 'Oh, mammy!' She ran over to the sink and jerked open the window. The stinking air from the rubbish-strewn, rat-infested back yard wafted in. She stumbled back to the bed, completely caught up in her mother's panic. She tried to hold on to her. Tried to calm her, comfort her, but her mother kept thrashing about, and now, crying out pitifully with the pain.

Just then Tam returned with the doctor. Virginia had never been so glad to see anyone in her life. The doctor took one look at Janette and immediately opened his case and began preparing an injection. Within a few short moments, he had administered it, and Janette began to subside, to calm down.

'Oh, thank you, doctor,' Virginia said. 'She looks so peaceful already. That was dreadful. My poor mother.'

Tam said, 'Aye, I've never seen her in as good a sleep as that for a long time. Her nights have been awful bad. Sometimes she hasn't been able to close her eyes at all.'

The doctor snapped his case shut. 'I've given her some morphine, but I'm afraid her heart's giving out. There's nothing more I can do for her now. The chances are she'll just slip away in her sleep. And if she does, I think it'll be a blessed release.'

Virginia was too shocked to say anything. Vaguely she heard Tam and the doctor talking together before he eventually saw the doctor out.

'Thank God he managed to come and stop her pain,' Tam said when he returned to the kitchen. 'I couldn't watch your mammy suffer like that any more. It's more than human flesh can stand. Poor old Janette.'

'But mammy isn't old,' Virginia said. 'She should be enjoying the prime of her life. It isn't fair.'

Tam sank miserably into a chair and started rolling a Woodbine with shaking hands.

'Fair? What's fair around here? Your Mrs Cartwright has a holiday home. She got all the rest and good food and fresh air she wanted and with you to pander to her every need. What has your mammy ever had?' Tears were welling up in his eyes and he angrily raised his voice. 'I can't even get a decent bloody cigarette!'

Virginia went over to the bed to check that her mother had not moved and was still sleeping peacefully. Then she said to Tam, 'I'll make us a cup of tea.'

'Aye, all right, hen. Sorry for the language.'

'It's all right. I feel like swearing myself at the unfairness of it all.'

She made the tea and they sat opposite each other drinking it in silence until Virginia said,

'That's the door.'

She went to answer it and then ushered in plump little Mrs Friel.

'How's your mammy, hen?' Then, catching sight of the still figure of Janette in the bed, she lowered her voice to a whisper. 'Aw, she's huvin' a wee sleep. Ah'll no' bother ye, then. You know where Ah am if she needs me.' She backed carefully, quietly, towards the door. 'Anythin' ye need, mind. Jist ask.'

Virginia nodded her thanks. Afterwards she said, 'When James comes, I'll tell him I'd better stay the night.'

'The bed through there'll take the two of you.'

'Yes, I expect he'll stay too. If that's all

right with you.'

'Of course hen. I'll be glad of your company. I hope Janette'll not take another turn, though. What can any of us do? It's just terrible.'

'Try not to think about it, daddy.'

'It doesn't bear thinking about.'

'I've got a couple of coppers left. Do you want me to go out and get you a paper?'

'No, hen,' he replied quickly, a note of panic in his voice, 'No, you just stay here. When did James say he'd be?'

'He should be here any time now, daddy.'

They had another cup of tea and before they'd finished it there was a knock on the door. Virginia went to answer it and came back followed by James's stocky figure. He took off his shabby homburg and unbuttoned his coat.

'How is she?'

'The doctor's given her something to ease the pain. She's sleeping now. There's tea in the pot.'

'Thanks.' He went over to the bed to stand looking at Janette. Then he bent closer. When he turned round again, the look on his face told them what he was going to say before he said it. 'Virginia, Tam, I'm sorry... She's gone.'

Both Tam and Virginia stared uncomprehendingly at him until he repeated, 'She's gone. She's died in her sleep.'

'Oh no.' Virginia began to weep and rushed over to the bed. 'Oh no, mammy!'

Tam sat on like a statue.

After a time, James took hold of Virginia and forced her back down on to the chair.

'There's things to be done. Arrangements to be made. It's a good job we're here. Control yourself, Virginia, for your daddy's sake.'

Virginia nodded and rubbed at her face with the apron she was still wearing. Suddenly Tam said, 'I'm not having any ministers or any of that damned religious mumbo-jumbo.'

'I know how you feel, Tam,' James said. 'But I think we should respect Janette's beliefs – mistaken though they might have been.'

'Yes,' Virginia said. 'Mammy was a true believer. She must have a decent Christian funeral.'

Tam said brokenly, 'I can't even afford to pay the minister.'

'Don't worry about that,' James said. 'I'll sort that out.'

Tam nodded, 'You're a good man, James.'

1920

30

'I'm so sorry about your mother,' Nicholas said. They were walking together alongside the canal. Earlier they'd made love and he'd agreed that it wasn't yet the right time for her to make the break and to start the new life they planned. They had waited for a number of weeks after the funeral before they even met. In a sense, Virginia knew that they should not be meeting at all – the memory of her encounter with Mrs Cartwright was still painfully fresh in her mind.

After a few minutes he said, 'I don't even know if this is the right time yet to tell you my good news. I don't want to appear insensitive.'

'Och, tell me, please. It'll maybe help to cheer me up.'

'My book has been accepted for publication. I didn't tell you before. I could hardly believe it myself. You had so many other things on your mind. The trial, and then your mother's death.'

'You mean you've been keeping this from me all this time? How on earth did you manage to contain yourself? Darling, congratulations, it's wonderful.'

'As I say, I can hardly believe it. It still hasn't sunk in but the publishers are rushing it out. They think it's going to be a great success.' He laughed. 'Fame and fortune. It looks like I'll have no money worries from now on, according to them. And it means I won't have to rely on my parents' support any longer. Perhaps we can buy that house in Edinburgh after all.'

'When's it coming out? You've been so secretive about this. I don't even know what it's called or what it's about.'

'It's called *Scenes from the Inferno*, and it's based on the experiences of myself and my comrades in the trenches. My editor has been saying such embarrassingly kind things about it – he reckons it's just about the best book to have come out of the war so far. He says he's never read anything so powerful and moving. I'm sorry I couldn't talk to you about it, as I did with my poetry. It's just ... I felt if I discussed it with anyone I would talk it out instead of writing it.'

'I'm so happy and excited for you, Nicholas.'

'They want me to do all sorts of lecture tours and personal appearances – all over Britain. There's even talk of America, but I won't have anything to do with that. I'll put them off until you're free and we can get married. Or at least until we are able to go together.'

'No, you mustn't, darling. Please. Maybe this is the answer to all our problems. While you're away, it'll give me time to get everything sorted out with James without a confrontation. With you, I mean. And it'll also be a test of your love.'

'Virginia, I don't need any test. I've had enough tests and for far too long.'

'What I meant was, you'll be meeting all sorts of interesting new people...'

'Virginia.' It was the first time she'd seen anger getting the better of him. 'Stop talking nonsense. I understand how you must be feeling at the loss of your mother. I understand all the problems you've had to cope with, but now you're beginning to make stupid excuses. You must take me for a fool.'

She was shocked. 'No, Nicholas. I was just trying to be fair. You deserve this success. I don't want anything to spoil it for you.'

'That's not what it sounded like.'

'Oh, darling, I'm sorry.' She wound her arm around his neck. 'I hardly know what I'm saying just now. All I know is that one day, I'll be free and we'll be married. The time will fly past if you just relax and enjoy your success. Go ahead and do whatever your publisher suggests. You can write to me while you're away and keep me up to date with everything. But you'll soon be home. The time will fly past.'

He sighed and shook his head. 'Has there

ever been anyone, I wonder, who has had a love affair lasting as long as ours?'

'Of course, hundreds. Some people have had affairs that went on for a lifetime.'

'Well, I've no intention of going on like this for a lifetime.'

'Nor have I.' She stood on tiptoe and kissed him. 'But all the time we've waited will be worth it in the end.'

'Are you sure you want me to go ahead with promoting this book?'

'Definitely. It'll give me a better chance to sort things out with James.'

'But we always said we'd talk to him together, Virginia.'

'No darling, *you* said we'd talk to him together. I know James, and that is what has been worrying me all along. I need to do this on my own, Nicholas, and in my own way. Trust me, please.'

Reluctantly he agreed. 'If you're absolutely sure that's what you want and that it's the best way.'

'Yes, I am.'

She felt elated afterwards. Here, at last, was the solution. It didn't make what she had to do any easier, for herself at least. But she didn't care about herself. As long as Nicholas and Richard were safe.

It wouldn't be any easier either to leave James. But she would try to make him understand that she didn't want to hurt him and had never intended to cause him any unhappiness. He would be angry at her. He would probably rage at her. He would threaten to confront Nicholas. But she would tell him that Nicholas had gone. Hopefully, by the time Nicholas returned from America, James would have calmed down and accepted the inevitable.

Meantime she would choose her moment carefully. And afterwards, her bolt hole would be in the Gorbals with her father until she and Nicholas could find a suitable home. Her father would not disown her now, she felt sure. She was the only family he had left...

She felt happy and relieved, just to be making a final decision. She wished now that she'd been able to make it long ago. John Maclean's wife had left him in the autumn of 1919 and one of his daughters had been put into the care of Maclean's younger sister. The other girl had gone to live with his wife's brother in Maryhill. According to James, there had been no ill feeling about the separation. It was simply a case of Maclean having no money with which to feed and clothe them. But he kept in contact with them by letter. He wrote especially to the girls. James said, 'He tells them to sing "The Red Flag" every day and never forget it. He tells them to remember every day that the masters rob the workers and that socialism is the only thing to stop the robbery.'

'That's a bit serious for such young children.' Virginia had said, 'I don't think I'd want my children to be singing "The Red Flag" every day and worrying about the masters robbing the workers.'

'That's the trouble with you,' James said angrily, 'you're not committed enough. You've allowed yourself to be corrupted by your contact with wealth and comfort.'

'What nonsense, James. Honestly, sometimes you talk complete rubbish. All I'm saying is that they should be enjoying children's songs and stories – daft rhymes and fairy tales and things like that. Things to stimulate their imaginations or make them laugh. They'll have to face the bad things in life soon enough.'

'Oh well, I'm sure he does that too. He's good with children. He's a teacher, remember. But he wants to bring his children up with the right beliefs and values. I remember asking him what he did about the religious instruction all the children got at school. He told me his daughters stood outside the class, along with the Jewish children. He warned them never to worry about the silly ghost stories in the Bible and the silly stories about a good God who lets soldiers kill other men to please the rich. I thought, "Good for him, and if I have any children, that's how

I'll bring mine up.'"

Talk like this confirmed Virginia in the rightness of her decision to leave James. She regarded herself as a socialist, but she would never expect her children to be exposed to so much politics so young. She wasn't even sure if she'd want to deny them religious instruction. Above all she would want them to think for themselves and to make up their own minds.

Mathieson was becoming more and more involved in the formation of a Scottish Communist Party, as well as helping Maclean and his ragged army of unemployed men in their campaign to force the Parish Councils to grant larger amounts of relief. Men who couldn't find work could be refused 'outdoor relief', which meant they had to live in the poorhouse in Barnhill, separated from their wives and families. Even when they got relief, it was barely enough to live on. He had been going on and on about the unfairness of it for weeks. So much so that something finally snapped inside Virginia and she knew she couldn't wait another day.

The crisis came as he was lecturing her about a down-and-out from Bridgetown called Matthew Fry, who'd been refused assistance and only offered the poorhouse. He was so distressed at the prospect of being separated from his wife and family, he'd gone to Maclean's house to ask for his help.

'Right away, John took Matthew in the tram-car to the City Chambers, marched in and demanded that the Chief Officer of the Parish Council be sent to speak to him. And when the officer came, John demanded that Matthew be given outdoor relief and if he didn't get it, there would be a gigantic demonstration in the square the next day.'

James laughed uproariously. 'Matthew Fry was sent at once to the cashier with an authorisation from the officer for a cash payment. They knew John would be able to do it, you see. They knew he was a man of his word.' He suddenly glanced at Virginia. 'Are you listening to me?'

'I've been listening to you for years!' she burst out. 'Politics, politics, politics. Nothing but politics! If only, James, you could have left them on the doorstep every time before you stepped into this house, we might have got on better.'

James stared at her in astonishment. 'We get on perfectly well…We're both interested in politics. It's something we've always shared. I don't understand what you're complaining about. What's got into you all of a sudden?'

'It's not all of a sudden, James. Talk about listening? You've never listened to me. Never thought about what my real interests are, what I really feel, what I really want. Never thought about me at all.'

'But ... but ... this is preposterous. Have you taken leave of your senses?'

'The only mad thing I've done is to talk myself into staying with you for so long.'

'What do you mean? What on earth have I done? I've always tried to be a good husband. I've always been faithful to you. And I don't drink. I don't smoke. Any money I earn I give to you. What more can I do?'

He was so genuinely uncomprehending that her anger fizzled out. 'You don't understand, James.'

'No, I don't.'

'It's not really that you've been a bad husband. Just not the right one for me.'

'But we've been happily married for years. We've never even had one argument.'

'As far as arguments are concerned, I've never had much of a chance to say anything except just agree with everything you've said about politics.'

'But you've always been a socialist – just like the rest of us.'

'I'm a socialist but not a revolutionary, James. I don't want a socialist revolution or any other kind of revolution.'

'But Virginia, John says–'

'I know what John says. And I know that most of what he says is right. I know he's an exceptional man, James, and a good man. I know he's everyone's hero, especially yours. So much so that you never stop going on and on about him. I've got to the point where I can't stand to hear his name.'

'Oh well.' James looked deeply hurt. 'If that's the way of it, I'll never mention him in this house again.'

'Damn it,' she said, frustrated. 'Here we go again! This isn't about politics. But it's where we always seem to end up.'

'Is that so. Well, what did you want to talk about then?' James was angry now. 'Go on then, I'm listening.'

31

'You know that I used to work for the Cart-wrights at Hilltop House before the war?'

'Yes, why?'

'While I was there I got to know their son, Nicholas.'

James' mouth twisted sarcastically. 'Oh yes, the big war hero. I know all about him.'

'No, you don't, James. You know nothing about him.'

'I know he's the product of a family that represents the worst elements of capitalism.'

'There you go again. You can't see past politics.'

'I'm just stating a fact.'

'Well, here's a fact for you. Nicholas and I

were lovers and I became pregnant.'

The colour drained from her husband's face. There was a kind of pleading in his eyes. She turned away to avoid his desperate stare.

'It was long before I knew you, James, and so it had nothing to do with you.'

'The usual story,' James said, through gritted teeth. 'A rich bastard taking whatever he wants from life. That's why you were flung out, of course. It's been the same for centuries. They use girls like you and then toss them out onto the streets. And you wonder why I'm such an ardent socialist. Why I'm all for a revolution. And a bloody one at that!'

'It's true that Mrs Cartwright dismissed me when she found out. But it wasn't Nicholas's fault.'

'How can you say that?'

'Because I know he pleaded with her to look after me until he returned from the war. He was sent to the front before he could do anything else to help me. I only told him about the pregnancy the night before he left.'

'And you believed that story? More fool you.'

'I had his child, James, and Mrs Cartwright took him and has looked after him ever since.'

'You mean, there's ... his ... bastard!'

'His name is Richard and he's a lovely little boy. You must keep this in your mind, James. All this happened long before you and I even knew each other. Then when I did meet you, as far as I knew Nicholas was dead. That part of my life was past. I was fond of you and I admired you and yes, we had our political beliefs in common. I married you in good faith, James, and I had every intention of staying faithful to you.' She forced herself to meet his shocked stare. 'But then when Nicholas came back ... you see, I've never stopped loving him. I tried to forget. I tried not to think of him. But when he came back, when I saw him again...' She hesitated then went determinedly on. 'We became lovers again, James. I love him and I want to be with him and my son. That's why I'm leaving you.'

James' mouth worked soundlessly for a few seconds. Finally he uttered, 'Leaving me ... for that Cartwright bastard!'

'James, please. He's not to blame for anything his father's done. Nicholas is as good and honest a man as yourself.'

'Don't you dare compare that capitalist bastard with me! All my life I've fought against ... fought against...' He staggered and fell against the fireside chair.

'James,' Virginia cried out. 'Please, I can't bear to see you in such a state. You'll make yourself ill.'

But it was already too late. His face, his whole body, had become contorted. His eyes were staring out of his head. He tumbled helplessly from the chair onto the floor.

'Oh James!' She wept as she tried in vain to lift him back on to the chair. 'I'll call the doctor. I'll run all the way there and back.' She struggled to her feet. 'I'll fetch the doctor. You'll be all right.'

Weeping in distress she flew from the house. In the streets clusters of women turned to stare at her and call after her, 'What's up, hen?'

After she'd called the doctor and was running back, they called to her again and she gasped out, 'I think my husband has taken a stroke. I was getting the doctor.'

'Oh my!' There were gasps of horror and sympathy. 'Is there anythin' we can dae, hen?' they asked as they followed her back to the house.

When she got there, she found two of the neighbours, Mrs McGann and Mrs Finniston, were dragging James across the floor towards the bed.

'Oh, there you are, hen,' Mrs McGann puffed out. 'We saw yer door open. Were ye getting the doctor?' They were both breathless with their exertion. Now they were attempting to hoist James up to the high bed and finding it doubly difficult because of their difference in height. Mrs Finniston was very tall, and Mrs McGann was very small. Virginia rushed to help them.

'Yes, he'll be here as soon as he can.'

It was a terrible struggle because James was sturdily built, but eventually the three of them managed to get him on to the bed.

'We'll help ye get his claes aff,' Mrs Finniston said.

'No, no, thanks all the same but I'll manage that. I'll see you later and let you know what the doctor says.' Virginia replied as she eased them towards the door.

'I reckon it's a stroke, hen.' Mrs Finniston shook her head. 'That's what the doctor'll say. The same thing happened tae ma sister's man. The very same. He didnae last long. The doctor gave him a month but Charlie didnae last three weeks–'

'Well, anyway, thanks again,' Virginia interrupted and shut the door. She hurried back to gaze helplessly at Mathieson's grotesquely twisted face. All she could think to do was loosen his collar and tie.

'The doctor'll be here in a minute, James. You're going to be all right,' she added, as much to reassure herself as him.

She felt as though she was going to collapse. Her mind was reeling with guilt and regret. Never for one moment had she thought that this could happen. It was just terrible. 'If he dies,' she repeated over and over again to herself, 'I'll have killed him.

God, don't let him die. I'll never forgive myself.' She was in such a panic-stricken state that she didn't hear the knock at the door at first. Then Mrs McGann's voice squeezed through the letter box, 'It's the doctor, hen. Come on, open the door.'

Virginia ran to let the doctor in. It only took him a matter of minutes to look at James and announce he'd arrange for the ambulance to remove him to hospital. The doctor left again and Virginia sat by the bed until the ambulance arrived and then she followed them as they carried James downstairs on a stretcher.

A crowd of men, women and children had gathered out-side the close. Women were also leaning on windowsills gazing out at the scene. Men took off their caps as the stretcher passed as if James was already dead. Women murmured, 'Poor Mr Mathieson. Such a guid wee soul.'

'Aye, like oor Johnny, wearin' hissel oot helpin' folk.'

'A guid soul. Aye. He disnae deserve this.'

It took all Virginia's strength to climb into the ambulance. She was beyond tears now. All she could do was pray. In the hospital, they took him away and she sat on her own for what seemed like an eternity before a doctor came to speak to her.

He explained that James had suffered a very serious stroke. Her husband was partly paralysed and had lost the power of speech. The doctor expressed his sympathy. They would do what they could but... She hardly heard anything else. She didn't need to. She could tell just by looking at the sympathetic young doctor's eyes that he wasn't optimistic about James' chances of recovery.

In a daze, Virginia allowed herself to be led by a nurse into a long ward and shown James' bed. A chair was brought and put beside the bed. She collapsed into it and stared at James. A trickle of saliva began to dribble out of his mouth and down his chin. She quickly fished out her handkerchief and dabbed his face dry. She didn't know what to say to him or even if he could hear her. She couldn't even meet his eyes.

For days after that she would sit beside the bed every afternoon in a strained silence. Sometimes she'd get up and dab at his face or arrange his pillow more comfortably or straighten the bed clothes. Then she'd sit down again. But as the days went by, there was no visible improvement in his condition.

Guilt consumed her. It wasn't only that she felt she'd caused his stroke. It was the fact that she had never really loved him and could not feel love for him even now.

She'd come back again every evening and sit in silence once more. It was truly terrible. She wanted to be miles away, anywhere but in the bleak hospital that smelled of sickness and death. She'd written to Nicholas several times – in England and then in America. At her request, he'd sent letters to her care of her father's address. At first her letters had been normal, full of all her news. But after James' stroke, they became short and strained. She'd stopped mentioning James, and had never told Nicholas about his stroke. She couldn't face putting her guilt into words. Nor could she risk Nicholas suffering the same guilt. He had suffered enough in his life.

Eventually, Nicholas asked in one of his letters if she'd told James yet. She replied that she'd told him long ago. She even lied about the way he had taken it. How he'd surprised her by being reasonable and understanding. He had been sad of course, and upset that of all people it had been a Cartwright but he'd come to terms with that. The separation had been perfectly amicable. Finally she wrote and told Nicholas that James was now ill and in hospital, as if it had just happened. She had to avoid the slightest hint of any connection with the real cause. For his sake, as well as her own. She said that she was now visiting James several times a week and she'd gone out to work to make some money to keep herself.

Nicholas immediately wired her a large sum of money and told her to stop working at once. He insisted there was absolutely no need for her to go out to work. He went on to argue that she could have no reason to refuse his money, since her separation from James was out in the open, and amicable... She could have replied that, just then, she welcomed doing jobs she loathed and detested, regarding them as some sort of penance, something that she deserved. But she didn't tell him.

She did confess, however, that she felt totally alienated from James. She couldn't even bring herself to speak to him. She knew it wasn't fair. He couldn't help looking so dreadful but she was repulsed by him. He wasn't the James she had known any more. The stroke had turned him into something grotesque, no longer even a man.

Nicholas was obviously shocked by her confession. She received a letter by return of post telling her she must try to imagine what it would be like to lie in that hospital bed unable to communicate. Especially for a man like James whose whole life had been spent communicating his ideas to others. She could understand where this depth of sympathy was coming from. Nicholas had once been in hospital and unable to communicate. He had been unable to remember even who he was. For months he had lain in a terrible no-man's-land of silent isolation. In a strange way this not only drew Nicholas closer to James, but distanced her from both men.

She began making excuses to herself for not going to the hospital every visiting time. What was the use, what good was it doing? Perhaps she could even be doing him harm. Her visits might be making him as uncomfortable as she, as they sat together through the long, terrible silences. He was probably relieved when she didn't turn up. And she was turning up less and less often. She tried to explain this to Nicholas, knowing at the same time that he would only grow more shocked at her. He didn't understand. But she had reached the point where she no longer cared. She wrote and told him that she couldn't cope any more. She simply could not force herself back to the hospital again. She had stopped going to see James because she felt he really was no longer there.

Nicholas by this time was on his way home from America. She couldn't even feel excited by this fact. She had lost her way completely, and felt she had made a complete mess of her life. Even worse, she had made a mess of everyone else's life. She should never have married James knowing that she didn't love him. Having done so, she should never have been unfaithful to him. Nor should she have kept Nicholas hanging on for all this time. He should have been free to turn to someone else who would have been willing to marry him and give him the happiness he deserved.

Day after day, she locked herself in the single end in the Calton and sat nursing her head in her hands. She felt the walls and ceiling pressing further and further in on her. Neighbours knocked on the door and she ignored them. Let them think she'd gone to the hospital. Let them think she'd gone back to live in the Gorbals. Let them think whatever they liked.

32

'Could I speak to Virginia, please,' Nicholas said.

Tam stared at him.

'And who might you be?'

'Hasn't she told you about me?'

'No.'

'Well.' Nicholas hesitated uncertainly. 'I'm a friend of Virginia's. I take it she's not in at the moment.'

'She'll be where she usually is – at the hospital visiting her husband.'

'Right.' Nicholas had not been asked in. He turned away from the door, then turned back again for a moment to ask, 'Have you been in to see him?'

'Just the once. That was enough. I don't

think he even knew me. Didn't make any sign. Couldn't speak or anything. There was no point in being there.' He shook his head. 'A terrible tragedy.'

'Yes indeed,' Nicholas thought in sudden anger. But he just said in a calm voice. 'Just tell Virginia that Nicholas called. She knows where to contact me.'

Nicholas went out of the close and found a crowd of children milling around his car. A few hunched-shouldered men, fists plunged deep into the pockets of their trousers, were viewing it as well. Nicholas bid them a polite good afternoon and managed a smile at the children as they cleared a path for him. He felt appalled at the place, at the close, at the buildings, at the street. No human being should be expected to live in such conditions. His heart went out to Virginia. How on earth had she managed to survive in such a place. The Calton wasn't much better. He remembered the area from when he'd given her a lift home. She had written to say that when she'd left Mathieson, she had gone to stay with her father in the Gorbals. He had been glad that at least she'd made the break but he could see that the Gorbals was even worse than the Calton and he felt he must do his best as soon as possible and get her out of here and into a decent house. There were nice areas in Glasgow, but it would probably be best to make a fresh start away from the city.

He was appalled at the slums but he was even more appalled at James Mathieson's situation. The poor man was lying alone and helpless, cut off from the world, out of touch with everything, not knowing what was going on. Despite what Mr Watson had said, he doubted that Virginia would be anywhere near the hospital. The thought of Mathieson's predicament haunted him because it inevitably reminded him of his own nightmarish experiences in hospital, lying there unable to communicate with his family or anyone else. He couldn't get it out of his mind. He couldn't get James Mathieson out of his mind. But Virginia might have come to her senses, and started visiting him again. He appreciated it was an awkward situation for Virginia, to say the least. But still the man needed to know that somebody cared about him. It was a case of common humanity. On an impulse, he turned the car towards the hospital, stopping en route to buy a few newspapers – the *Glasgow Herald* and a couple of socialist papers. Once in the hospital, he asked what ward James Mathieson was in and was given directions.

He had never seen such a depressing place. It was even worse than the military hospital where he'd spent his lost time. A nurse pointed out Mathieson's bed.

Nicholas fetched a chair and sat down at

the side of the pathetic, propped-up figure. He touched the withered arm. 'I hope you'll forgive me if I've done the wrong thing by coming here, James. I've had a similar experience in hospital, you see, and I know what you must be feeling. And when Virginia wrote to me and said that she had stopped visiting you, I felt I had to do something. She's just upset to see you suffering. It's not that she doesn't care about you. Even though you and she are separated, I'm sure she still cares about you. And I would like to say how glad and grateful I am that you have behaved so reasonably regarding the separation. I know it must have come as something of a shock that she and I have a child, but it's wonderful that you've been so understanding. I've always admired anyone who stands up for their principles as you do, but I must say my respect for you has increased greatly on account of the way you have behaved in this matter.'

He spread the newspaper on the bed. 'Anyway, I thought you'd feel out of touch with what's been going on. So how about if I read all the news to you?'

He read through every word in the *Herald* – even the sports pages. Then he ploughed through the socialist papers. There was still a few minutes left of the afternoon visiting time so he simply talked to Mathieson about all sorts of things, his own beliefs and opinions. He told Mathieson that since being away at the war, his views on a lot of things had changed dramatically and he now considered himself something of a socialist. He was also now very much anti-war.

'I've written a poem that goes some way to expressing my feelings about the war. I'll come back this evening and read it to you. You might find it interesting.' He rose and touched James' arm again. 'Try to keep your spirits up. You'll come through this. From what I've heard about you, you're a fighter. Keep fighting, James.'

He drove back to Hilltop House to an enthusiastic welcome from Richard, as well as a warm one from his mother and father. They were making a real effort to be more affectionate towards him than they'd ever been before in his life. It was almost pathetic. He wasn't used to seeing them like this. But he did appreciate that they were giving Richard a far better childhood then they'd given him. They doted on Richard. They would miss him when he and Virginia took the little boy away.

He and Richard had a game of football and then they all enjoyed tea together. Nicholas was constantly amazed at how different his parents were with Richard. He vividly remembered when he was a child, before he was banished to boarding school, how he had been given a frugal tea in the nursery by his ghastly nanny. She had missed her vocation, she would have been more suited to being a prison warder. A very strict, severe and unloving creature she'd been. He'd never allow anyone like that near Richard. Now, there was a plump, jolly girl in the nursery, and Richard had the freedom of the house for most of the day when he wasn't at school, skipping happily through whatever room took his fancy.

Nicholas decided that it would be better to look for a house with a garden so that Richard could have somewhere to play outside. Either that or a house near a park. As yet he hadn't told his parents of his plans. He wished that they would stop trying to persuade him to go with them to the Highlands. He'd told them that he would be happy to visit them, to spend holidays with them, but that he was not going to take up permanent residence there.

Yes, it was a lovely estate, he agreed. Yes, the castle they'd bought had an interesting history and was most impressive. Yes, it could make an ideal background for a novel. But he was not going to live there.

They insisted that the peace and quiet of such a remote and beautiful place would be much more conducive to his writing than life in a busy city like Glasgow. They had gone from one extreme to the other, becoming suffocatingly, irritatingly possessive towards him. He supposed it was understandable to a certain degree, after thinking he was dead and then suddenly finding him again. He tried to understand and be patient, but he knew he would be very glad to get away – to feel free to live his own life.

After dinner, avoiding their questions about where he was off to, he drove back to Glasgow and the hospital. He took his poem and his novel. He would not normally have imposed his work on a captive audience, but the circumstances weren't normal. He thought it might help James to understand that everything in life wasn't either black or white, that there was more to Nicholas Cartwright than just his name or his background. From what Virginia had told him about Mathieson, he was very bitter and full of hate towards anyone who wasn't of his class.

'My poetry, and particularly my novel,' he thought, 'should at least show James that I'm just an ordinary human being like himself.'

He also took some lemonade and a few bottles of beer. He didn't know whether James would be allowed the latter but he could always check with the nurse. He didn't see a nurse in the ward at first and so after greeting James, he put the bottles on the bedside locker.

'I'll check with the nurse before I leave. To

see if you're allowed any of this,' he explained. 'I hope they will allow it.' It suddenly occurred to him then that Mathieson might not drink. Many fervent socialists were also strong temperance men. 'On the other hand,' he added, settling himself down on the chair, 'you might be TT. If you are, the nurse can always give it to someone else.' He brought out his poem, *Tagged*.

'I hope this might interest you as an expression of what war means from the point of view of an ordinary soldier. My novel gives a more detailed vision of the effect war can have on people. I know you were strongly anti-war and I thought it might at least pass the time if I read a bit to you on each visit. For a week anyway. I'm thinking of looking for a place in Edinburgh – but I could still come and see you from time to time. I'd have to come through to see my parents anyway.' He smiled. 'They dote on my little boy. They'll want me to bring him as often as possible. In a couple of months, their place up north will be ready and they'll be selling Hilltop House and moving up there.'

He sighed. 'They want me to go with them but Virginia and I have already talked about the possibility of settling in Edinburgh. I haven't seen her yet since I've been back from America. I understood when you and she separated she went to live with her father in the Gorbals. I went to see her there but she wasn't in.' He sadly shook his head. 'That was an eye-opener to me – seeing that place. It's a disgrace that decent people are forced to live in such terrible conditions. When I think of the men coming back from the war to places like that...' He shook his head again. 'It's absolutely disgraceful. Do you know, something has just occurred to me, James. Perhaps I should stay here in Glasgow, and write a novel about things like that – about the terrible gulf between the rich and the poor.'

He was suddenly beginning to feel quite excited. 'The good and the bad in both – but exploring the effects that environment has on people. The unfair advantage in life that money gives... I wish you could tell me what you think of the idea. I'll have to discuss it with Virginia. She could be of help to me, couldn't she? When you think of it, she's had experience of both kinds of life. Or at least she's seen what life is like in a big house. And she knows all about life in the slums. I must speak to her about this right away.'

He looked puzzled for a moment. 'I wonder where she is. I only had a few words with her father but I gathered she hadn't told him anything about me. I expected with her having left you to live with him, she would have had to explain. Anyway, I hope you don't mind me inflicting my writing on you. This poem simply illustrates how the war changed me from the man that I was when I went off to war thinking of it as patriotic duty. The poem is called 'Tagged'.

The tag tied
To the bloodless toe
Bears only his name and number.

And registers nothing
Of youth consumed by the bullet's bite
Or sorrow and forced loathing
As another's gun stormed
At the brief candle of his light.

It should read
In carnage red
Of war's pity and waste
But would be delivered
By those who would ignore

To those who cradle
A corpse's smile
Desiccated heart
Fruitless seed

Like diamonds drained
Of light and clarity
Diamonds that bear razor edges.

Hastings, Crimea,
Passchendale...

'Now...' he said after a few moments of silence, 'I don't know what you'll think of that as a piece of poetry. You were a teacher and I expect you'll have good critical judgement in these matters. All I can claim is that it expressed my true feelings when I wrote it. But as I told you earlier, I think I've explored my feelings in more depth and with more success in the novel.'

He cleared his throat. 'Well here goes, my friend. Chapter One...'

33

'You did what?' Virginia cried out incredulously.

'I went to see him. And I'm glad I did, Virginia. He's a poor soul lying there alone. I don't know how you can bear *not* to go and visit him. After all, he has been so understanding about your love for me. His generosity of spirit is an example to us all.'

They were in the hotel, and at first everything had been wonderful. For a few brief moments she had been able to forget the overwhelming sense of guilt she felt about what had happened to James. And the way she had kept the truth from Nicholas. It had been so good to see Nicholas again. He had grabbed her and whirled her around in his usual joyous way and then covered her mouth with kisses before she could utter a word. Passion had overcome her. She forgot about everything else except his passionate love-making. He'd never been so wildly passionate. Afterwards she laughed and said,

'Talk about absence making the heart grow fonder!'

'I'm so happy to see you again and to know that at last our lives are coming together as they should – as I've always wanted them to. All I've to do now is confront my parents and tell them of my plans. I've already told James.'

She was horrified but Nicholas went on to say, 'He couldn't tell me what he thought, of course, although he was fighting to try. Happily his voice will come back in time. I told the doctors to give James any specialist treatment available – at my expense. Not to let on to him though that I am paying for it. I thought it was the least we could do, Virginia.'

'It's one thing to pay his expenses but how on earth do you think you're helping him by going into the hospital, Nicholas. I don't understand.'

'I can see you don't. But try to think of the situation from his point of view. He's a man of action. Despite his terrible state, I'm sure he's still committed to everything he believed in before. How do you think he feels lying there deserted by everybody who thinks of him as written off, as already dead?'

'But...' Tears welled up in her eyes. 'He might as well be dead. He can't talk or move. He doesn't know what you're saying or even if you're there at all.'

'You're wrong, Virginia. His eyes are full of expression and he is beginning to regain some movement. I think one of the most important things is to channel his strong spirit, give him a reason to live, a reason to fight to get back the kind of life he was so passionate about.

'His politics, you mean.' Virginia could not hide the bitterness in her voice. James' passion had never been for her. 'Why are you doing this, Nicholas?'

Nicholas stared at her. 'I've told you, it's the least I can do, the least *we* should do, to help the man. It's just common humanity. I'd do it for anybody. But I think we especially owe it to him. You should visit him, Virginia. You could go every afternoon and I could go every evening. It's only for an hour at a time.'

She felt a tremor of horror again. She desperately wanted to tell him that she'd lied about being separated and living apart from James. That James had not known about her affair until the last moment, and it had been the shock of that which had caused his present condition. The doctor had said that overwork – and his previous head injuries – could also have been factors. He'd certainly been pushing himself too hard, and he'd suffered severe blows to the head on more than one occasion, but deep down she knew that finding out about Nicholas Cartwright was what had finally broken him. The mere mention of the name Cartwright in connection with her had almost killed him. Now she had the added guilt about how James would be feeling at having Nicholas visit him. It was all her fault for lying to Nicholas. She had only meant to protect him, but now she would never be able to make him understand that. Nor would he ever be able to forgive her. He thought he was helping James when in actual fact, because of her, he was making him suffer all the more.

She could only hope that James was not able to understand or feel anything. Then she immediately felt ashamed and even more guilty for thinking that. Nicholas was right. It was the least she could do to conquer her feelings and visit James, and try in whatever way she could to help him.

'All right,' she said. 'I'll go in the afternoons.'

'Good.' He kissed her. 'There's no reason

why we can't all be civilised about this. I've been telling him my views on the war. And I was saying that I hoped that perhaps, one day, we could be friends. After all, there's enough hatred in the world without us adding to it.'

They were staying overnight and had ordered dinner in the small dining room downstairs. As they went in and sat down to have their meal, Nicholas said, 'It feels good, doesn't it, that we no longer need to hide away and be so secretive?'

Virginia smiled ruefully. 'We wouldn't feel so good if your mother and father walked in and found us sitting here. At least I wouldn't.'

He shrugged. 'Perhaps. But in any case I think it's time I told them that I'll be leaving soon. Well, they know already. They just don't want to accept it. I don't mean they know about our plans, but I have told them I'm definitely not going with them to their Highland estate. I'm going to be living my own life. By the way, I've been telling James that I'm thinking of setting my next novel in Glasgow and–'

'Why have you chosen Glasgow?' Virginia interrupted.

'Well, I was thinking that I might explore how social conditions have changed since the war. I'd also like to show what life is really like – for both rich and poor. Maybe, in some small way, I can help to heal the divisions in society that ruin so many people's lives. If I'm going to do this, it would help if we looked for a house in Glasgow – perhaps in the West End near the Botanic Gardens. It would be good for Richard, and convenient for the Mitchell Reference Library whenever I needed to do research there.'

'Yes, I'd like that. There are some lovely flats in the West End.'

'And terraced houses and villas.'

'I'd be quite happy in one of those big roomy flats.'

'Well, we can begin to look and see what's available. Tomorrow I'll clear things up with my parents and I'll meet you here in time for dinner in the evening, after I've been to see James. All right?'

'Yes, all right.'

'And don't forget you said you'd go to see him in the afternoon.'

'Don't worry, I'll go.'

To change the subject she steered the conversation back to his new novel and soon they were both enthusiastically discussing the project. Virginia could see how she would be able to help Nicholas with his research and she was looking forward to working with him. Yet all the time, at the back of her mind, the ordeal of the next day's hospital visit remained to haunt her.

Nicholas left the hotel after breakfast to

return to Hilltop House. She took her time, pottering about the bedroom, going down to the dining room for coffee, going for a walk along the canal, having a leisurely lunch. Eventually she could delay the evil hour no longer and she went to catch a bus to Glasgow and then a tram to the hospital.

Once there she braced herself to walk into the ward and face James. But she could only briefly allow her eyes to meet his before sitting down beside the bed. Eventually she broke the silence to say,

'Nicholas persuaded me to come, James. I was terribly shocked to hear he'd been visiting you. You see, he's under the impression that we've been separated for some time. I even let him think that it was an amicable separation. He has no idea that your illness had anything to do with...'

Her voice faded into silence. At last she managed to continue, 'I know what's happened to you has been my fault. The shock of me telling you. I didn't tell Nicholas the truth because I felt he had suffered enough without knowing what really caused your stroke. He looks all right, James, but he still hasn't fully recovered from the war. He has nightmares and ... and ... I just felt I couldn't add to them by burdening him with the same terrible guilt that I feel about you. I'm so sorry about everything. I didn't mean to hurt you. But I had to tell you. I

352

can't help loving Nicholas. And I've never stopped longing for my baby.'

Tears escaped and ran down her face. 'I've been too ashamed and guilty to come in and see you like this, knowing all the time that it was my fault. And now for you to suffer Nicholas coming here. I know how you must hate him but I don't know what to do. He thinks he's helping you.'

After a long silence, Virginia rose. 'I'll go now. But I'll be back tomorrow. Nicholas made me promise to come in every afternoon and he's coming every evening. I'm so sorry, James,' she repeated. She could see James' mouth moving but only strangled, incomprehensible grunts emerged. She couldn't bear to listen, and she turned and walked away.

Nicholas took in the day's newspapers and read them to James. He detected a twitching of James' eyelids and one of his hands, and felt cheered about this. After the newspaper reading, he told him how he'd now seen Virginia and they'd arranged to take turns visiting him. They were also going to start looking for a place in the West End. A flat probably. He said how he thought Richard would enjoy playing in the Botanic Gardens. Nicholas said he hoped that they could become friends after he got out of hospital and he'd always be welcome to visit them.

'Now, I'm going to be selfish again and read you another few chapters of my novel.

By the time I've gone through the whole book, hopefully you'll be fully recovered and you can discuss it with me – or you can at least tell me what you think of it! And any criticism and comments would certainly be of value to me when I'm writing my next novel. I've been talking to Virginia about my ideas and I can see she's going to be a great help. But then she's always inspired me and encouraged me with my writing. Long ago, before the war when she worked at Hilltop House, we used to meet secretly in the woods and I'd give her my poetry to read. She was the first person who knew I'd written anything. My mother and father have always had their own plans for my life and they certainly never included being a writer. A soldier, yes. The heir to my father's business empire, yes. But a writer?'

Nicholas laughed. 'I knew they'd squash that idea right away. But Virginia changed my whole life. She was such an inspiration and a help to me. She gave me the self-confidence to believe that I could be and should be a writer. I'll always love her and be grateful to her for that. But I'd better get on with our reading or it'll be the end of visiting time before I've even started.'

However, he did manage to finish the reading in time. There were even a few minutes to spare.

'I had the most dreadful time this morning,' he said. 'I told my mother and father about my plans for setting up home with Virginia. They were absolutely furious. Then when they saw that I wasn't going to budge, my mother became tearful. It was awful. Before Richard, she used to be a cold and unfeeling woman. All my life that's how she seemed to me. My God, James, I thought even my father was going to weep. It was terrible. I can only hope that in time they'll get used to the idea. But they're going to live up north – I think I told you – and then they'll be far away from Richard. That's what really matters to them – I don't think they really care all that much about me.'

He sighed. 'But it's their own fault. All those grandiose ideas about a castle and an estate in the Highlands. It's like a whole different world – but it's their world, not mine, I'm afraid, and they'll have to inhabit it without me and without Richard. Oh, if they come to think of Virginia differently and accept her for who she is, then maybe things will improve between us. But I doubt they'll ever change.' He laughed. 'I'm afraid we'll never convert them to socialism, James.'

He rose. 'It's time to go now. See you tomorrow night.'

Again he felt sure there was a response from James. 'Progress at last!' he thought, as he made his way cheerfully to the stairs and out to his car.

34

Each day, Nicholas read the newspapers to James. Then after chatting to him for a time, he would work his way through whatever socialist papers he was able to find. One day, he came in with a copy of *The Vanguard*. In it there was an article by Maclean, entitled 'The Irish Fight for Freedom'. Nicholas marvelled at men like Maclean and Mathieson who could have such passionate belief in a cause that they devoted their whole lives – practically every waking moment – to it. Speaking all over the country, writing so many articles and pamphlets, teaching the thousands of working men who filled their classes. He confessed to James that, although he had become more politically aware than he used to be, his overriding interest was in people. That was what he wanted to write about. People were his passion, not causes.

'It takes all kinds, I suppose,' he told James. 'It would be a dull world if we were all the same. But although I could never be like you or Maclean, I can admire your dedication. And the energy you put into it.'

He glanced at his watch. 'Anyway, here's Maclean's latest pamphlet. I haven't time to read it all now but I'll give you a summary instead.' He began, 'He points out that the recent war was supposed to be fought to defend the rights of small nations. But in the General Election of 1918, and at the municipal elections and county elections of 1920, Ireland voted with a huge majority for an independent republic. Instead of that Ireland got an army of occupation with aeroplanes, tanks, etc. He compares what the British are doing in Ireland with what Churchill did in Russia.'

Nicholas shook his head. 'Apparently Churchill spent two hundred million pounds in direct and indirect attempts to overthrow the Russian Republic because he said it was "a dictatorship by terrorists". Two hundred million pounds!' Nicholas repeated. 'That would have been enough to clear away all the slums in Glasgow and build decent houses for everyone. Anyway, Maclean goes on to describe some of the repressive measures taken against the Irish and claims that it's impossible to expect the Irish to suffer this kind of terrorism without some kind of retaliation. He wants Scotland to protest about it.'

Nicholas and Virginia continued with their house-hunting. They had looked at quite a few flats and had recently fallen in love with a beautiful house in Kirklee Terrace, just next to the Botanic Gardens. It would cost more than he'd originally planned to spend, but his book was doing well, and after he and Virginia had discussed it, they had decided they could afford it.

Once they'd put in an offer for the Kirklee Terrace house and it had been accepted, Nicholas felt it was time to take Virginia to visit his parents. He said to her,

'I want to introduce you to my father and I want to show both my parents how proud of you I am.'

'Darling, your father has met me. It was both he and your mother who persuaded me to allow them to bring up Richard.'

'Nevertheless, I want them to see how much we love each other and want to be a family together with Richard.'

She agreed to accompany him but when she looked so worried and unhappy, he said, 'There's nothing to worry about, darling. It doesn't matter what they say. They can't come between us.'

'It won't be just class differences they'll find a problem with, Nicholas. It'll be the morality. Or immorality, as they'll see it, of us living together without being married.'

'Well, they'll just have to put up with it until you and James are divorced. They'll not be the only ones to say we're living in sin. But I don't care what anyone thinks or says. Do you?'

'Then there's the fact that I've nothing

decent to wear.'

Nicholas tossed back his dark head and laughed.

'Ah, that's what's really worrying you, is it? Well, we'll soon fix that. You'll go to the best shop in Sauchiehall Street and buy the most fashionable outfit you can find.'

Later he told James about all this, describing the smart outfit she'd bought and how it had helped her self-confidence when they set off to visit Hilltop House.

'She looked really lovely, James. It was a pale blue outfit with a wide-brimmed hat. The colour matched her eyes. And oh, that beautiful golden hair of hers. I'd never seen her look so beautiful. Or so dignified. I was really proud of her.'

It hadn't been an easy visit. His parents had been stiff and cold. Polite of course, but they'd tried to freeze Virginia out at first by addressing any remarks to Nicholas and ignoring her. Virginia had put a stop to that herself.

'Mr and Mrs Cartwright,' she said firmly, 'I know how you must feel and you have my sympathy. You have been wonderful with Richard and I thank you for that. But you're not getting any younger and, apart from anything else, it wouldn't be easy to continue what you've been doing.'

'We neither need nor want your thanks.' Mrs Cartwright looked down her long nose at Virginia. 'And we are perfectly capable of continuing to see to our grandson's welfare.'

'Mother,' Nicholas said. 'Neither you nor father have thought this through. You're going to live in the Highlands. If we left Richard with you, what about a school for him out in the wilds? What about friends of his own age? But anyway, the fact is, Richard is our son and he's coming to live with us.'

Virginia said, 'You will be welcome to visit him as often as you like. There's plenty of room in our house in Kirklee Terrace for you both to stay. And if you wish we can bring Richard to visit you during the summer holidays. It would be so much better for Richard if there was no unpleasantness or ill feeling between us.'

Mrs Cartwright didn't reply but she rang the bell for tea. To Virginia's surprise, it was Mrs Smithers, the housekeeper, who pushed in the tea trolley. Virginia greeted her with a smile.

'Hello, Mrs Smithers. It's nice to see you again. I hope you're well.'

Mrs Smithers fussed with the tea cups and made no reply. Plainly, she was deeply embarrassed.

'That will be all, thank you.' Mrs Cartwright dismissed the housekeeper from the room.

Virginia knew that in Mrs Cartwright's eyes she had committed a social faux pas, but she didn't care. It was Mrs Cartwright who was at fault by not moving with the times. No wonder girls were refusing to go into service nowadays.

They drank their tea in silence except for the heavy tick tock of the grandfather clock in the corner. Eventually Nicholas said, 'Virginia has told me, mother, how well you looked after her when you were both in Helensburgh and how wonderful you were at the birth.'

Virginia could see that he'd found a soft spot.

'I did my best. And it's good to know I helped my grandson into the world.'

'Yes, you really were wonderful,' Virginia said. 'I don't know what I would have done without you.'

Mr Cartwright cleared his throat. 'My wife has always been a very capable woman.'

'You seemed to get on together then, mother,' Nicholas said. 'And I'm sure you and Virginia can get on well together again. If you'll just give her a chance.'

'You talk about living as a normal family, Nicholas,' Mr Cartwright said. 'But Virginia already has a husband.'

'They have been separated for some time now, father. And it has been very amicable. He's ill in hospital at the moment. The poor fellow has taken a stroke, but both Virginia and I are visiting him regularly. There will be a divorce as soon as it's possible. Then Virginia and I will just have a quiet wedding.'

'Why don't you wait until Virginia is free,' his father said. 'And see how you feel then.'

'Father, have you not been listening to what I've been saying. We love each other. We've already set up home together. All we need to complete our happiness is our son.' He replaced his cup on the tea trolley. 'I've already spoken to Richard and told him he'll be coming to live with us. He's quite excited about the prospect. He's looking forward to it.'

'We have a lovely room all prepared for him,' Virginia told them eagerly. 'Do come and see it. Please come and visit him.'

Despite sitting rigidly straight-backed in her chair, Mrs Cartwright was now visibly trembling. 'How can you do this to us? We've loved and looked after the child for all these years. I'll never forgive either of you.'

'Oh mother,' Nicholas groaned. 'What's the good of talking like that. It was your choice to take Richard. Virginia didn't want to part with him. You should be glad that he'll be reunited with his mother now in a good home.'

Mr Cartwright said, 'You must appreciate that this isn't easy for your mother, Nicholas. I think it really would be better if you gave us more time to–'

Nicholas rose. 'I can see that there's no point in continuing this conversation. Please tell the nurse to have all Richard's clothes and belongings ready. We'll call for him on Friday after Virginia's hospital visit.'

Virginia followed Nicholas to the door, turning for a moment to say before leaving, 'Please remember that it's not a case of you never seeing Richard again. I meant it when I said you'd always be welcome.'

On the way back to Glasgow, Nicholas said, 'You were very generous, darling. After all you've suffered. I haven't forgotten that my mother dismissed you the moment my back was turned.'

'Oh, I don't believe in harbouring resentments. I saw enough of that when I lived with James.' She sighed. 'He was so full of bitterness and hatred. He absolutely seethed with it at times.'

'That's what could have made him a candidate for a stroke. It's not healthy to be like that.'

'No, I suppose it isn't. I used to warn him about getting so worked up about everything.'

Before going to visit the Cartwrights, she'd made her usual visit to the hospital. She still found it difficult to talk to James or even to look at him. Unlike Nicholas – who seemed to treat James as if he was perfectly normal.

Even more than that, he treated him like a close friend. When she did look at Mathieson, she wondered what was going on in his mind. She was beginning to think Nicholas was right, that James was able to understand everything. His eyes were those of a thinking, feeling person trapped in a useless body. Yet she was never sure what the expression in those eyes meant. Or how to interpret the twitchy movements he could now make.

Nicholas believed Mathieson's eyes were expressing interest and enthusiasm when he read to him. He could see fire and anger too, but Nicholas said that was in response to some of the terrible things that were happening in the world.

She couldn't help feeling uncertain and worried though. Especially on the Friday afternoon when Nicholas came for her at the hospital. He arrived early and marched right into the ward – he was so eager and excited about going to collect Richard.

'Hello, old chap,' he greeted the twitching figure in the bed. 'This is the happiest day of our lives, the day Virginia and Richard and I start a proper family life. Maybe you'd like to meet Richard? We could bring him in one day. Anyway, I'm sorry I can't stay longer. Come on, darling.' He grabbed Virginia's hand and hauled her away, calling out to James, 'See you later, old son.'

On the way outside, Virginia said, 'Do you

think it was wise letting James see us together like that, Nicholas?'

Nicholas looked surprised. 'Why on earth should you feel that? He knows all about us.'

Perhaps it was because she'd felt like that about James so often before. Suddenly Nicholas shouted, 'Good God, look at this!'

The streets were seething with hordes of cloth-capped men. It was the biggest crowd Virginia had ever seen.

'It must be some sort of demonstration.'

In the middle of the mob a man had been hoisted far above all the others. A sturdily-built man in a shabby homburg. As he spoke, he was waving one fist high in the air. In the other he was clutching a huge red flag which was snapping violently in the wind.

Virginia felt faint. 'For a moment,' she said shakily, 'I thought it was James.'

Above the noise of the crowd that surged all around them, Nicholas shouted back joyfully,

'One day it will be James,' he said. 'Just you wait and see.'

The publishers hope that this book has given you enjoyable reading. Large Print Books are especially designed to be as easy to see and hold as possible. If you wish a complete list of our books please ask at your local library or write directly to:

Magna Large Print Books
Magna House, Long Preston,
Skipton, North Yorkshire.
BD23 4ND

This Large Print Book, for people
who cannot read normal print,
is published under the auspices of

THE ULVERSCROFT FOUNDATION

... we hope you have enjoyed this book.
Please think for a moment about those
who have worse eyesight than you ...
and are unable to even read or enjoy
Large Print without great difficulty.

You can help them by sending a
donation, large or small, to:

**The Ulverscroft Foundation,
1, The Green, Bradgate Road,
Anstey, Leicestershire, LE7 7FU,
England.**
or request a copy of our brochure for
more details.

The Foundation will use all donations
to assist those people who are visually
impaired and need special attention
with medical research, diagnosis
and treatment.

Thank you very much for your help.